A Bird's Eye View

What You See Is Not Always What You Get

Sharron McKinnis Fowler

AuthorHouse™
1663 Liberty Drive, Suite 200
Bloomington, IN 47403
www.authorhouse.com
Phone: 1-800-839-8640

This book is a work of fiction. People, places, events, and situations are the product of the author's imagination. Any resemblance to actual persons, living or dead, or historical events, is purely coincidental.

First published by AuthorHouse 3/30/2009
ISBN: 978-1-4389-4216-2 (sc)

Library of Congress Control Number: 2009900563
Printed in the United States of America
Bloomington, Indiana

This book is printed on acid-free paper.

Cover illustration by Gread McKinnis, Jr.

Forward

"But when that which is perfect has come, then that which is in part will be done away. When I was a child, I spoke as a child, I understood as a child, I thought as a child; but when I became a man, I put away childish things. For now we see in a mirror, dimly, but then face to face. Now I know in part, but then I shall know just as I also am known. And now abideth faith, hope, love, these three; but the greatest of these is love."

NKJV

I Corinthians 13:10-13

Acknowledgements

This book is dedicated to the memory of my late father Gread McKinnis, Sr.

To my family, who always supports me and gives me enough material for a million books; especially my mother, Naomi McKinnis who is the most intelligent woman I know. Finally, to my husband William, whose love, faithfulness, generosity, and patience inspires me everyday.

Prologue

"Cheryl, you better hurry up girl! Mama's gonna kill you if you don't get your butt back in here. And get back off that screen before you fall down and break your neck!"

"Okay, I'm comin." Cheryl jumped back off the huge screen that ran from one end of the concrete terrace of the sixteenth floor to the other end. Each floor above the first had the same type of screening; a safety mechanism to keep the residents of the Marshall housing project, and others like it, from falling off the concrete terrace.

The George Marshall Housing Project consisted of a cascade of four stately apartment buildings, each standing sixteen stories high. From the city's main expressway, they appeared to be majestic architectural monuments with coveted views of the city's beautiful tree lined lakefront. But once the huge rod iron fences that stood as a barrier between the complex and the expressway were entered, the cold reality of crime, poverty, and isolation was blatantly evident.

Cheryl Marks and her family had moved into the housing project just three years earlier. It was one of the best days of their lives, or so they thought. The Marks were one of the first families selected to move into the large Chicago housing complex. On the day they moved in Cheryl, along with her two sisters and twin brothers, raced from one end of the small apartment to the next in sheer excitement. Her mother marveled in the kitchen at the brand new basic grade appliances as her father stood proudly at the front window, peering down at the newly landscaped lawn.

The sixteenth floor was considered the "penthouse" floor, as it was the highest and had the best view of the city. Being located less than a mile from the lakefront, the view was absolutely spectacular. While her father continued to admire the view, and her mother continued to check out the new appliances, Cheryl and her sisters were excited for yet another reason. They would be getting their own bedroom. In their old two bedroom apartment, they had to set up a cot in the living room for Pearl, and Tischa and Cheryl shared one twin bed in the extra bedroom, with their younger brothers sharing the other.

Pearl the oldest, was turning thirteen, Tischa was eleven, and Cheryl was going to be entering the fourth grade the next school semester. The idea of three preteen girls even though Cheryl wasn't technically a preteen yet, getting their own room was a dream come true, even if they would have to share it. Looking back on that day three years later, it seemed like an eternity had passed, given how swiftly the novelty of the complex had faded into the reality that remained today.

"Mama will be here any minute and you know she told you not to go outside." Pearl snapped.

"I was just standing on the terrace, I didn't really go outside." Cheryl explained to Pearl, even though Pearl wasn't buying Cheryl's explanation.

"If you go out that front door, you go outside. You better be glad I'm not gonna tell Mama you went out."

Cheryl rolled her eyes at her older sister as she fell down into the overstuffed chair facing the front window. Pearl was always making empty threats to tell Mama on somebody. The actual truth was nobody wanted to be the cause of Mama being in a funky mood when she came home from work. Like they say, if Mama wasn't happy, nobody was happy. Cheryl sat staring out of the window.

Though it wasn't the same as standing in front of the long screen over the landing, the view from the front window would have to suffice.

It was amazing how different the world appeared from the top of the complex. Cheryl and her siblings weren't allowed to go downstairs once it started getting dark. That was usually the time things jumped off in the neighborhood, and her parents were determined to keep their family as safe as feasibly possible. The strange thing was, the project was located just a couple of blocks from one of the most upscale neighborhoods in the city, Diamond Row.

The residents of Diamond Row had been lobbying the mayor for the last few years to have the housing project removed, as they weren't thrilled about having to share their prime real estate with the city's underprivileged population. But regardless of how her upper class neighbors felt, Cheryl's favorite past time was looking down from her perch at the project at their comings and goings. From her bird's eye view, she could see the luxury cars stream up and down the boulevard. Porches, BMWs, and Mercedes Benzes were the standard mode of transportation to the restaurants and designer shops that lined the boulevard. Luxury condominiums and magnificent homes sat on the far end. Everything seemed so close from the top of the complex, almost as though once she left her family's small apartment and took the rickety elevator down to the first floor, she would step into a whole new world. But the reality was, once she stepped out of the tall complex building, it was clear the view from the window had created quite an illusion. Even so, Cheryl would imagine herself living in one of the mansions and driving a metallic blue Porsche in the future. She had already picked out the make and color. For a twelve-year-old, she had a vivid imagination. But actually, her selection of that particular car wasn't just based on imagination alone.

Her obsession with the car started after Pearl decided to make a detour on the way home from school one day and take a brief excursion to Diamond Row. Of course if she was going, Tischa and Cheryl had to tag along too as she couldn't take the risk of them

3

getting home from school before she did and her parents finding out. Pearl loved roaming up and down the shops that lined the row and imagining she really belonged there. As Pearl was peering into the window of her favorite boutique, Cheryl remembered being distracted by the slam of a car door. She turned around and saw a beautiful young woman checking the car door to make sure it was locked. As the young woman started to walk away from the car, she glanced back at the car with a somewhat proud look and headed toward the boutique door. Standing at the door was a tall young man, looking at her the way she looked at the car. Cheryl stared at the shiny car parked in front of the boutique. She remembered hearing Pearl announce the shiny blue car was a Porsche. It didn't quite register to Cheryl the significance of the model of the car, but in her mind she associated it with the young glamorous couple, and imagined that one day, she would be in the same situation as the young woman the car belonged to.

She didn't know how she was going to afford it, but one thing was certain, she wouldn't be a resident of the George Marshall Housing project when she grew up. She just knew one day, she'd meet the perfect man, not too different from the young man who stood waiting lovingly for the young woman who drove the shiny blue car. And he would look at her in the same way the young man looked at that young woman, with pride and admiration, and they would live happily together in their beautiful mansion on Diamond Row....

Chapter One

"Cheryl, get up off that chair and help me with these groceries." Mrs. Marks snapped as she walked in the door.

"Okay Mama, I'm coming." Cheryl replied, snapping back into reality.

"Did y'all clean those dishes yet? I hope that kitchen is clean, because I'm ready to start cooking dinner."

"Yes Mama, we cleaned the kitchen a long time ago." Pearl chirped, running into the living room to grab the grocery bags from her mother. Pearl was such a kiss up Cheryl thought, always going out her way to prove to everybody that she was the dependable oldest child.

"Good, cause I'll be ready to get started cooking once I change these clothes. Put these groceries away before I get back." Mrs. Marks ordered as she walked out the living room and disappeared through her bedroom door.

Cheryl and Pearl began taking the groceries out of the brown paper grocery bags and placing them in the kitchen cabinets, just as Tischa walked out of the bedroom door. "Did I hear Mama come back?" she asked. Tischa had been watching the small black and white television in their bedroom as she usually did every evening after school.

"Yeah you did. Get over here and help us put these groceries up." Pearl ordered, trying her best to sound like her mother.

"I know, you don't have to tell me what to do." Tischa snapped. She hated being bossed around by Pearl as much as Cheryl did. Cheryl and Tischa looked at each other and rolled their eyes in silent unity over Pearl's bossy attitude. Who did Pearl think she was anyway? Just because she was the oldest, she thought that gave her the right to fill in for their mother when the real one wasn't around. But if the truth was told, their parents did place a lot of responsibility on Pearl because she was the oldest. And if anything did go wrong, they would most likely blame her for it. That fact didn't make Tischa and Cheryl any more sympathetic towards Pearl's dilemma though.

"Your Daddy's not back with the boys yet? How long have they been gone?" Mrs. Marks inquired walking past Pearl, Cheryl and Tischa as they continued to unload the groceries. "They sure have been gone a long time."

Mrs. Marks already knew the answer to her questions. She just had a habit of asking them anyway. Mr. Marks usually got home from work long before Mrs. Marks, as he left early in the morning, before anyone was even up yet. When he came home, sometimes he would take the boys out just to get them out of the apartment. He never liked the boys playing in the playground in the housing complex because of the gang activity in the neighborhood.

"No Mamma, you know how Daddy gets when he's out at the park with Ralph and Carl. He always loses track of time. You know they gonna all come in here smelling like God knows what when they get back." Pearl walked over to her mother shaking her head as she leaned on the kitchen counter watching Mrs. Marks pull out the pots and pans in preparation for cooking. "You need some help with something Mamma?"

"Yeah, you can peel about six of those large white potatoes. Cheryl and Tischa, get a couple of onions out and peel them for me."

"Okay Mamma." Cheryl and Tischa said at one time, a little less eager than Pearl.

The girls sat in the kitchen watching their mother cook. Pearl liked to ask her mother how she would make certain dishes, mentally preparing herself to care for the family she hoped to have one day. And Mrs. Marks loved to answer questions about her cooking, as cooking was one of her favorite things to do. Nothing pleased her more than cooking a large meal for her family and having them heap accolades and compliments on her for the rest of the night. Everyone could tell she would get really irritated if they sat down to eat one of her meals without stopping every couple of bites to tell her how good it was.

Just as Mrs. Marks was putting the finishing touches on dinner as the girls sat around watching, the front door swung open and in bounced Ralph and Carl followed by Mr. Marks.

"Go straight to the room and take off those clothes and clean up before we eat. Y'all smell like fresh puppies after playing in that park all day." Mrs. Marks yelled.

"Ah Dorothy, we don't smell that bad." Mr. Marks protested. "We weren't even out there all day. We didn't leave until about five, and the boys finished their homework first too."

"Well y'all smell like y'all been out there all day. Don't come in this kitchen!" Mrs. Marks fussed as Mr. Marks grinned at her.

He didn't care if she fussed. The smells coming out the kitchen were more than enough incentive to make him want to get cleaned up as soon as possible. There was nothing that pleased him more than coming home to find his wife putting the finishing touches on a good home cooked meal.

"Umm smells like fried chicken to me." Mr. Marks sighed.

"Alright, Mamma cooked fried chicken for dinner tonight!" Ralph yelled to Carl. "Hurry up and clean up so we can eat!"

Ralph and Carl ran towards their bedroom slapping each other's hands and taking their coats off on the way.

"You too!" Mrs. Marks snapped at Mr. Marks with a grin. "You smell like a puppy too."

"I'm going. But you better have that chicken laid out when I get back because I'm ready to eat." Mr. Marks ordered back. Mrs. Marks looked at him and rolled her eyes, not taking his order too seriously.

Earl Marks was a tall middle aged man with graying temples and wide broad shoulders. He was a former high school athlete, and had received a scholarship to run track in college, but he injured his leg in a car accident and was not able to run the same again. He never made it to college either.

Dorothy Marks was tall and slender and always wore her thick long black hair pinned up in a roll on top of her head. She'd met Earl when they were both on the high school track team in downstate IL. They ended up getting married right after graduating from high school, and eventually moved to Chicago after Pearl was born.

Pearl, Tischa, and Cheryl smiled as they listened to their parents interact in a way that only they could. They had a unique way of communicating with each other that was born out of years of familiarity and deep affection. The girls cherished the times when their family was together like this, sharing one of their mother's good home cooked meals and enjoying each other's company. Those times were the best. For during those times they didn't have to listen to their parents complain about how many bills were sitting on the dresser in the their bedroom, or the fact that there were five children in the family that needed clothes, lunch money, bus fare and God knew what else.

But Cheryl noticed there was something uniquely different about Mr. and Mrs. Marks that night. Mr. Marks seemed especially giddy for some reason, almost to the point of being excessive. Mrs. Marks kept making faces at him as though she was trying to keep him from letting the cat out of the bag too soon. Finally, after Mr. Marks could no longer contain himself, and Mrs. Marks could no longer keep him under control, he made an announcement that took everybody, other than Mrs. Marks and him by total surprise.

"Well your Mamma and I have some news for you all. You know we been talking about moving out of the projects once we got able to. Well, we been saving for the last couple of years, and we finally got enough money to move. We just put a down payment on a new house on the far south side, a long way from here. It's a brand new house, and we going to be moving at the end of this month!

"What! We're getting a brand new house?" Everyone seemed to be screaming at once.

"Can I have my own room in the new house?" Pearl screamed making sure she was the first one to take dibs on any available house space.

"As a matter of fact you can have your own room in the basement since you're the oldest. Tischa and Cheryl can share the one upstairs. There'll be a separate room for the boys, and one for us. We have three bedrooms, four including the one in the big basement, two bathrooms, a large kitchen, dining room and living room." Mrs. Marks said proudly.

"Two bathrooms!" All three of the girls squealed in unison.

They didn't really hear much else past that point. Sharing one bathroom with six other people was no fun when you were a teenage girl. Cheryl wasn't quite a teenager yet, but at twelve, she was well aware of Pearl's ability to hog a bathroom. Pearl loved to stare at herself in the mirror in the bathroom, and got a huge attitude if someone else seemed interested in using the facilities while she was in there.

9

"Yes, we're moving into a brand new house at the end of the month. Praise the Lord! Make sure you children thank the Lord for blessing us with a new home before you go to bed tonight. Now help me to clear the table of the dishes. Whose time is it to wash?" Mrs. Marks asked, smiling as she walked away from the table with her and Mr. Marks' plates.

"We will Mama. It's Cheryl's time to wash, and mine's to dry." Tischa said as she walked to the kitchen carrying her plate.

Once all the plates were in the kitchen and scraped off by Pearl, Cheryl stood on the stepstool placed in front of the sink for her and began to wash them. She wasn't quite tall enough yet to reach the sink without the stool. She had asked her mother a couple of years ago if she could begin washing the dishes like Pearl and Tischa did. It made her feel as though she was as old as they were. It hadn't taken long for the thrill to wear off, but for some reason she didn't seem to mind the dishes as much this night. They were going to be moving to their own house. She wondered if it would resemble the huge houses that lined Diamond Row.

Later that night, Cheryl knelt down on her knees and thanked God for blessing her family with a new house just as her mother had asked. Then she climbed into the bed she had to share with Tischa, turning away from Tischa's feet. She would soon have her own bed in the room at the new house. No Pearl getting on her and Tischa's nerves anymore about how sloppy they kept the bedroom. No more of Tischa's feet in her face every night. She laid imagining how she would arrange her part of the bedroom in the new house and wondering how different life would be there until she fell asleep. She didn't know why, but she had this strange feeling that something good was going to happen, and her life would never be the same.

Chapter Two

Cheryl stared at herself in the mirror approvingly. It was important that she looked good today. She gave the bangs on her newly relaxed bob hair cut another once over with her thin black comb. She'd worn a more natural style through grade school, but this was her new high school look. She continued to stare into her large brown eyes looking back at her in the mirror. Today she was likely going to be running into Matthew Robinson, whom she was sure was going to be the finest boy in the freshman class, much less the entire school if you asked her. The first time she laid eyes on him was her first day of eighth grade. Deborah, the girl who lived across the street, had tried to tell her how fine he was, but Deborah's animated description of Matthew's attributes in no way prepared her for what she was going to behold when she walked into that classroom.

It was a beautiful sunny day when the Marks family moved into their new house in Ridgeland, a working class neighborhood on the far south side. The citizens of Ridgeland prided themselves on the cleanliness of their neighborhood, and Ridgeland was known for its manicured lawns and the effort its residents put forth to keep the streets clean and litter free. They would actually devote weekends out of the year to pick up trash from the grass and tree lined streets. The Marks family loved trimming their new lawn as well, as it was the first time they'd actually had a lawn. But Mrs. Marks would occasionally get a little put off by some of the neighbors and their obsessive fixation with grass. It was obvious Ridgeland was a long way from the George Marshall Housing Complex, and the community had somewhat of a ghetto bourgeois' mentality.

Cheryl was sitting one late summer evening on the bench in front of their freshly trimmed lawn, when a girl who looked to be about her age, came bouncing up the sidewalk that led to the Marks front porch. She was tall and lanky with short fuzzy brown hair.

"Hey, my name is Deborah. I live in that house across the street with the big brown awning in the front window." She said swiftly pointing at the big house directly across from theirs. "What's your name?" She asked without taking a breath.

"Cheryl..." Cheryl replied slowly.

"Hey Cheryl, what grade you going into when school starts? I go to McArthur, and I'll be in eighth grade this year. But I really can't wait until next year...'cause I will actually be in high school!" Deborah gushed rapidly.

"I'm in eighth grade too, I think I'll be going to McArthur...at least I think that's what my mother said." Cheryl replied still speaking slowly.

"Oh yeah? We can walk to school together then. I've been shopping for school clothes all day. You know I gotta look good this year since I'll be in eighth grade and everything. I got to get me a new boyfriend." She said laughing. "Girl, you know who the finest boy in school is? Matthew Robinson! Girl, that boy is f-i-n-e." Deborah gushed. Cheryl sat looking at Deborah amazed at how quickly she spoke, and trying her best to take in all the information she was disclosing all at once.

"Uh, okay I guess. I'll ask my mother if it's okay."

Cheryl had been a Marks child way too long not to know she needed to clear everything with Mrs. Marks, who kept a pretty tight leash on her kids. While her control at times felt a bit claustrophobic, the Marks kids understood their mother loved them, and if she was somewhat controlling, it was for their own good. After all, they hadn't always lived in the best of neighborhoods, but Mr. and Mrs. Marks had always done the best they could for their family.

"You got to get permission from your mother to walk with me to school? Are you for real?" Deborah asked obviously having a lot more choice over her selection of friends. "Well, if you can, I usually leave out around eight thirty to get there by nine. Let me know and I'll come by and pick you up on the first day…Oh, well I'll see ya. My mama gave me some money to get some new shoes for school and I need to catch the mall before it's closed."

After that Deborah turned, waved, and bounded down the sidewalk as quickly as she came up.

It turned out on the first day of school Cheryl couldn't walk to school with Deborah after all. Mrs. Marks actually had to take the kids to school on the first day since they were transferring from another school. Papers had to be filled out and transcripts had to be delivered. The kinds of things only a parent or guardian could do. Cheryl just didn't know how her mother would have taken Deborah anyway. She could come across a little odd, but Cheryl could tell she was okay, and she was usually a good judge of character.

Poor Mrs. Marks had to spend most of the morning getting the boys in class since they were going to a different school and Cheryl would be going to McArthur, which was the neighborhood middle school. Luckily, Pearl and Tischa were able to go to school by themselves because they were going to stay in the high school where they were already enrolled. Pearl wasn't thrilled about switching schools in her senior year and this was going to be Tischa's sophomore year there. Pearl had already shown her the high school ropes, so everything was under control for them. But by the time Mrs. Marks made it back home for Cheryl, it was already noon. Cheryl would have to walk in class after the kids returned from lunch break, and she was a little apprehensive about walking midday into a classroom full of strange kids. Cheryl stood at the door of the class peering in while her mother and her new teacher talked. As she surveyed the room, she grew more and more nervous, anxiously waiting for her mother and Mrs. James to stop talking so she could go inside and get the impending humiliation over with already. She'd been new in class before and knew how the drill went. Mrs. James would stand her in front of the class and go, "Class, this is Cheryl Marks, she's new to our class, please welcome her!" And she would have to stand there looking and feeling stupid wishing she could evaporate in mid air.

After finally bidding Mrs. Marks goodbye, Cheryl and Mrs. James walked into the room. "Class, this is our new student, Cheryl Marks. Welcome Cheryl to our class. Who has an empty desk next to them?"

"I do Mrs. James." A youthful masculine voice called out from the back of the room.

"Great, thanks Matthew. Please raise your hand so Cheryl will know where to go. Cheryl, it looks like we have a seat for you in the back. Once my seating chart is completed tomorrow, however, I will be assigning new seats."

Cheryl glanced at the raised hand and began to walk in its direction, not really looking at the body to which it was attached. All she could think about was getting seated as quickly as possible. Once seated, she turned to the occupant of the seat next to her.

"Thanks." She mumbled.

"No problem Cheryl." He replied.

At that point, Cheryl looked up into the face of the person seated next to her. For a brief moment she sat and stared blankly. It was the most handsome face she'd ever seen that wasn't on the television or movie screen. The young man looked at her and smiled briefly. His caramel colored face was framed by jet-black curly hair. He had piercing dark brown eyes that sparkled when he smiled. He also had an unusual amount of facial hair for a boy not yet in high school, even though it was just the light trace of a mustache. Cheryl smiled briefly and turned her head towards the front of the room.

Unfortunately, that was the closest contact she had with Matthew Robinson that year. The next day, Mrs. James informed Cheryl she would actually be switching seats and would sit in the front of the class. Matthew settled somewhere in the middle of the classroom, and Cheryl never really got an opportunity to get to know him any better that year. Their level of conversation would basically consist of "Hi" as they were passing each other. Matthew was usually with his A list friends, one of the perks of being the best looking boy in school, and she was usually with her more B list ones.

Cheryl continued to stare at herself in the mirror. Now that she was about to enter high school, she was beginning to feel a lot better about her looks. The gawkiness of grade school had begun to wear off, and she had actually filled out enough to wear some of Tischa's, and even Pearl's clothes, which she, of course, thought were way cooler than her own. Even though the official age for makeup in the Marks household was sixteen, she still managed to sneak on a little bit of eye shadow after her parents left for work. And she'd learned how to smear a drop of petroleum jelly on her lips to give them a nice shiny look, a tip she'd picked up from her best friend Charity. When she was feeling really adventurous, she and Charity would burn the tip of a black eyebrow pencil and line the top of their eyelids. She knew Mrs. Marks would kill her if she ever caught her with that black stuff on her eyes, but she always managed to wipe it off before her mother saw her. Cheryl took one last look in the mirror, smoothed her beige turtleneck sweater over her dark blue jeans, then she slung her brown leather shoulder bag over her shoulder and grabbed her notebooks. She couldn't believe Charity was already at the front door ringing the doorbell. She could hear Tischa opening the living room door.

"Cheryl! Charity's here!" Tischa yelled.

"Okay, I'm coming!" Cheryl yelled back.

Charity was standing in the doorway with a half smile, half frown. She hated having to walk all the way to the Marks house. Cheryl and Charity agreed to meet each other at the bus stop every morning before school, but if Charity stood for over five minutes past the agreed upon time, she would began to walk to Cheryl's house just in case something happened or Cheryl wasn't going to school that day. If, however, she walked all the way to the door and Cheryl was going to school, she was rightfully perturbed.

"Sorry, I'm just running a little late. I couldn't find my brown shoes." Cheryl lied. She didn't want Charity to know that she had to walk all the way to the house because she was busy staring at herself in the mirror and rehearsing what she would do if she ran into Matthew that day.

"That's okay." Charity responded halfheartedly. "Where'd you get those shoes? What size are they?"

"I got these at Bakers a couple of weeks ago. They're size seven and a half. You can borrow them if you want to." Cheryl replied, trying to smooth things over.

"Cool. Those would look nice with the new brown suede skirt I just bought." Charity replied looking as though she might be thawing out a little.

Nothing could get Charity to forget the reason she was mad quicker than the prospect of borrowing a new pair of shoes. Charity was meticulous about her appearance, as was just about everyone in Cheryl's little group, but Charity was obsessive about two things, shoes and hair. She loved coordinating all her outfits with the perfect pair of shoes, and every week she'd spend practically all her allowance on maintaining her short tapered haircut. She thought the short cut made her resemble Halle Berry, even if that thought was not totally shared, and was almost paranoid about keeping her edges straight. By the time they got to the school, Charity had forgotten all about her walk to the Marks house that morning. That's one of the things Cheryl liked about Charity. She couldn't stay mad for long.

When Cheryl first started going to McArthur, after moving to Ridgeland, she didn't know anyone other than Deborah across the street. While she liked Deborah, she just wasn't the type of girl Cheryl cliqued with. Cheryl didn't diss Deborah or anything when she ran into her at school because the girl did live across the street. It's just that Cheryl found she had more in common with Charity and the group of girls she soon gravitated to from her eighth grade class. It was Charity who first showed Cheryl how to apply eye shadow in class without Mrs. James finding out. After Mrs. James assigned seats as she promised on that second day of school, Cheryl was assigned the seat next to Charity near the front of the class. Every day, right after the morning bathroom break, Mrs. James would stand in the hall for a few minutes and chat with the teacher in the classroom across the hall. In those few minutes Charity and Cheryl, along with Vanessa and Jennifer who sat behind them, would pass the blue eye shadow from one to the other. By the time Mrs. James made it back in the classroom, the girls would be all made up.

But it wasn't as though they were fixing themselves up for any of the boys in the eighth grade. They weren't interested in any of them, other than Matthew. They just didn't think the eighth grade boys were mature enough for them. They considered the boys in their class goofs whose level of conversation basically consisted of whose turn it was to pitch in the next softball game. The girls would usually hold much deeper discussions about what happened on their favorite soap opera, or what fresh outfits they were going to be picking up at the mall next. On the walk home from school, they would pretend they were in high school, making eyes and flirting with the high school boys as they got off the bus after school. Now that they were actually in high school, they were looking forward to meeting a higher class of boys. As far as Cheryl was concerned though, the only boy she wanted to see today was Matthew.

"Hey Cheryl, hey Charity, give me a hug, I haven't seen ya'll in months!" Vanessa squealed as she came running toward Cheryl and Charity. "What bus did you catch? I tried to wait for you two but I didn't want to be late on the first day of high school."

"Cheryl couldn't find her shoes, so we took the 8:10 bus. What's up girl! I like your jacket. That is the bomb!" Charity grabbed Vanessa and gave her a hug.

"How long you been here Vanessa?" Cheryl asked hugging Vanessa as well. "Girl, that *is* a bad jacket!"

"I just got here about ten minutes before you did. Maria and Jennifer just went in the school. I told them I was going to try and wait for you. All the new freshmen are supposed to go to the study hall first for some kind of orientation." Vanessa explained as she started walking quickly toward the entrance of the school.

Cheryl and Charity followed close behind. They weren't familiar yet with the large school and wanted to stick together until they were required to part. Cheryl looked around the enormous building as they entered the door. Brian Henry High School was huge in comparison to the small grade school they'd graduated from. Since Tischa was still attending the high school she and Pearl attended before moving to Ridgeland, she wasn't there to give Cheryl advice like Pearl was for her. So Cheryl was feeling just a little lost. Pearl had already graduated at the end of the prior semester, and was now attending the city college.

Cheryl, Charity and Vanessa noticed Maria and Jennifer waving trying to get their attention and holding seats for them in the large auditorium. Once seated, they surveyed the room trying to locate other members of their graduating class who were no doubt just as overwhelmed by the new experience as they were. They sat and listened intently as the administrator instructed them on how to navigate the school and where to pick up their class schedules. As they were leaving the large auditorium, Cheryl glanced across the room and locked eyes with a familiar face. It was Matthew Robinson! She could feel her face began to heat up and hoped she wasn't out and out blushing. After all, she didn't want to give Matthew any indication that she'd obsessed over him all summer. Or that she'd obsessed over him since the first day she'd laid eyes on him. Nor that he was the last thing she thought about every night before she went to sleep.

She glanced away briefly, and then looked back. But it was too late. By the time she returned her gaze, one of Matthew's friends had grabbed him and pulled him into a large mob of their friends. That figures. As fine as Matthew was, of course he'd be just as popular in high school as he was in grade school. Now he just had a larger crowd to mingle with.

"Cheryl, would you come on! We have to pick up our schedules and make it to class before the bell rings. As big as this school is, it's probably gonna take us about thirty or forty minutes to walk from the admissions office and find our class rooms!" Charity said. Charity was always exaggerating.

"I'm coming! It's not going to take us that long. Calm down Charity!" Cheryl said rolling her eyes.

She pretended she wasn't disappointed that Matthew hadn't come running over to her, wanting to know how her summer had been, and asking her if they could get together after school, just like she'd imagined he would while staring at herself in the mirror that morning. The truth was Matthew never paid much attention to her after that first day in eighth grade, when he politely pointed out the empty desk next to him. Why did she think things would be so different in high school? Guys like Matthew were out of her league, she told herself. As she followed Charity and the other girls down the long halls of the new school, she could hear the mocking voices in her head telling her she'd set her sights too high. If she'd wanted to avoid ending up at the end of high school pining over a guy that was out of her league, she'd better get real. Otherwise, she was going to end up one of those girls who didn't even have a prom date at graduation! She told herself if she wanted a high school boyfriend she should set her sights on someone else, maybe someone from the B list.

Chapter Three

The dynamics of the Marks family had undergone significant change since moving into the Ridgeland community. After finishing high school, Pearl had decided to drop out of college, much to Mrs. Marks dismay, and moved to Georgia with a couple of her friends. Pearl turned out to be somewhat of a free spirit, and wasn't quite sure what she wanted to do with her life. She was more interested in traveling and seeing the world before settling down into whatever she decided to do. Tischa was attending the city college and working part-time at a boutique in the mall. She loved working in the boutique, and Cheryl loved her working there too, for she used her employee discount to keep the Marks girls' closet well stocked. The boys, Ralph and Carl were in their first year of high school and were busy playing sports, and learning how to "mack" the ladies, if the amount of phone calls coming into the Marks home by young girls were any indication.

It hadn't taken Cheryl as long to fit into life at Henry High School as she thought it would. It seemed like the last four years had flown by. She'd made lots of new friends at school, and while she wasn't anywhere near being the most popular girl in the place, she'd grown comfortable with the school and the people, and was looking forward to graduating in the spring. Life at school had changed since freshman year in other ways too. While she and Charity were still the best of friends, Charity had been dating Mike Fields, one of the varsity football players since sophomore year, and was actually talking about getting married after high school. It seemed as though their relationship developed out of nowhere, but that was Charity. She was never shy about going after what she wanted. Everyday after school Cheryl, Charity and their girls would walk home together. They would all stand around in front of the school building waiting to hook up. One particular day while Cheryl and Charity were waiting for Vanessa and Jennifer, Cheryl noticed Charity kept glancing at the park across the street from the school. Cheryl also noticed the freshman and sophomore football team was practicing in the park, as they usually did during football season. When Vanessa and Jennifer finally made it out, Charity suggested they should cross the street and cut through the park instead of staying on the sidewalk the way they usually did, which was a quicker route to the bus stop.

"Why are we walking through the park?" Vanessa asked, "We're going to miss the 3:15 bus if we do that!" Vanessa was a little on the plump side and wasn't interested in exerting herself any more than she had to.

"It's nice out today, we can walk home." Charity suggested. "It's really not that far anyway."

"Since when do *you* want to walk?" Jennifer asked. "I don't want to run over the heels on my new shoes. I just bought these shoes last week." Jennifer then reached down and wiped the dust off the side of her black leather pumps.

"Nobody told you to wear your church shoes to school anyway. You always have to try to look cute don't you?" Charity said rolling her eyes at Jennifer.

"I think it has something to do with the football team over there." Cheryl said, grinning at Jennifer and Vanessa, and eyeing Charity suspiciously.

Charity rolled her eyes at Cheryl and grinned back. "Okay, so what, you got me. But that Mike Fields is so f-i-n-e!

"Which one is Mike Fields?" Vanessa asked.

"He was in my Algebra class last year. I don't know what happened to him over the summer, but the boy looks good this year. I mean, look at him! He's the one standing by the tree talking with that guy with the long green socks on. Girl, would you look at those shoulders? And those football pants are fittin' nice too!" Charity said shaking her head.

The girls looked over toward the tree at the same time. Okay, the boy looked good everyone agreed. Mike was an average height with a fair complexion. He had broad shoulders, then again, it could have been the shoulders pads Cheryl thought, but for some reason, she could tell they were broad even with the shoulder pads on. His football pants fit to reveal a pretty cute butt just as Charity had suggested. He briefly took his helmet off to wipe the sweat from his forehead and then pulled it back over his crop of curly brown hair. His hair looked like it would be soft to the touch by the way he pulled it back and placed it effortlessly under the helmet. Cheryl glanced back at Charity and shook her head up and down approvingly, while Vanessa gave Jennifer a high five.

Charity didn't say anything to Mike that day, but the girls decided to walk home everyday that the football team practiced in the park. Mike began to grow suspicious of the girls' trek through the park, especially since they would usually stare at him giggling and pointing, and looking back the entire time. One day, after Charity couldn't take it anymore she asked one of the other football players to tell him she said hello. She didn't know what it was about teenage boys. But they always seemed to need the girl to make the first move. The move paid off though, because it turned out Mike was into Charity as well and the next time the girls took their walk through the park, Mike shyly said hello to Charity first. Charity stopped and they chatted for a while as the other girls stood around pretending not to listen.

Mike and Charity made plans to see a movie together the following Saturday, and they were inseparable after that date. They dated all the rest of sophomore and junior year, and were still dating as the end of senior year approached. Cheryl always admired how Charity went after what she wanted. She wished she could be that aggressive, but it just wasn't in her to make the first move.

Charity's situation wasn't the only change in Cheryl's group of friends. Things had changed regarding Vanessa too. Actually, Vanessa was no longer a part of their little clique since she was forced to transfer schools after getting pregnant at the beginning of junior year. Cheryl never forgot the day not long after the beginning of the fall term that she, Vanessa and Jennifer were walking home from the bus stop. Charity was also with them that particular day since Mike was busy practicing with the football team. It wasn't quite clear how the conversation got started, but the subject suddenly turned to sex. Since Charity was the only one in the group with a steady boyfriend, the attention quickly turned to her. Everyone was interested in whether she and Mike had actually done anything yet, or if not, if they were thinking about doing it.

"Well, we've come pretty close, but no, we haven't actually done it yet. I mean Mike's a man and everything, and he's brought it up more than once, but I'm scared to do it right now, you know. I don't want to get pregnant before I get out of school. I mean look at Teresa Blackwell, you see how she has to walk around school with that big belly. I do not want to end up like that." Charity said.

"You all could use some protection, I mean a rubber or something, or you could go on the pill. Pamela Brown told me you can get them without your mother finding out at the free clinic. I know a lot of girls who have them." Jennifer suggested. "I mean I've never done it or anything, and I don't know if a rubber really works, but I don't blame you. I wouldn't want to have to walk around school with a big belly either. I feel so sorry for Teresa. My mother would just send me down South if it was me anyway." Jennifer said laughing.

"I hear you girl, me too." Cheryl agreed.

24

Cheryl knew that wasn't even an option for her. The Marks were known in the neighborhood as being a devout Christian family. Mr. Marks had served on the deacon board at First Avenue Church for the last couple of years, and Mrs. Marks was the president of the Missionary Board. There was no way a child of theirs was going to end up pregnant if they had anything to do with it. Needless to say, after years and years of hearing about how important it was to keep their virtue to ensure getting a decent husband one day, and how men respected women who learned how to keep their dresses down and their legs closed, Pearl, Tischa, and Cheryl were well programmed. "Why buy the cow when you can get the milk for free?" Mrs. Marks would say. And she made sure she quoted that cliché as often as possible given the fact she was raising three girls. She didn't have to worry, though. She'd done her job well. It was safe to say she had put the fear of God in all three of them.

As Cheryl and the girls continued to walk home talking about sex that day, everyone noticed Vanessa, who usually dominated the conversation, was being uncharacteristically quiet. Charity glanced at Cheryl and Jennifer, and as only she would have the nerve, asked Vanessa the question everyone was thinking.

"Why are you so quiet today Vanessa? What, you ever done it?"

Charity could be so blunt sometimes Cheryl thought.

Vanessa's eyes darted at Charity as though she was abruptly called on in class while daydreaming and didn't hear the question. She then glanced back and forth from Cheryl to Jennifer and said slowly… "Umm….maybe…one time."

"What!" Everyone yelled in unison.

The girls stopped walking and stared at Vanessa. Her eyes looked down at the ground. She looked uneasy, like she didn't really want to discuss it, but relieved at the same time, like she really needed to discuss it with someone.

"What! ....When? Who did you do it with? You never told us anything!" Jennifer said.

Her eyes were wide open. She stared at Vanessa as though a total stranger had appeared before her, and she didn't know where she'd come from. This couldn't be the friend she'd known and shared just about everything with since the fifth grade withholding this kind of information.

"...It was right before school started this summer when I stayed at my Aunt Justine's house for a couple of weeks. I met this guy named Jeremy. He lived a couple of doors down from my aunt's house, and would hang out sometimes with my cousin Ronnie. Well, one night when my aunt was out, he came over and we were just hanging out watching TV." Vanessa was speaking quickly and the girls were trying to hang on to her every word. "Ronnie needed to step out for a minute. He really was sneaking out to see his girlfriend Angie before Aunt Justine got back, and he left Jeremy and me at home alone. Anyway, we didn't plan it, we just started fooling around and one thing led to another and that's about it."

Vanessa still looked uncomfortable telling the story. When she finished speaking, Cheryl remembered thinking she hadn't realized how short Vanessa was. The way she was standing, with her shoulders hunched over, she suddenly appeared really small.

"I don't believe it. You've been holding out on us." Cheryl said, trying to break the silence.

"Well...how was it?" Charity asked. "What!" She said to Cheryl and Jennifer. "Ya'll know ya'll want to know too."

"It hurt!" Vanessa exclaimed to Charity. "It hurt, that's how it was! I was expecting it to be different. But all I can say is I was glad when it was over, even though it didn't last that long anyway. And we only did it that one time."

"I hear the first time usually hurts anyway." Charity said. "That's another reason I'm not in a rush to do it. But the second one is supposed to be better." She said laughing.

"Well I'm not going to be having a second time, at least not with him. I didn't really like him that much anyway." Vanessa said, glancing towards the ground again.

Cheryl stared at Vanessa. She couldn't imagine having that experience with someone she didn't even like. And it was obvious Vanessa hadn't heard from Jeremy since then. She began to feel sorry for her. They ended up walking the rest of the way home making awkward small talk in between awkward silence. It wasn't really clear why everyone was so shocked Vanessa had done it. It wasn't like a lot of the others girls at school hadn't done it already. Once in Health class, the teacher, Ms Klein had made the mistake of asking the class if any of them were sexually active already. Cheryl actually began to feel a bit out of place since she hadn't raised her hand, given the number of hands that suddenly went up in the air. Most likely everyone with their hand up wasn't telling the truth, but Ms. Klein, who was single, suddenly looked like she'd opened Pandora's Box. She obviously wanted to have a healthy, chaste discussion with the girls about the cons of having sex too early, how important their sexual health was, etc. Instead, based on the sudden graphic turn the discussion was taking, it was obvious some of the girls had a lot more experience than even she had. No, the issue wasn't that girls their age weren't having sex…it was just that no one from their group had done it yet.

It wasn't long after that conversation that Vanessa dropped another shocking bomb. She hadn't gotten her period that month. Vanessa ended up staying in school until the end of her second trimester, until she could no longer hide the fact she was pregnant. She then decided to transfer to a school for pregnant high school girls for the duration of her pregnancy. Cheryl and Jennifer tried to keep in touch with Vanessa ever so often, to find out how things were going with the pregnancy, but it got to the point with everything going on at school, they began to lose touch. It was just beginning to feel like they were in two different worlds. Cheryl could not imagine having to learn how to take care of a baby at this point in her life.

And Charity wasn't even making an effort to keep in touch with Vanessa. She seemed a little disgusted that Vanessa had gotten herself in the situation in the first place. Cheryl and Charity were the best of friends but sometimes she felt Charity could be so critical. For one thing, as soon as Cheryl got home that evening after Vanessa told them about her experience with Jeremy, her phone rang, and it was Charity yelling into the phone, "Girl, did you hear that? I cannot believe that Vanessa was that stupid!" In Cheryl's opinion everyone was entitled to make mistakes in life. What was important was not being stupid enough to repeat the same mistakes over and over.

After she realized she hadn't heard from Vanessa in a while, Cheryl decided to give her a call. Her mother answered the phone. When Cheryl asked to speak to Vanessa, she was informed that Vanessa was going to be staying with her uncle and his family in Alabama for a while. She later decided to stay there and go to school even after the birth of her baby. They never heard from Vanessa again.

Chapter Four

By the time senior year rolled around, Cheryl was beginning to think everyone else was hooking up except for her. Even Jennifer now seemed to be going nuts lately over this new guy she'd met at church named Robert. Robert was the new choir director at First Avenue, and Jennifer thought he was the finest thing she'd ever laid eyes on. She was already planning on taking him to the prom, even though she hadn't told him yet. But if Jennifer was really interested in a guy, most likely she got what she wanted. She was the prettiest one in their little clique. Cheryl wasn't quite as pretty as Jennifer, but she could still attract her fair share of male attention. She just tended to move a lot slower than her friends. She'd gone on a couple of double dates with Charity and Mike with some of Mike's friends, but nothing she considered earth shattering. There was a group date here, and a football game there, but nothing romantic. It just seemed like the guys *she* was really interested in weren't usually the ones asking her out, they were usually already dating someone else, like Matthew.

Cheryl couldn't believe that after four years of high school Matthew Robinson had never noticed her. For one thing, he was going with Donna Johnson, one of the prettiest pompom girls at school. Usually if you saw Matthew, Donna was usually hanging on his arm like one of her pompoms. But even if he weren't that into Donna, it wouldn't have mattered, because he still didn't pay any attention to her anyway.

Sure, he would usually acknowledge her presence if he passed her in the hall or in class, but a friendly greeting or nod seemed to be the extent of his interest in her.

It wasn't like Cheryl couldn't get a date if she really wanted to. Lots of guys were interested in her. And one of them, Tom Morgan, had even asked her to go to the prom with him. Tom was in her English class, a member of the debate team, and incredibly smart. He was also pretty cute, so she accepted. After all, she didn't want to be dateless for the senior prom, even though in her fantasy world, Matthew and Donna would have this huge fight and break up just before the prom. Matthew would finally discover how fabulous she was, express his undying love, and take her to the prom instead. But that was Cheryl's world. While everyone else was busy doing, she was busy dreaming.

At least she was looking forward to attending college in the fall, even though she still wasn't sure where she was going. Her parents weren't the richest people in the world and didn't have the money to send her to school. So she'd have to take the same route as Pearl and Tischa and go to the city college. A lot would depend on how much financial aid she could get. Mr. Marks was planning to retire from the post office after twenty-five years of delivering the mail. Even though he'd draw a pretty decent pension, money was still going to be tight, and not a lot left for college. Good thing Pearl was pretty resourceful and was just about supporting herself, and Tischa wasn't doing badly either. Tischa loved working at the store in the mall so much, she had applied for a management position with the retail chain, and she was still taking classes in the evening. Cheryl was hoping to attend DePaul University in the fall, but if necessary, she would start with the city college, like Tischa, and work during the day, then transfer after a couple of years. At least she'd be pursuing some form of college.

One of the good things about going to Henry High was the employment training program. In the program, graduating seniors were allowed to attend classes in the mornings and hold part-time jobs in the afternoons as a way of gaining employment experience.

Even though she was just a part-time file clerk, Cheryl loved going to work everyday after school, pretending she was just like the other business people maneuvering in and out of the tall office buildings. There was nothing more exciting to her than the hustle and bustle of the downtown area. It was so different from the neighborhood. Everyone downtown seemed important, like they were busy doing important things. Cheryl loved people watching on her way home from work, and would make up stories in her mind about them and what line of business they were in, even though she was sure a good number of them were probably file clerks or typists just like she was. However, if she saw a man or woman wearing a nice navy blue or black pinstriped suit and carrying a briefcase, she just knew he or she had to be an attorney, or the president of a corporation. Each day after last period, Cheryl would catch the express bus and head downtown, carrying her books in a canvas briefcase and wearing her sneakers with her heels in the bag. She used to carry a large book bag to school, but after she started working downtown, she began carrying the briefcase because it made her feel like a real businessperson.

Not long after Cheryl began working, Jennifer got a part-time job downtown as well as a relief receptionist at a small law firm. Cheryl would walk over to Jennifer's office after work and wait for her to complete her shift and they'd catch the bus back home together. Jennifer was petite and pretty with large brown eyes, a fair complexion, and long sandy brown hair which she usually wore pulled back in a pony tail. She was on the smart side, but everyone just assumed she got the receptionist job because of the way she looked. Being a flirt by nature, she enjoyed the extra attention she got from some of the attorneys at the firm. Even though most of them were married, she flirted back with them shamelessly just because she could. Many of them were old enough to be her father, so the thought of actually getting together with them grossed her out. But there was one of them that she didn't find gross at all. He was also married, and he was her boss.

Chad Phillips was about thirty-three years old and he was the head partner at the firm Phillips, Willis and McKenzie. He and

Mark Willis, one of the other partners, had built the firm from nothing a few years earlier. Steve McKenzie, the newest partner had joined the firm recently, and together they were building one of the most prominent corporate law firms in the city. And Jennifer was in complete awe of Chad. He was not really tall, sort of short if you asked Cheryl, but when he entered the room he commanded attention. So she could understand how a young high school girl, who was used to hanging around with teenage guys in jeans and sneakers on a regular basis, could be awestruck by him.

As Cheryl was sitting in the reception area waiting for Jennifer's shift to be over one afternoon, Chad walked out of his office. His starched white shirt was rolled up at the sleeves, but the monogram with the letters CSP on the cuff was still visible from the other side. Attached at the collar of the shirt was a red, white and gray silk tie, which was loosened slightly at the neck. Chad had an olive toned complexion and he wore his black curly hair neatly combed away from his face, showing off his chiseled features. He also had intense blue gray eyes that he would fix directly on the eyes of whomever he was speaking with, at times, causing the other person to look away.

"Jen please make sure this package is messengered over to Bob Keenan's office before you leave today. He's probably gone for the day, but I want to make sure he has it first thing in the morning." Chad asked.

"Sure Chad, no problem!" I'll make sure Arrow picks it up before I leave today." Jennifer said looking flushed. "You think Bob's gone already?"

"Yeah, I think so. Today's his golf day you know." Chad said with a grin, revealing a deep dimple in his cheek. His eyes sparkled for a brief second. Then he disappeared back into his office as quickly as he appeared and closed the door.

Jennifer grinned back staring as he walked back into his office, then looked at Cheryl and mouthed the words "F-I-N-E!"

Cheryl looked at Jennifer and shook her head giggling low enough so that Chad couldn't hear her.

"Guess what?" Jennifer said. "I might be taking a full-time job at the firm after graduation. I was talking to the office manager the other day in the restroom, and she told me they were going to be looking for another paralegal in a couple of months. I told her my graduation was in a couple of months and I might be interested in applying for that job after I graduated. She told me if I was really interested, she would put in a good word for me with Chad, Tom and Steve. She said she knew they were pleased with the job I've been doing with the front desk, and I should have a good chance of moving up."

"What! Are you for real? But what about college, I thought you wanted to go to Grambling in the fall? That's all you've been talking about since junior year. And didn't you say that's where your parents wanted you to go because they met there? What are they going to say?" Cheryl asked.

"I know, but I really like the law firm. It's a fun place. Plus, I would start off in a paralegal training program. It's a six-month program and the firm will be paying the tuition for the training. After six months, I'll be a certified paralegal, and who knows, if I still want to, I can go on to school and even law school. The firm has a tuition reimbursement program and they like to promote from within. I know Chad likes me so I'm sure he'll give me the job if I apply for it."

"Girl, Chad is married. What do you mean you know he likes you?" Cheryl asked. "Plus he's w-h-i-t-e!"

"So what...I'm not prejudiced...I like em all shades and colors." Jennifer said laughing. "Plus, I wasn't talking about like me like that anyway. I was just saying I know he likes me as a person and I do a good job and everything. He would probably rather give the job to someone he's comfortable with already anyway. You know, he's kind of reserved that way."

Cheryl looked at Jennifer. She knew exactly what she meant. She realized that she'd spent the last few years pining away secretly over Matthew, but Matthew Robinson was just a schoolgirl crush. Chad was a different matter altogether, and she hoped Jennifer wasn't trying to get herself into something that was over her head. Like her mother would say, she hoped she wasn't writing a check her behind couldn't cash. At that point Jennifer grabbed the phone to call the messenger service.

"Anyway, girl let me make this phone call. I don't want to have to be here all night. What time is it anyway? We don't want to miss the 5:30 bus."

"It's almost 5:05 so I hope they can get here in the next fifteen minutes." Cheryl responded dryly.

"No problem. Once they know it's for me, they'll be here in ten minutes. Those boys will do anything for me." Jennifer said with a smug grin.

Cheryl looked at Jennifer, shook her head and grinned back. Jennifer was so full of herself, but she was her girl anyway.

❧❦

"Girl, can you believe graduation is in three weeks and the prom is Friday? It seems like this year just flew by. I know one thing, Mike better be able to pick up his tux on Thursday. I told him to get measured before last week, but all he could think about was hanging out with the football team. Football season has been over since January, but they just can't seem to part with each other. Did you get the ivory shoes you were looking for to match your dress Jen?" Charity asked.

"Yeah girl, I found the freshest shoes at Penny's last Saturday. I was going to have them dyed to match my dress, but my mother said ivory would work better." Jennifer replied.

"You're still going with Robert, right?" Cheryl asked slyly.

"Of course, who else am I going to go with?" Jennifer asked rolling her eyes at Cheryl.

"Oh, I don't know, I thought maybe Chad had asked his wife if he could take you." Cheryl responded looking at Charity laughing.

"You know what? You are beginning to get on my last nerve with all that Chad stuff, I should never have told you anything. I'm getting so I can't stand you!" Jennifer said to Cheryl still rolling her eyes.

"So what, I can't stand you either!" Cheryl replied shaking her head from side to side and jumping in Jennifer's face.

"Both of you need to just shut the heck up! And don't be trying to start nothing in my mother's house. I just colored my nails and I'm not about to mess them up trying to break ya'll up. Anyway, you know you're both lying." Charity said jumping in between Jennifer and Cheryl.

"I know I am." Jennifer said grinning then pushing Cheryl backwards causing her to land on Charity's bed. "You believe everything I say don't you?"

"Not really, I hardly ever believe anything you say." Cheryl replied smiling. "....Well, since you two already have everything you need for the prom I guess I need to jet. I still need some rhinestone earrings. I was going to wear my mother's but they look a little tired. Tischa said she saw some at the mall that would go with my dress, and I'm supposed to meet her in about thirty minutes, so I'm outta here." Cheryl jumped up off Charity's bed. "I guess I'll see you all on Friday, then. What time is the car supposed to pick Tom and me up? He said his brother was dropping him off at my house around six."

"Don't worry, we'll be at your house at six too. " Charity replied.

"That's cool. I'll talk to you later then. I love you Jen!" Cheryl said giving Jennifer a quick peck on the cheek as she ran out the bedroom door.

"I love you too heifer!" Jennifer yelled after her still rolling her eyes.

Chapter Five

Everyone in the Marks home was gathered around Cheryl gawking at her as though she was a masterpiece on the wall of the Art Institute or the Picasso in Daley Plaza. Mr. Marks stood back proudly holding her hand and looking down at her in her sleeveless lavender satin prom dress.

"Look at my baby girl! She is gonna be the prettiest girl at the prom!" He said grinning.

"Aw Daddy, please." Cheryl said bashfully. She really hated being the center of attention.

Mrs. Marks rubbed her fingertips lightly up the back of Cheryl's hair making sure her up do was firmly in place. She then fluffed out the full bottom of Cheryl's dress with one hand while holding the camera in the other. "Stand over by the stairs. I want to get a picture of you by yourself before Tom gets here."

"Too late, I think that's him pulling up right now. Cheryl does Tom's brother drive a blue Cavalier?" Tischa yelled.

"Yeah, I think that's him, don't just stand there looking Tischa, let him in. Mama, are you finished with the pictures yet? You already took about a hundred." Cheryl exaggerated. She was beginning to feel warm from all the satin material and started fanning herself with her hand.

"Hey Tom, come on in. Man, you are lookin' too cool with your lavender shirt and black tux and tie." Tischa said holding the door open.

Tom walked in the door grinning and looking down admiring his clothes.

"Thanks Tischa. I went with the black tux since Cheryl wanted to wear lavender. You know, I couldn't be going to the prom in a lavender tux. How are you Mr. and Mrs. Marks?" Tom asked still grinning. Tom was always extremely polite, and he knew how to carry himself well, which is why Cheryl's parents adored him.

"Just fine Tom, you do look handsome, come on over here and let me take a picture of you and Cheryl, doesn't she look beautiful." Mrs. Marks asked as though she wasn't really asking a question but making a statement.

"Thank you Mrs. Marks, and yes, Cheryl always looks beautiful." Tom said grinning at Cheryl. "Hi Cheryl, you really do look nice, I brought this for you. I hope it's the right color." Tom handed Cheryl a plastic box with a lavender corsage in it.

"It's perfect!" Mrs. Marks said reaching for the box. "Here let me help you pin it on." Tom looked relieved as he didn't want to have to fumble with pinning the corsage on Cheryl's chest in front of her parents.

Just as Mrs. Marks was about to take another picture, Tischa yelled once again, "I think that's Charity and her boyfriend in the tan Cadillac in front of the house."

Good, Cheryl thought, I cannot take another picture. "Let's just go outside. It's getting hot in here in this dress." She wined still fanning.

"Okay, everybody go outside, I want to get a picture of Charity and Jennifer with their dates too." Mrs. Marks said picking up the back of Cheryl's dress. "Cheryl, be careful! You don't want to get the bottom of your dress dirty before you even get to the prom."

Finally, after all the poses of Cheryl and her prom group Mrs. Marks could possibly shoot were taken, they piled into the car and drove away. Everyone was thrilled to be riding to the prom in Mike's father's Cadillac. While Charity and Mike sat in the front of the car, it was a little snug in the back with Jennifer, Robert, Cheryl and Tom. But they weren't complaining since it wasn't often a bunch of eighteen-year olds got to ride around wearing formal wear in a Cadillac. But once they reached the ballroom of the downtown hotel where the prom was being held, everything seemed just about perfect. Cheryl felt like Queen for a Night, and Tom made sure she did. He went out of his way to be attentive, getting her chair before she sat down and jumping up to pull it out when she got up. He also made sure she stayed well hydrated, asking if she wanted anything else to drink whenever her punch glass looked like it was about to get empty. And she was beginning to look at Tom in a whole new light. He did look exceptionally handsome in his black tuxedo. His short black hair was neatly trimmed and lined, and he was freshly shaven. He was also wearing the freshest fragrant cologne Cheryl had ever smelled, and just enough of it. Cheryl noticed how the chandelier lights in the ballroom reflected in his eyes. She'd never even noticed the beautiful shimmer of hazel in his eyes, until that night.

The truth was she had been so obsessed with Matthew that she hadn't really allowed herself to really see Tom or anyone else for that matter. And she knew Matthew was at the prom somewhere. The room was so large and there were so many people there that she couldn't see where he and Donna were. But the strange thing was she didn't seem to care. Maybe it was the fantasy of the prom and all, but for some reason, Tom seemed to be suddenly commanding all her attention. After the prom was over, as usual, a good portion of the senior class was headed for rooms at some of the downtown hotels. Some just assumed it was the rite of passage for prom night. But their group opted to go to the large afterset that was being held at one of the dance clubs instead. They danced until the early hours, and then stopped in one of the all night restaurants for a late night snack.

As the morning hours approached, they finally headed home pretty much exhausted. Charity and Mike dropped Jennifer and her date off first, then drove to Cheryl's house to drop her off since Tom lived closer to Charity. When the car stopped in front of the Marks' home, Tom jumped out of the car, and let Cheryl out on his side.

"I'll walk you to your door and see you inside. Don't want anything to happen to you." He said grinning.

"I doubt anyone's up at this hour, but okay, I guess you can walk me to my door." Cheryl smiled. "Thanks Char and Mike, we had a ball didn't we?"

"Yeah girl we did! I'll call you tomorrow okay?" Charity said grinning at Cheryl and then winking at Tom.

"Okay, I'll talk to you tomorrow then. See ya Mike." Cheryl said grinning back.

"See ya Cheryl. All right Tom man, try not to get too comfortable, I got to get this baby back to my old man in one piece. He's probably gonna be waiting at the door when I drive up anyway." Mike said.

"Be back in a minute." Tom said, not really looking back at Mike.

Tom stood at the door as Cheryl fumbled through her purse for her key. Once she found it, she placed it in the keyhole and opened the door. The living room was completely dark and she could tell everyone in the house was long asleep. Tom was standing awkwardly at the door as she stepped in.

"You want to step in for a minute?" She asked.

"Um…sure, I can step in for a while. I don't think Charity and Mike will mind too much." Tom whispered as he stepped in behind her not really caring that much if Charity and Mike did mind.

Cheryl turned around and looked toward the Cadillac sitting in front of her house. She pushed the front door as though attempting to close it, but didn't quite close it all the way. "I had a really good time tonight. I'm glad I went with you after all."

"I'm glad you went with me too. I had a really good time too." Tom said a little nervously looking into Cheryl's eyes. He then reached out and took her hand. He stared at her in silence for a brief moment, then without saying anything else he leaned forward and kissed her lightly. Cheryl leaned into him and placed her arms around his neck. It was hardly the first time she'd been kissed. She'd given a goodnight peck or two to a couple of Mike's football friends after a movie or football game. But she'd never actually felt quite the way she felt when Tom kissed her. It was as though she could feel tiny jolts of electricity flow through her body. She leaned in closer to Tom when he suddenly pulled away.

"Good night Cheryl." He said softly.

"Good night Tom." Cheryl answered whispering.

Just as Tom was about to step out of the door, he turned back around and asked, "Is it okay if I give you a call tomorrow? Maybe we can get together with Charity and Mike and go see a movie or something?"

"Yeah…okay, that sounds good Tom." Cheryl answered quickly.

"Okay then…. I'll call you tomorrow." Tom replied.

Tom turned, opened the door, and walked out closing it behind him. Cheryl locked the door and leaned back against it for a moment, not wanting to move just yet. She then grabbed the bottom of her dress and reached down and slipped off her shoes. She suddenly realized the pointy shoes were killing her, but for some reason, she hadn't noticed until after Tom left. As she walked up the stairs towards her bedroom door carrying her shoes, she began to reflect on the events of the evening. Her prom night wasn't anything like what she'd long dreamed it would be, but it had been perfect just the same.

Once her lavender satin dress and heels were finally tucked away in the closet, Cheryl climbed into bed and pulled the covers up to her shoulders. That night when she went to sleep before she closed her eyes, she glanced at the clock on her dresser and wondered if Tom had made it home yet.

ॐॐ

By the time graduation day rolled around Cheryl could not wait another minute to get out of high school. She was graduating with honors, and Mrs. Marks made sure she called all of their relatives, some even long distance, to let them know, even though there were only enough invitations for the immediate family. Unfortunately, Pearl was not going to be able to make the graduation ceremony. She'd gotten a new job with a small television station in Atlanta and they were sending her to New York that week on an assignment. She was training to be a reporter, and was going to research a story, so she didn't have time to fly back to Chicago that week. Tischa was going to be there though, and she was going to be bringing her new boyfriend.

She'd met Steve at a retail industry seminar, and during a break, they shared a cup of coffee together. Turned out, he was a manager at a men's wear clothing store downtown, and just as into fashion as Tischa. They both walked into the graduation together looking like they'd just stepped out of a discount fashion magazine. Mr. and Mrs. Marks, and Ralph and Carl, who had become rather handsome young men, sat in the front of the auditorium, waving and snapping pictures as Cheryl walked down the aisle along with the other graduates.

After graduation, there was a lot more change in store for everyone. During the summer, Cheryl started working fulltime at the insurance firm downtown, and taking classes in the evenings. In the fall, she'd

42

enrolled in the city college as she'd planned. Even though she had a 3.0 grade point average, she still didn't have the money to start at a university just yet. Jennifer decided to do as she'd planned, and after taking a couple of weeks off during the summer, decided to enroll in the paralegal program at Phillips, Willis and McKenzie full-time. Mike ended up getting a football scholarship to Jackson State and Charity followed him there. The night before Charity left for Mississippi, Cheryl and Jennifer surprised both Mike and her with a going away party that mainly had Mike's football teammates as guests. Some of them were fortunate enough to be playing college ball that year like Mike, but others weren't as lucky and would be staying behind trying to figure out something else to do with their lives.

The next day, there were a lot of tears as Cheryl and Jennifer said goodbye to Charity before her mother took her to the airport. It seemed like they'd all grown up so quickly. It was difficult to believe they wouldn't be hanging out together just about everyday, and were about to experience a taste of the real world. They could just tell life was going to be a lot different for them from there on. It was as though they were about to embark on a new journey and didn't quite know where it was going to lead them. While it was an exciting period, it was also a scary one at the same time.

Cheryl's relationship with Tom had begun to develop as well. She'd gone all four years of high school without a steady boyfriend, but after the prom date, it was all about Tom. True to his word, the next day after the prom, Tom called Cheryl and they agreed to meet Charity and Mike for a movie. During the movie, Tom placed his arm around the top of Cheryl's chair resting his hand on her shoulder. Whether real or imaginary, Cheryl remembered feeling that same jolt of electricity she felt when he kissed her when his hand touched her shoulder. They shared a large bag of popcorn and laughed at all the funny parts of the movie. Tom kept making little comments during the movie causing Cheryl to laugh even when the movie wasn't supposed to be funny. Cheryl couldn't understand why every time she was with Tom, she didn't seem to think about anything or anyone else. And Tom always made her feel as though she was the only one in the world who mattered to him.

It was hard to believe she hadn't even noticed Tom at school. The only reason she agreed to go to the prom with him in the first place was because Charity and Jennifer had already had their dates, and she didn't want to be dateless or a charity case having to be fixed up with one of Mike's friends. Mike was a sweet guy, but his friends weren't really her type. Not that she really knew what her type was. But she knew they weren't the smartest guys in the world. The basis of their conversations usually consisted of what this ball player was doing or what the score of last night's game was. No offense to Charity and Mike, but she was just not that into sports. She just kept up the pretense in order to fit in. Tom was different though. He was smart and funny and she could actually talk to him for hours at a time, almost like she did with one of her girlfriends. But her conversations with Tom weren't based on what shoes they'd just bought, or which girl looked nasty in school that day.

Tom had received a scholarship to Northwestern and planned on majoring in Journalism. He planned on getting his degree and working on a major newspaper after graduation. And most likely, he was going to end up doing just that. It was difficult not to believe that Tom could do anything he set his mind to do. He seemed to know everything about anything, as he spent most of his spare time reading novels and magazine articles. Cheryl found herself mesmerized and hanging on every word when he would get on his soapbox and start debating about what was wrong with the world and how he would fix it if he could. Tom was a debater, but Cheryl could lean toward being opinionated herself. She loved purposely irritating Tom by disagreeing with him just to get a stimulating conversation out of him, and she was going to miss their friendly spats when he was away at school. It was going to be difficult to stay on the phone all night once they began to get into college life and classes. The one good thing about him going to Northwestern though, was he would only be an hour or so away by car, so Cheryl could visit him, or he could visit her at least a couple of times a month.

Cheryl wasn't sure, but she had a feeling that she and Tom would be together forever. At least that was what she'd planned.

Chapter Six

The elevator door swung open to reveal the signage reading Phillips, Willis and McKenzie. Jennifer stepped through the elevator doors into the lobby of the tenth floor, and stared at the large gold block letters. She felt as though she'd never actually seen those letters before, even though she'd only been away for a couple of weeks. But this was her first day as an actual full-time employee of Phillips, Willis and McKenzie, and in six months, she would be a paralegal, working side by side with the attorneys. This could possibly be the beginning of an exciting law career for her if things worked out. As Jennifer stood staring at the sign, imagining that one day it could possibly read Phillips, Willis, McKenzie and Thompson, as in Jennifer Thompson, Attorney at Law, she heard a familiar voice.

"Well good morning Ms Thompson, how are you today? Are you ready to get started working harder than you ever have in your life?" Chad asked.

Jennifer swung around startled at the sound of Chad's voice. He was smiling at her with his usual intensity. He had a way making you feel as though he was looking through you while looking at you at the same time.

"Chad! Good Morning! I didn't see you over there. You're early this morning aren't you? I mean I know you usually don't get here until around 9:00." Jennifer said trying to sound calm, yet sounding completely rattled.

"I know...I'm a slack off." Chad grinned. "I have John Morris of Morris and Green coming in this morning so I wanted to get in early and review a couple of documents before our meeting. We're going to be working on a project together. I know you've got other exciting things to do today, so I won't keep you. That Jill is a hard taskmaster I hear. She likes to crack the whip so you'd better get going. First day of training, exciting stuff, huh?" Chad said still smiling. Then he turned and walked toward his office.

"You idiot." Jennifer thought to herself. "How dare you question the head of the firm about what time he gets here in the morning? It's his firm and he can get here anytime he wants to."

"Yes it is. I, uh, I better get going. Have a good day Chad. I hope your meeting goes well." Jennifer said turning quickly and pushing open the glass door leading to the main office floor.

She raced down the corridor into the open large room filled with small cubicles. The walls of the large room were lined with glass doors revealing offices of various shapes and sizes. She could hear the muffled voices of workers on telephones and private conversations as she walked by. Jennifer found the small cubicle with her name engraved in white on the black shiny nameplate attached to the outside wall of the cubicle. Inside was a large desk with a computer on it that took up most of the space and a hook attached to the inside wall of the cubicle. She took off her thin jacket and hung it on the hook, placed her new brown leather bag in the desk drawer, and sat down in the small gray chair behind the desk.

"I can't believe I had to run right into Chad first thing in the morning and make a fool out of myself. I didn't even have time to go to the ladies' room and comb my hair, which is probably all over my head." She thought, running her hands over her hair and combing it back into place with her fingers.

She set motionless for a moment trying to gain her composure. Then she looked around the small cubicle, the reality that she was actually sitting in her own cubicle on her first day as a paralegal trainee was setting in.

"Hey, are you the new paralegal trainee? I heard you were starting today." Said a strong feminine voice peppered with a touch of a Latin accent. "You used to work at the front desk in the afternoon right? I remember seeing you as I was making my mad dash out the door in the evening. Hi, I'm Rachel Lopez. I sit in the cubicle right behind you."

Jennifer looked up at the young Latino woman standing at the entryway of her cubicle. She was slender with long dark hair and large dark brown eyes. Jennifer sized her up quickly, looking her over from head to toe. She was pretty and wearing a simple white blouse tucked into a short dark green skirt and simple black pumps. Jennifer noticed the black pumps were the same ones she'd seen at the mall and started to buy, and was suddenly grateful she hadn't bought them after all. She couldn't be wearing the same shoes as the woman sitting right behind her. She took her reputation for being the best-dressed woman in the room way too serious for that.

"Hi, I'm Jennifer. Jennifer Thompson, I guess you already knew that from my name plate though. I think I do recall seeing you running out of here in the evenings. I guess now we'll be running out together." Jennifer said standing up to shake Rachel's hand.

"I'm sure we will. Everybody just about breaks the door down at five around here. Of course, there will be times when that won't work though. You'll find that out soon enough, so enjoy your training period while it lasts. Once you become an actual paralegal they'll start to work your butt off. Chad and the boys don't play. They do compensate well though as long you do what's expected." Rachel looked Jennifer up and down examining her brown and tan ensemble. "That's a nice outfit you're wearing Jennifer. I see I may have a new shopping buddy. There are a couple of nice shops downtown, and sometimes I spend my entire lunch hour shopping on State Street.

Maybe we can go together sometime." Rachel said still looking at Jennifer's shoes.

"Sure, I love to shop. That's one of the reasons I was looking forward to working full-time downtown. Before, by the time I would get here after school, I just had time to run in and start manning the phones, and after work, my girlfriend and I would be running to catch the five thirty bus, so we didn't have a lot of time for shopping. Now I actually get a lunch hour along with a larger paycheck too, life is good!" Jennifer said laughing. She then lowered her voice and leaned toward Rachel. "So, how is it really working for Chad? I mean, I dealt with him as far as doing his mail and answering his calls when I was a part-time receptionist in the afternoons, but how is it *really* working with him?"

Rachel leaned in a bit as well. Jennifer could already tell she was the type that liked to share information.

"Um, Chad's cool. He's tough but he's fair. Just don't piss him off, because if he gets mad there'll be hell to pay. He walks around looking really easy going, and he is as long as everyone is doing what they're supposed to do, but he will bite your head off if you mess up. Once, one of the associates screwed up a deal and cost the firm a lot of money and Chad went off! The poor guy was almost in tears. Luckily, Chad didn't fire him, but gave him another chance. But I doubt he's going to make that mistake again." She whispered.

Jennifer's eyes widened. She was surprised by what she was hearing. She couldn't believe her Chad had such a mean side to him, but she could understand how he could. She'd noticed how just his presence commanded a lot of respect and everyone seemed to jump whenever he spoke, and seemed tense around him even when he was being nice. But instead of putting fear in her, this news just made her more in awe of him than she was before.

"But everyone really likes Chad around here...especially some of the ladies." Rachel said slyly. "The man is good looking, and there are a couple of girls in the office who have been rumored to have tried to get with him if you know what I mean. The jury's still out on whether he took them up on it or not. But there was this one girl who was really into him. I mean everyone could tell, even though she thought she was hiding it. She was always running in his office asking him questions about how to handle certain cases when there were other attorneys in the office she could ask and not have to bother Chad. The man is the principal partner after all. But she wanted him to notice how smart and ambitious she was. You know, trying to get some brownie points. Well, I guess it paid off, because Chad started inviting her to attend client meetings when she didn't really have anything to do with the case. She also started getting assigned a lot of the more prestigious clients. She was Chad's "it" girl, or so she thought. There were all kinds of rumors flying. The gossip going around was Chad's wife found out about an affair between them and made him let her go. No one really knows for sure, but all we know is she was here one day, and the next, we were told she got another position with Morris and Green." Rachel said winking one eye.

At that point, Jennifer's telephone rang. She reached down and placed it to her ear.

"Hello, Jennifer Thompson speaking."

"Jennifer? Hi, this is Jillian Reed. How are you?"

"I'm just fine Jillian, how are you?" Jennifer said quickly.

"Great. I wanted to give you time to get settled in first, but after you're settled, please come by my office. I think you know where I'm located correct?" Jillian asked.

"Yes, of course I remember. I'll be right in." Jennifer said.

"Good, thanks Jennifer, I'll be here waiting for you." Jillian replied.

Jennifer placed the phone back on the receiver and grabbed a memo pad and pen.

"I have to run Rachel, that was Jillian Reed, but we will definitely have to talk later. I look forward to working with you!" She said smiling.

"Uh oh, now it's time for the fun to start. We'll chat some more when you get back. It's going to be nice having you here Jen." Rachel said stepping aside to let Jennifer run past.

Jennifer strolled down the long corridor looking anxiously at the nameplates on the wall as she walked. She hoped she did remember where Jillian's office was. She didn't want to come across looking like a ditz to Jillian on her first day. But her mind kept replaying her interesting conversation with Rachel, especially the part about Chad. So, she wasn't the only woman who was enamored with Chad Phillips. That wasn't so shocking. But apparently, he had a bit of a roaming eye for the ladies too. She didn't know exactly how she felt about that piece of information yet, but she decided to tuck it away in her memory until a later time. Life in the real world was going to be very interesting.

Chapter Seven

"Hey Jen....it's Cheryl. Let me know if you can get away for some serious shopping at lunchtime this Friday. Megan just informed me I need to go to Vegas next week for this huge insurance industry meeting and I need to pick up a new pants suit. It's been a while since I've bought a new one, and since I've been traveling so much lately, my other ones feel played out." Cheryl said. Then she whispered into the phone. "I know one thing I'm really getting sick of living out of my suitcase lately. Ms Thing insists that I go to this meeting even though I just got back from Washington on Tuesday. Anyway, give me a call when you get this message and we can talk then. And by the way, it would be nice if you were at your desk sometime."

Just as Cheryl placed the phone back on the receiver, she glanced at the entrance of her cubicle in time to see the tailored young woman standing in front of her. "Where in the heck did she come from?" She thought. "I know she wasn't there a moment ago. I swear her ability to appear out of nowhere is uncanny."

"Megan, is there something I can do for you?" She asked.

The young woman stood silently for a moment, looking around Cheryl's work area, then pointed at the large brown file on the credenza behind Cheryl's desk. "Is that the Petersen file?" she asked.

Cheryl backed her chair up and took hold of the file folder. "Yes it is. Do you need it for something?" Cheryl asked, struggling to hold up the huge folder.

"Chuck wants to get an update on how this account is coming. Have you been in touch with Petersen yet? This account is on the hot list you know." Megan replied.

"Well, I stayed late last night to review the file and I feel pretty comfortable with everything. I'm having the pricing unit work up some preliminary numbers just to see where we are. Not sure if we're competitive yet, but I hope to know something today, tomorrow morning at the latest. Do you need me to speak with Chuck about it?" Cheryl asked feeling slightly annoyed.

"No, I'll stop by his office and give him an update on the status myself. Thanks." Megan then took the file out of Cheryl's hands. "Are your notes in here?" She asked.

"Yes, there should be an analysis of the account right in the front of the file." Cheryl replied.

"Great." Megan said and turned quickly and started to walk out the cubicle, then she swung back around and said, "Cheryl, by the way, I need you to attend the meeting with the claims unit this afternoon. I'm going to be way too busy to attend. Take notes and be prepared to give me an overview of the meeting tomorrow morning, thanks." Megan called over her shoulder, and then disappeared as quickly as she appeared.

"That woman is starting to really work my nerves." Cheryl said to herself. "Who does she think she is anyway? Take notes and give me an overview tomorrow. I'm too busy to attend." Cheryl mocked. "Well we're all busy Ms Thing. What does she think I do all day, sit here and pick at my nails?"

Cheryl took a deep breath, composing herself. Megan had a way of bringing out the worst, and best in her.

It had been four years since she'd finally finished her degree in Communications at DePaul University, and after graduation, she was offered an opportunity to go into the account executive training program. It had taken ten years, but Cheryl couldn't believe how far she'd come since starting as a file clerk in high school and taking classes part-time. And it had taken her six long years to finally complete her degree, but she'd finally done it. It hadn't been easy by any means. She'd cried a couple of times watching everyone else in the world, other than herself, quickly finish school and climb the corporate ladder. But her inability to go straight through college after high school had held her back a while. As usual, she had to do things the hard way. Some nights after putting in so many hours at the insurance firm, she really didn't feel like going to class. There were days when she would leave the building after work, not sure if she was even going to class that night, but something inside of her would push her forward. Before she knew it, she would be standing in front of the school building, and at that point, she'd have no choice but to go in.

She especially started to feel a little discouraged when she'd hear about her friends and others she'd gone to high school with getting their degrees after just four years of college, and starting exciting new careers, while she just felt like her life was in a deep rut. Charity and Mike both graduated from college after four years, and were now living in a suburb outside Jackson, MS. After graduating from Jackson State, Mike asked Charity to marry him as everyone expected he would. They had a huge fairy tale wedding in Chicago, with Cheryl and Jennifer as bridesmaids. After the honeymoon, they packed up everything and moved back to Mississippi where Mike had taken an assistant coaching job with Jackson State. While Charity had earned a degree as well, she decided to stay home for a while to take care of the new baby. It was unbelievable how quickly Charity moved, but then again, that was typical of Charity. She always knew what she wanted, and always went after it.

And Jennifer had shocked just about everybody with what she'd accomplished. She'd started as a paralegal, and after breezing through the training program, decided to take advantage of the college tuition reimbursement program. She finished her degree in Business Administration and went on to complete law school. Because the law firm had such a commitment to education, they gave her a great deal of flexibility so she was actually able to carry full-time class loads, which is the reason she finished as quickly as she did. Cheryl, on the other hand, had to work full-time and take classes in the evenings on a part time basis. But it seemed like things were finally beginning to turn around for her. Getting prior work experience had at least allowed her to already have a foot in the door after she finally graduated. So when the opening came available for the associate account executive, she was at least in the right place at the right time.

She really did owe a lot to Megan, even if she did rub her the wrong way sometimes. She could tell the first day she met her that things were going to be real interesting with her around. After a couple of years at the firm, she applied for and was promoted to an executive assistant. She'd heard a new account executive was starting at the firm and they would need a new assistant to work with her. She was supposedly some hotshot young thing that had just moved to Chicago from Los Angeles. And she was going to need someone who'd been with the company for a little while to show her the ropes, at least from an administrative perspective. Cheryl thought that would be a good opportunity for her to at least get more involved in the actual insurance side of the business, so she applied for and got the job. On her first day in the new position, Cheryl was busy setting up her desk in her new workstation when a tall attractive young woman, who appeared to be not much older than she was walked up behind her.

"You must be my new assistant. Hi, I'm Megan White." She said reaching out her hand and smiling revealing a perfect set of straight white teeth.

Her long black hair was neatly pulled back into a bun at the nape of her neck, and she was smartly dressed in a navy blue pin striped pants suit with a small strand of pearls around her neck. Her eyes slanted when she smiled, revealing her partial Asian heritage. Cheryl later learned Megan's mother was from the Philippine Islands and her father was African American.

Cheryl turned around and smiled back. "Hi Megan...my name is Cheryl Marks, and yes, I am your new assistant. It's nice to meet you."

"It's nice to meet you too. Well Cheryl we're going to have to get together later so you can tell me what I need to know. I'm not yet familiar with how you guys do things around here." Megan said still smiling.

"Oh don't worry. You'll catch on in no time. Just let me know when you're ready, and I'll come in your office and we'll talk. Anything I can do for you just let me know. I can let you know the ins and outs, you know, who's easy to work with and who to avoid if possible." Cheryl said jokingly.

"Oh, don't worry about that." Megan said smiling slyly. "If anybody doesn't cooperate with me, I'll just have someone from my old neighborhood take care of them."

Cheryl looked at Megan for a second. "Your old neighborhood.... you're from Los Angeles right?"

"I was raised in Compton." Megan responded proudly, waved and walked back to her office.

That was Cheryl's first clue that, while Megan was the picture of professionalism, she still had a bit of home girl in her, and she wasn't about to take any crap off of anybody. Megan also turned out to be the epitome of ambition and driven to a fault. And she tended to project the same nearly impossible expectations she placed on herself on everyone else. It was not uncommon to find her bent over her desk at seven o'clock in the morning and still in the same position at seven o'clock at night. Some of the other employees would joke behind her back about receiving messages from her at eleven- thirty at night. One even got one at two-thirty in the morning. Her persistence and dedication did pay off for her, however, because it wasn't long before Megan had made a name for herself at the First National Insurance Company. And senior management rewarded her efforts with a series of promotions. She went from being an account executive, to staff manager, and finally the position she held today as Megan White, Vice President of Sales.

To some extent Cheryl admired Megan's ambition and drive. Here was this young minority woman who'd come from humble beginnings, who was polished and professional and commanded respect from mostly everyone who came in contact with her. There was a lot to admire. But working for Megan could be rather difficult too, especially if things didn't go the way she thought they should. She also enjoyed being in the spotlight and had a way of turning her subordinates' accomplishments into her own. Just the same, Cheryl knew if her path hadn't crossed with Megan White's she wouldn't be as far as she was at the company. Megan recognized Cheryl's potential and desire to do more, and she pushed her constantly to get out of her comfort zone. Cheryl found herself picking up some of Megan's drive and ambition, and it wasn't long before she was glancing at the clock on her desk at seven or even eight o'clock at night herself.

❧❦

Jennifer waved her arms frantically trying to get Cheryl's attention. Cheryl strained her eyes searching the small crowded cafe, finally noticing her friend's frantic wave. She smiled and walked in her direction, squeezing through the other customer's chairs while trying not to bump them with her shopping bags.

"Girl, I was trying to hold this table by putting my bags in the other chair, but everyone was looking at me like they thought I was trying to hog a whole table for myself. You know this place is so tight. If it wasn't for their soup I would've picked somewhere else for us to eat lunch. How much time you got left?" Jennifer asked, taking a small cup of soup from Cheryl's tray.

"It's Friday, I have all the time I need." Cheryl responded dryly. "I've been working my butt off all week and if I want to sit down and have a cup of soup, I'm going to sit down and have a cup of soup."

"Well, I heard that!" Jennifer laughed. "Megan's really been cracking the whip, huh?"

"I tell you, that girl acts like she's working at the Big House and Master's gonna kick her back to the curve with the rest of us if she doesn't whip everybody else back into subjection." Cheryl said laughing.

"It's a shame we have to act like that when we get to the top. It's like we never really feel comfortable with our accomplishments or something. As if we have the mindset that if we don't continue to do more and be better than everyone else, someone's going to come along and take everything that we've worked for back." Jennifer said taking a sip of the creamy soup. "Man, they have the best baked potato soup here!"

"Yeah, this is good soup." Cheryl agreed reaching down and slipping her high heel pump off her foot. "I need to take this shoe off first so I can enjoy it though. The price of looking good while working is a lot of pain."

Jennifer laughed at Cheryl as she removed her shoe.

"Cheryl, you are getting way too tense. You're beginning to act just like Megan. I mean it's a wonder that girl has a man at all. When does she have time to be with him anyway? She's always out of town or at the office. I wonder what her poor husband thinks about all the hours she puts in. It's one thing to be driven and successful but you have to have some type of balance in your life. Your life should be about more than just the kind of work that you do. I mean, at the end of the day, what really matters, you know?"

Cheryl sat a moment and pondered over what Jennifer was saying. Jennifer could come across a bit superficial, but sometimes she could get occasional spurts of deepness. And what she was saying made a lot of sense. To everyone who saw her, Megan appeared to have everything, success, prestige, status and respect, and a good man. But was she really happy? As Cheryl listened to Jennifer continue to exhort on the true meaning of life, she realized that those things, the status, prestige and respect...those were the exact things she'd always dreamed about having and wanting for herself. Ever since she was a young girl staring out the window of the George Marshall housing project, spying at the people coming and going up and down Diamond Row, and dreaming about one day becoming one of them. And she appeared to be on her way to where she wanted to be. But was *she* really happy?

"I haven't heard from Charity lately, have you? What's going on with her and Mike? Can you believe they have baby number two?" Jennifer asked.

"Not since last month some time. No, I can't believe it. If you had asked me in high school which one of us would have ended up a suburban housewife with two kids, it would not have been Charity. Life is a trip isn't it?" Cheryl replied.

"Girl, tell me about it. I mean look at us. Who would have thought that I would have finished law school and be working at a law firm as an attorney instead of as the receptionist? And look at you Ms Big Time Account Executive. And we have the nerve to be working our gold cards too! Long way from Ridgeland, huh?" Jennifer said laughing and pointing at the shopping bags occupying the spare chairs across the table.

Cheryl grinned in agreement. They had come a long way. But just as she was about to revel in the reality of their rise as two sisters from the hood, Jennifer asked a question that put the party on hold.

"So I haven't heard you talk about Tom in a while Ms Cheryl. Whatever happened with him anyway?"

Chapter Eight

Jennifer's question definitely took Cheryl out of her element for a moment. Mainly, because she couldn't even remember the last time she'd even spoken to Tom.

After going to the prom together and graduation, they were practically inseparable for the remainder of that summer. And even after Tom went off to Northwestern, they continued dating long distance. Tom would come home on the weekends whenever possible, that is, if he wasn't scheduled to work that weekend at the university's bookstore. It didn't pay a lot of money, but he'd taken the job anyway to help supplement the scholarship that he received from the university. On occasion, she would make the trip to Northwestern to visit him, but Mr. and Mrs. Marks had a real problem with her spending the weekends away from home to visit her boyfriend. She had to convince them that she was actually staying with a female friend of hers from Henry High, which in actuality was truly the case, since Colleen from her Sophomore PE class was going to Northwestern too, she had the perfect alibi.

The Christian ideals she was taught as a child regarding sex outside of marriage, even though she wasn't that sure Pearl and Tischa were still sticking to that philosophy, were firmly embedded in her psyche. She tried to avoid discussing the issue with anyone as much as possible, even though somehow her girlfriends just knew, but she held firmly to the ideal that she would reserve sex for the man who would be her husband. She knew she was a rare commodity in that day and age, and didn't want everyone looking at her as though she was some strange being from a distant galaxy or something. But no matter how the years began to pile up, she found herself still holding on to that conviction. But it turned out sex wasn't the fundamental issue between her and Tom. While it was true he did sometimes have difficulty maintaining their 'celibate until marriage' relationship, he loved her anyway and respected her convictions. But it was another ideal that Cheryl held firmly to that would prove to be more detrimental to the continuation of their relationship.

Everything was fine for the first three years Tom was away, but as his graduation got closer, things began to change. It wasn't just that Tom began to change, but she was changing as well. After completing a couple of years of college courses, even though she was doing it on a part-time basis, and had quite a few to go, things were beginning to pick up for her at First National Insurance. By that time, she had received the promotion to executive assistant and had just started working for Megan White. Cheryl would spend hours at a time in Megan's office, talking about the inner workings of the industry. Megan loved nothing more than talking about herself and basking in her own accomplishments. She'd constantly point out how she'd turned the department around and how much money she'd brought into the company. She had established herself as the go-to person whenever there was a prestigious account the company wanted, as clients seemed to love her, and senior management knew she would do just about anything to seal the deal.

Her new assistant's eagerness to sit at her feet and learn was not lost on her either, as it was obvious Cheryl held Megan in the highest esteem and would hang on to her every word. And it wasn't long before she soon began to emulate everything she did. Cheryl started to dress like Megan, even though she couldn't afford the high priced designer suits Megan strutted around the office in. She did, however, spend a lot of time at the discount designer outlet malls with Jennifer, doing her best to knock off Megan's style.

There was one piece of advice Megan gave her that she never forgot. Back then, she was pretty much willing to do anything she needed to do to follow in Megan's footsteps. Late one evening while they were sitting in Megan's office shooting the First National breeze, she told her in no uncertain terms that her goal was to one day be in her position. Megan, of course, wasn't the least bit intimidated by that fact, as she had no intention of being in that position much longer. She was always reaching for the next best thing. Cheryl, on the other hand, was desperate for any help she could get. She wanted to know the number one thing she needed to be concentrating on to start her upward mobility track and she was a little surprised by the simplicity of Megan's answer.

"Cheryl, you're an attractive girl. If you'd just learn how to sell your ass, you could get anywhere you want."

Cheryl stared at Megan speechless for a moment. Partly because her comment was a little crass coming from someone so posed and professional, but mainly because she didn't exactly know where she was going with it. But Megan wasn't telling her the way to get ahead was to start turning tricks. The point she was making was that hard work and drive was just a portion of becoming a success. If she wanted to get anywhere, she was going to have to put herself out there. In other words, its not just about what you know, it's just as much about who you know, and whether or not you knew them well. And it wasn't long before Cheryl found out, unfortunately, that was the way most of the business world worked. She could name a number of people at the firm who worked really hard, but they had been slaving away in the same position for years, and most likely, would remain that way. They just didn't seem to have that "it" factor, the thing that got someone like a Megan White noticed.

It wasn't long after that conversation that Cheryl started asking to sit in on meetings with Megan and attending lunches and after work functions with important clients. She would watch intently as Megan interacted with the high-powered clients and senior officials at the firm. She was clearly learning a lot from her mentor and Megan was growing increasingly proud of her protégé. Not only did her relationship with Megan create a change in her work life, but soon the changes began to carry over into her personal life as well. For Cheryl was beginning to grow more and more fascinated with Megan's entire lifestyle.

Megan's husband, Richard, was a senior vice president at one of the largest brokerage houses in Chicago, and he was just as driven as she was. They lived in a luxury condominium on the near North side with a spectacular view of the lakefront. Not long after Cheryl and Megan's work relationship began to evolve, Megan invited Cheryl to a surprise party she was giving for Richard's thirty-second birthday. When Cheryl received the invitation she was thrilled and felt as though she had finally arrived. She was actually going to be socializing with Megan White on a personal level, even visiting her home no less. The invitation made her feel as though she was one of her peers and not just her assistant.

Later that night, as she sat on one of Megan's plush Italian leather chairs, sipping on club soda and enjoying the view from the top, she realized how far her life had come from the little girl who would sit and stare out of the window at the Marshall housing complex. At that moment, Cheryl discovered she did not just desire the type of professional life Megan had, but the type of life Megan had period. She sat and imagined the day she would step off the elevator, after a long day of wheeling and dealing and calling the shots, to her condominium in the sky and live the glamorous life with the man of her dreams. It was just as she'd imagine that girl on Diamond Row lived all those years ago.

Unfortunately, Tom was beginning to look less and less like that man of her dreams. Prior to graduating from college, Tom began to consider which career paths he would pursue. Cheryl, of course, tried to push him in the direction of those that would provide the most compensation and prestige, but for some reason unbeknownst to her, Tom didn't seem to think money and prestige were the most important things in the world. Tom had this idealistic view that only one's true calling in life would provide one with true happiness. And Cheryl just wasn't trying to hear that. She could not believe that after spending four years of college on the Dean's List, rather than choosing a lucrative career, Tom opted to accept a position as a writer for a small newspaper in New York. His reasoning was he'd always wanted to live in New York, to experience the city and obtain the life knowledge he needed to become a great writer. He didn't want to get bogged down with some high pressured, competitive job, as he wanted the flexibility to concentrate on writing his great American novel. The problem was there was no way he was going to be able to afford the luxurious lifestyle Cheryl desired on his nominal salary, especially given the cost of living in New York. And Cheryl just didn't find struggling with Tom in his matchbox apartment in the Big Apple appealing.

After graduation, Tom asked Cheryl to move to New York with him, hoping she could get transferred to First National's New York branch. He hadn't said anything yet, but Cheryl could tell a marriage proposal couldn't be far behind. When Tom first went away to school, all she could dream about was the day Tom would get down on his knee and pull out a brilliant princess cut diamond and place it on her finger. A proposal of marriage from Tom would have been her dream coming true. Unfortunately, it wasn't coming in the package she'd expected. All her life, she had dreamed of the perfect life and being married to the perfect man. But, after all the work she'd put into developing her own life, she just didn't see the same type of growth in Tom. They just seemed to be going in two different directions.

On the day Tom left for New York, she offered to drive him to the airport. Before Tom stepped out of the car, she leaned over and kissed him goodbye. They promised each other they would call as often as possible and she made plans to visit him in New York as soon as she could get away from work. That was six years ago, and while they made an effort to keep in touch the first few years, she couldn't remember the last time she'd spoken to him.

Jennifer's eyes widened, examining Cheryl's face for a response. "Well? When's the last time you heard from him? How's he doing?"

Cheryl shrugged her shoulders glancing out the window next to their table. "I don't really know. I haven't talked to Tom in a while. I think the last time I heard from him he was still working at that paper in New York, but that was a couple of years ago. We tried to keep in touch after he moved, but it just got to the point I was never home when he would call, and being so busy, it was hard to always return his calls. I guess he finally got tired of being the only one calling and not getting a response. I don't know. I assume he's met someone else by now anyway."

Jennifer stared at Cheryl for a moment. "Probably, I mean what's it been about six years since he left? I'm sure he's got somebody else by now...but then again, you don't." She said laughing.

"Well just because you'll date anything with facial hair doesn't mean I have to." Cheryl said rolling her eyes.

"Hey, what can I say, I like a little male companionship once in a while, and if the boys like to keep me company too, then, so be it." Jennifer replied laughing. "But seriously, I know it took a lot for you to let Tom go after all that time together. But you two obviously had different goals in life, maybe it was for the best."

Cheryl shook her head in agreement. She had set standards for herself and regardless of how she felt about Tom, if he wasn't willing to work with her to reach those standards than he obviously wasn't the man for her. She couldn't believe how much she was beginning to sound like Jennifer. She told herself she was not being superficial just because she wasn't willing to compromise what she wanted out of life. If she lowered her expectations just to please Tom, she would have never forgiven herself. There was no way the two of them would have worked together anyway. She kept telling herself she'd done the right thing letting him go.

ॐ

"Cheryl, it's Megan, I need to confirm that you've made your reservations for the Vegas trip."

Cheryl rolled her eyes. "Yes, Megan, I had Rose book a seven a.m. flight for me on Tuesday. That was the earliest I could get out. I should be arriving there about nine a.m. Nevada time. That should give me enough time to check into the hotel and catch a cab over to the conference before the first session. "

"Good. Let me know what hotel you'll be staying at and what your itinerary is before you leave. By the way, I hear Bob Connor is going to be there. You should try and set something up with him while you're out there. We want to make sure no one else tries to woo him before we get a chance to for that Braxton account, even if it doesn't come up until November."

"I know. I have it under control. I spoke with Bob's assistant the other day and set something up with him for dinner Tuesday night."

"Great, what restaurant are you meeting him at? Make sure its someplace decent. We don't want to come across looking like the company's strapped for cash."

"Megan, we'll be dining with a colleague of his at a restaurant in the Bellagio. I've heard the food there is pretty good. Don't worry, you've taught me well. The last thing we'll do is come across looking cheap, as long as you sign off on the expense report."

"When it comes to Bob Connor and Braxton, we will spare no expense. But I expect you to come back with an assurance that Braxton is ours, though. So, don't neglect to sell it."

"I'll do my best." Cheryl glanced at her watch. "Is there anything else?"

"No, I'll be in Los Angeles next week, so if you need me for anything just call me on my cell. Otherwise, I'll try and touch base with you during the evening after your dinner with Bob. Good luck in Vegas. Thanks."

Cheryl placed the phone down on the receiver and sat back in her chair. Megan's demands were beginning to get a bit old. "She's going to be in Los Angeles next week?" Cheryl thought to herself. "Didn't she just get back from Texas yesterday? When does she even get to see Richard? What, does she give him the same 'check-in' phone call once a day that she gives her staff?"

She continued to sit back in the chair staring blankly. Then she glanced over at her computer screen for a moment, looking at the endless listing of open and unopened email messages on the screen. She thought to herself she should probably clean out the opened messages, but was afraid to really get rid of them. What if she needed them later for some reason? She was beginning to feel that way about a lot of things in her life lately. It was beginning to feel like her life was in overload and needed cleaning out…like she needed to let a few things go. But she wasn't quite sure yet what those things were, and if she did know, would she regret letting them go later?

Chapter Nine

Jennifer gave herself another once over in the mirror. She moved in to get a closer look, just to make sure there wasn't anything caught in between her teeth, or that there weren't any stray hairs sticking out of place. She stood back and gave herself a satisfactory gaze just as the door to the restroom swung open.

"Jen, everyone's in the conference room. Do you have everything you need for the meeting?" The young assistant said sticking only her head in the door.

"Thanks Beth. Yes, I think I have everything I need, I'm just supposed to be sitting in with Jill. Is Jillian Reed already in the conference room too?"

"Yes, I believe Jill just walked in. Chad and John Morris walked in a second ago also."

"Okay, I'll be right there then. Thanks Beth."

Jennifer quickly grabbed the leather bound memo pad she'd placed on the ledge in front of the mirror, and rushed out the restroom door. She couldn't have Chad waiting on her to start the meeting. She really should have gotten there before him and John Morris anyway. The last thing she needed to do was to walk in a meeting to find the principal partner and the firm's most important client waiting on her. Hopefully, they were still making small talk and wouldn't notice that she wasn't there yet. This was a great opportunity for her, getting a chance to sit in on a meeting with Chad Phillips and John Morris, and that reality wasn't lost on her.

John Morris, president of Morris and Green was one of Chad's closest friends, and the firm's largest client. Morris and Green were considering entering into a merger with another firm and had retained Phillips, Willis and McKenzie to draw up drafts for the contracts and agreements pertaining to the merger. She couldn't believe that Jill had suggested she accompany her to this meeting as she was just an associate, but Jill had been impressed with the way Jennifer had breezed through the paralegal program and finished law school in record time, and had taken a professional interest in her.

Jillian Reed, a small blonde woman in her early fifties, had a great deal of pull with Chad and the other partners, even if she was a woman. She was a seasoned attorney who everyone, men and women alike, looked up to. Jillian was responsible for the training and supervision of most of the associate attorneys at the firm, and she was well respected in the field based on her years of experience and knowledge of corporate law.

"There you are Jen. John, I don't think you've actually met Jennifer Thompson. Jen is one of our newest associates." Jillian said extending her hand toward Jennifer. "Jen, this is the infamous John Morris." Jillian then pointed toward a distinguished looking middle-aged man with thinning mixed gray hair, wearing black horn-rimmed eyeglasses.

"Hello John. It's a pleasure to finally meet you. I've seen you in the office and spoken to you briefly on the phone before, but I've never actually met you in person." Jennifer said extending her hand to John Morris and trying to hide any bit of nervousness.

"Hello Jennifer, it's nice to meet you as well. I understand you are one of the up and coming attorneys at the firm. I hope Chad isn't driving you too hard." John said winking at Chad.

"Oh, you know how it is John. Of course we're driving her hard. We only expect the best from our attorneys. Isn't that right Jen?" Chad replied smiling at Jennifer.

Jennifer smiled back at Chad and tried to remain cool. "Of course it is Chad. Everyone knows you're a slave driver, and your reputation's safe with me. I can't even remember the last time I had a day off." Jennifer joked.

"Shame on you, Chad, you should give this young lady a day off every now and then. She needs to have some fun too. Life can't just be about work you know." John Morris admonished Chad winking at Jennifer.

"Oh, I'm just kidding John." Jennifer interrupted. "Chad's actually great to work for. Why, I can't imagine having a better boss."

Jennifer smiled at John Morris, and then glanced nervously at Chad.

"Well, shall we get started? We have a lot to discuss." Chad said quickly turning towards John. Jennifer thought she noticed a slight smile forming on the side of his mouth.

Jennifer sat and listened intently as Chad, John and Jill discussed in detail the impending merger, taking notes on key points of the discussion. She occasionally interrupted the conversation, to ask questions about the potential structure of the merger, and the proposed language for the drafts of the contracts, as she wanted to impress Chad, John and Jillian with her knowledge of Morris's corporate structure. She also wanted to make sure they knew that she clearly understood what was needed, and why it needed to be done and wasn't at all confused by the discussion. As the meeting drew to a close, Chad suggested to John that they make plans for drinks and dinner later that evening to continue the discussion. He then turned to Jillian and asked if she was available for dinner.

"Sorry Chad, unfortunately, I promised Bill I'd be home around six tonight. We have a meeting with our accountant...tax issues, you know. We need to figure out where to hide that boatload of money you guys are paying me." Jill joked.

"Oh, well in that case, you'd better make that meeting then." Chad said laughing. "By the way, tell Bill I said hello. I haven't seen him in a while. We'll have to set up a golf date soon."

"I will." Jill replied then turned toward Jennifer. "What about you Jen? Are you available to accompany Chad and John to dinner tonight? It would be great if you were then you could fill me in on everything tomorrow. I can't trust the boys to go alone or there won't be any business discussed at all." Jillian joked.

Jennifer stared at Jillian. "Um... I don't think I have any plans tonight."

"Great, I agree. It would be a good idea for you to come, since you'll be instrumental in drafting the language for the agreements." Chad said looking at his watch. "I have a couple of calls to make. John, we'll plan to meet you around six at Rossi's Café on Dearborn. Does that work for you?"

"That sounds good. I'll meet the two of you at Rossi's at six. Jennifer, it was a pleasure meeting you."

"Thanks John... I'll see you tonight." Jennifer replied.

Chad stood up and walked out of the conference room with John and Jillian following him. Jennifer remained seated for a while longer. What the heck just happened, she thought. Was she actually going to have dinner with Chad and the firm's biggest client? While Phillips, Willis, and McKenzie was not a huge firm, it still meant a lot to be asked to work on the firm's most important client. Jillian would be the lead attorney, and she would most likely involve some of the other associates if the work proved to be too tedious, but she was the one having dinner tonight with Chad and John Morris. At that point, she wished she'd reconsidered her choice of outfit that morning.

࿇

The minute number on the digital clock on Jennifer's desk slowly flipped from eight to nine. Jennifer sat staring at the clock. She'd already cleared off her desk ten minutes ago and was anxiously waiting for time to pass. Chad's assistant had called and informed her that Chad would meet her at the elevator at five forty, and she did not want him waiting on her. It should take them about fifteen minutes by cab ride to get over to Rossi's Café by six. She'd already made a last minute run to the ladies room to make sure her appearance was on point.

"Why didn't I wear my black pants suit today?" She thought to herself. "It would have been much more appropriate for an evening out."

She'd just have to settle for the navy skirt suit she was wearing. "Jennifer, what are you doing?" She suddenly asked herself. "This is a business meeting. Chad and John Morris probably won't even notice I'm at the table once they start discussing the merger and slipping off into guy talk. He only asked me because Jill suggested it and he didn't want to insult her. And Jill just wanted to make sure she was kept in the loop on everything and didn't want to have to rely on Chad for that." Jillian was a self- sufficient woman and didn't like having to rely on the boys at the firm for anything. "You are insignificant to this situation." She told herself. She just felt that if she kept telling herself she was unimportant, she could relieve some of the pressure she was feeling.

Jennifer quickly grabbed her small Gucci handbag from her desk drawer and leather portfolio and strutted briskly toward the elevator lobby. When she reached the lobby, she saw Chad with Mark Willis standing near Chad's office talking. Chad was wearing his black cashmere wool suit jacket and carrying his trademark black leather briefcase, looking as impressive as ever. Jennifer stood to the side and waited for the two men to wrap up their discussion. Chad was obviously discussing with Mark the John Morris meeting and the upcoming dinner. Since Morris was the firm's most important client, all the partners were interested in anything that concerned him. While Jennifer waited patiently for Chad, a few late leaving employees walked past her on their way to the elevator. She noticed a couple of them watching Chad and Mark as they waited for the elevator, then once they noticed her lingering nearby, they started to stare at her, obviously wondering what she was doing hanging around them. A couple of women who were standing in the lobby began to whisper as they stepped on the elevator. Jennifer began to feel awkward standing around waiting for Chad and Mark to stop talking, so she moved in closer toward them in order to get their attention, which turned out to be a good move.

"Oh there you are. Are you ready to go?" Chad asked as if just noticing her.

"Yes, I've been standing here for a while. I didn't want to interrupt you two. You looked like you were discussing something really important." She said smiling and turned to Mark. "How are you doing this evening Mark?"

"I'm fine Jennifer. You guys have a good dinner." He responded as he waved and walked over to his office door.

"Thanks Mark. I'll fill you in tomorrow morning." Chad called out as he walked to the elevator door and pushed the button to go down to the building's lobby.

"Well we'll buy John a nice juicy thick steak, and a couple of glasses of wine, and hit him up for more business for the firm, how's that sound Jen?" Chad joked.

"Sounds like a plan to me Chad. He won't know what hit him when we're through with him." Jennifer responded smiling.

The elevator doors swung open and Chad stepped back to let Jennifer on the elevator first. Jennifer began to feel a little less anxious. She was glad Chad appeared to be in such a mellow mood. There was something about stepping into the elevator away from the activity of the firm that felt relaxing…. freeing. They were lucky enough to catch a cab right in front of the building. During the cab ride, Chad made small talk with Jennifer asking about how things were going for her at the firm or if she had any problems with anything. Jennifer knew that it was customary for management to ask those types of questions, to show an interest in their staff, so she was selective about what her responses were. When they got in front of the restaurant, Chad handed the driver a bill and instructed him to keep the change. He opened the door, stepped out, and held the door for her. Jennifer's mind immediately started playing tricks on her and she began to feel for a second as though she and Chad were on a first date or something. She began to uncontrollably wander back to the school girl crush she'd had on him so many years ago. Looking back to then, it was hard to believe that she was in the position to be at an after work dinner meeting with Chad Phillips. She quickly dismissed those thoughts.

John Morris was already at the restaurant when Jennifer and Chad walked in, and was already seated. The hostess showed them to John's table, smiling at Chad as she walked away. Jennifer fully understood and gave the hostess an "I know exactly how you feel" glance as she left the table. It was completely understandable that other women found him just as attractive as she did.

The rest of evening went by smoothly and quickly. While Chad and John spent most of the evening discussing the merger and sharing tidbits of inside information, they made an effort to include her in the conversation, asking her what her thoughts were on certain issues. After the business aspect was out of the way though, the conversation turned more casual, and personal. After the steaks were finished off, and he'd polished off a couple of rounds of wine, John's attention turned toward Jennifer, and he wanted to know more about her from a personal level. He asked her how long she'd been at the firm, how she liked working there, where she'd gone to school, where she lived, and whether she was married or single. It was clear his interest in her was much more than professional. Jennifer was used to getting that type of attention and was well versed in how to handle flirtation from middle-aged men. While John's flirting in front of Chad was somewhat uncomfortable for her, she went along with his advancements, given his importance to the firm. She also felt he was harmless since he was almost twice her age. She and John were engaged in a round of lighthearted conversation when she noticed Chad was strangely quiet. She glanced over at him, and noticed he was glaring at John with a relative degree of irritation.

"John, I'm really happy I got an opportunity to meet with you today. It was truly an honor and a pleasure. I hope we can do a good job for you and all goes well with the merger." Jennifer said trying to get the conversation back on a professional track. She looked over at Chad again. He was still looking irritated, and she was beginning to feel more uncomfortable than before.

"Well Jen, I must say, I am happy you came along. You are indeed an impressive young lady. Chad needs to let you out of the office more often and stop working you so hard." John said. He was beginning to slur his speech just slightly.

"Thanks John, it's nice to have someone of your caliber in my corner." Jennifer responded looking at Chad smiling nervously.

"We already know Jennifer is one of our brightest associates and we are happy to have her. As she said, she started with us when she was just a kid in high school, and has worked really hard to get to where she is today." Chad said looking at John, then glanced at Jennifer and smiled briefly.

Jennifer sat silently for a moment as Chad and John finished off the bottle of wine. It was nice to hear him being so complimentary of her. She tried not to blush, but she could feel the color rising in her face. It was a good thing they were taking a taxi home after the dinner, because they obviously had way too much to drink to do any driving. After settling the bill, Chad flagged down a cab for John since he lived in the northern suburbs and had the farthest to go. And since the restaurant was slightly north of downtown, he suggested he and Jennifer share a cab back to the downtown area, where he lived, and Jennifer take the cab the rest of the way home. As they sat in the back seat of the cab, Jennifer noticed Chad was still a little quiet. The atmosphere on the way back from the restaurant was a lot thicker than the ride over, and she couldn't shake the uneasy way she was feeling.

"John's really a nice guy. I was a little nervous about meeting with him today, but I'm glad I got to come along. Thanks for inviting me Chad." She said, trying to break the tension.

"You're welcome. I'm glad you came along too Jennifer. It's good to get that type of exposure sometimes." Chad responded. He had that intense look on his face as though he had something serious on his mind. There was a moment of awkward silence again. As the cab driver pulled over to the curb in front of Chad's high rise building, Chad paused for a second then turned to Jennifer and looked her in the eye.

"Jennifer, I would like you to get even more exposure with working with some of our more high profile clients. The firm has a number of lucrative clients that bring a good deal of revenue into the firm. John Morris is just one of many. I have a couple of meetings coming up next week, and I would like you to accompany me to a few of them."

"Um…sure Chad…that would be great. I enjoyed observing you interact with John today, and I feel as though I've learned a lot about handling clients of his caliber." Jennifer was surprised by Chad's offer but tried to answer as calmly and as nonchalant as possible.

"Good, I'll have my assistant give you the information regarding the meetings next week, you know, who the clients are, and where we'll be meeting. I think we'll set up another dinner meeting for next Tuesday. I assume you're free that evening." Chad asked as though not really asking.

"I look forward to hearing from her, and yes, I'm pretty sure my schedule is open for next week." She responded.

"Then it's a date. Have a good weekend Jen. I'll see you next week." Chad then reached in his pocket, took out a small leather wallet, opened it and took out his corporate credit card, and then handed it to Jennifer. "Here you go. Will you be okay from here?" He asked. His eyes were still fixed firmly on hers.

"Sure Chad, I've taken cabs home after a few of those ten hour work days. Don't worry, I'll be fine." She replied.

"Then have a safe ride home, and I'll see you next week. Enjoy your weekend." He then reached out and touched her arm softly and smiled.

Jennifer looked at him and smiled back. "Thanks Chad." She whispered. She was suddenly having difficulty speaking. Chad then picked up his briefcase, opened the door and stepped out onto the curb.

As the cab pulled away from the curb, Jennifer turned and watched as Chad walked to the entrance of his building. The doorman nodded at him with casual familiarity, Chad nodded back and disappeared into the building. Her heart was pounding inside her chest and her mind was racing. Could this day have really happened? She never would have imagined it, but she'd spent most of the entire day and evening with Chad Phillips, the man she'd practically worshiped since she was a teenager. She'd eventually grown up and let those feelings go over the years, telling herself it was just a silly crush, but now could there possibly be something happening between them? Or was it all in her head. Her mind went back to her high school days as the part-time receptionist for the firm, when she would sit at her desk and practically have a breakdown every time Chad came out of his office or said anything to her. She thought about her first day as a paralegal trainee when she ran into him in the elevator lobby, and how awkward she'd felt after that meeting. Then she thought about the conversation she'd had with Rachel Lopez that very day regarding the rumors concerning Chad and some of the other female attorneys. Now she began to wonder if those rumors were actually true. She glanced down at Chad's platinum credit card in her hand and rubbed her fingers over the raised letters. And she couldn't help but wonder... had she just been appointed Chad Phillip's new 'it' girl?

Chapter Ten

"Ladies and Gentlemen, we have begun our descent into Las Vegas, NV. The pilot has turned on the Fasten Seatbelt sign. Please make sure your trays are stored and your seats are in the upright position. The weather in Las Vegas is sunny and warm and the temperature is about eighty-eight degrees. We should be landing in about thirty minutes. Please enjoy your stay in Las Vegas, NV and thank you for flying with us today."

Cheryl peered out the airplane window. She could see a mixture of mountains and cactus and dry heat, and the tips of the massive hotels and casinos lining the strip were beginning to come into view. The glare from the sun started to hurt her eyes, so she pulled the shade over the window down. She always hated this part of the flight anyway and didn't care to watch the plane land. The only part of the actual landing that appealed to her was the feeling of relief when the wheels touched the ground and screeched to a complete halt. She turned towards the file she'd pulled out of her tote bag and took another quick glance at the documents. She'd practically memorized everything she could about Braxton Corporation, which was domiciled in San Diego, CA, had been incorporated since 1967, whose CEO was a gentleman by the name of John Richardson, who'd received his MBA and an undergraduate degree in Psychology from Yale University. John had been the CEO for the last five years and had quickly turned the company into a multi-billion dollar corporation. Yes, she knew everything there was to know about Braxton, including the fact she needed to land this account. Megan wanted Braxton for First National and Cheryl knew there was no way she could leave Las Vegas without a commitment from Bob Conner that they were going to be given serious consideration.

Bob Conner was a scraggly middle-aged insurance broker who worked for the largest insurance brokerage firm in the country, Global International, and it was his responsibility to place the insurance for Braxton. Bob had been an insurance broker for the last twenty years, and was a crafty and seasoned salesman. She admired Bob's reputation, but selling First National to him was not going to be easy. Her competitors were most likely pulling out all the stops to get him to give them the business just as she intended to do. She gathered all the documents she had laid across her lap and placed them back in the folder, then put the folder back into her tote bag. Then she pushed the tote under the seat in front of hers with her foot just in time for the flight attendant to walk by and give her an admonishing look. As the plane rolled across the runway, Cheryl glanced at her watch. She had just enough time to grab a cab to the hotel, check in, and then grab another cab to the conference. It seemed like she was always in a crunch for time regardless how much she tried not to be. Once the plane stopped rolling, she jumped up even though she had to wait for the passengers at the front of the plane to disembark before she could even move out of her seat and get her suitcase out of the overhead storage.

"Come on people!" she yelled to herself. "Why is it taking so long to get off of this darn plane?" Finally, she was able to step out of her seat and grab her small suitcase. She struggled with lifting it out of the storage unit. Why did she pack so much stuff for just two nights anyway? She stepped off the plane and headed toward the ground transportation signs, glancing around the airport as she walked through. The heat was permeating through the airport walls and her gray silk pants suit was beginning to feel like a heavy weight against her body. The people sitting around the airport looked so laid back and comfortable. Most of them were wearing shorts, tank tops and sandals, and looked like tourists who were on their way to hit the casinos or whatever else Vegas had to offer.

Cheryl rolled her suitcase with one hand and held her tote bag with the other, fumbling through it to find a copy of her itinerary. She was absolutely lost without it as it was the only way she could remember where she was supposed to be next. She searched the piece of paper and found the exact address of her hotel so she could give it to the taxi driver. As she walked through the airport, she could hear the click of her high heeled pumps against the tile of the airport floor. The leather felt tight and rubbed against the sides of her feet. As Cheryl continued to watch the tourists at the airport, she began to feel a little envious. Everyone looked as though they didn't have a care in the world and she couldn't remember the last time she'd felt that way. Lately, if she did take a trip, she'd just been traveling for business, which wasn't exactly the same thing. Even when she did take a couple of days off, she found she was checking email and voicemail, or checking in with her assistant to make sure nothing had blown up while she was away. Even though she was doing well at work, she never felt totally secure with her job.

The taxicab swerved in and out of traffic as quickly as possible given the parking lot of cars and other vehicles stretched across the wide boulevard. Luckily, her hotel was off the strip in a less congested area, or she would never have time to check in before catching the first session of the conference. Cheryl grabbed a twenty dollar bill out of her wallet and handed it to the driver.

"May I please have a receipt?" she asked. Megan was a stickler for the expense report, and while she wanted her staff spending money for business, she also wanted an accounting for every dime spent.

"Thanks, keep the change." She said and stepped out the cab.

The driver jumped out and took her suitcase out of the trunk and handed it over to her.

"Thank you ma'am, have a good day!" He said smiling. Cheryl smiled back nodding her head and running into the hotel entrance.

The hotel lobby was cool and the décor was cozy and upscale. Cushy plush chairs with small ivory tables were scattered across the atrium. The floor was covered with plush beige and burgundy oriental carpeting throughout the center of the room and the floor of the registration area was covered with shiny beige marble tile.

"May I help you?" The registration clerk asked.

"Yes, thank you. I would like to check in please." Cheryl said pulling out her corporate credit card and handing it to the clerk. "My name is Cheryl Marks."

"Oh yes, here you are Ms Marks. So, I see you're here for the National Insurance Conference. We've had quite a few people check in today for that conference." The young and bubbly registration clerk said.

"Really, I wonder if anyone I know is staying at this hotel." Cheryl said raising her eyebrow.

"Well, let's see, we have a Johnathan James, Rachel Lee, Timothy Hayes, and Matthew Robinson. Do you work with any of those people?"

"Um…yes, I do know Johnathan and Rachel…did I hear you say Matthew Robinson?" Cheryl asked slowly.

"Yes, there is a Matthew Robinson staying here. Do you know him as well?"

"I'm not sure. I went to school with a Matthew Robinson, but I haven't seen him in years. Probably not the same one though, that's such a common name." Cheryl responded.

"Well here is your keycard Ms Marks. You will be staying in room 502. Just take the elevators to the right to the fifth floor. Have a wonderful stay!"

"Thank you." Cheryl smiled and took the small envelope from the clerk.

Well, that's a name I haven't heard in years, she thought to herself. Matthew Robinson. Could that be the same Matthew Robinson she knew in high school? No way, it couldn't be. What would the odds be that Matthew Robinson would be here in Las Vegas, and attending the same conference as she? It's probably someone else, she thought. And even if it is Matthew, he probably wouldn't remember me. I'm sure he's married by now to some gorgeous woman and they probably have a couple of beautiful kids and live in the suburbs like Charity and Mike. The thought that it could be him did peak her interest slightly though. She was curious to see how everything had turned out for him, and to let him see she hadn't done so badly for herself. "Reality check!" she told herself. "You're a grown woman now for God's sake. It's been ten years since high school and you haven't thought about Matthew in years, and he's never thought about you." She suddenly realized she was beginning to babble to herself like she had a couple of screws loose, then grabbed her suitcase and headed for the elevator.

છ૰ન્

Cheryl glanced at her watch quickly and tried with difficulty to focus her eyes on the speaker. "Well this one was a total waste of time." She thought to herself. If she heard one more lecture about how to evaluate risk, and the climate of the current marketplace, she was going to scream. She wasn't hearing anything she hadn't heard before. The market was softening and in order to pick up new business the carriers were going to have to get more creative. Well, she'd pretty much exhausted all her creative efforts to pick up business, and was wondering if she was going to have to resort to putting on her hooker outfits, or loosening a couple more buttons on her shirts. She found that scenario amusing and suddenly realized she was smiling. Anyone who knew Cheryl Marks knew that she would always remain the ultimate professional. That was one thing she learned from her mother years ago. The woman sitting across the aisle from her looked at her as if she wanted to know what was so funny. It obviously couldn't be anything the speaker had said.

At least this was the last session for the day. No one really came to these things for the sessions anyway. These types of industry affairs were mainly about schmoozing with clients and getting as much visibility in the industry as possible. She checked her watch again and wondered if it would cause too much commotion if she excused herself a couple of minutes early. She wanted to have a little bit of down time before her meeting with Bob Conner. That way, she could run back to her hotel and look over the Braxton file yet again before meeting with him. Good thing she'd switched the dinner to the restaurant in her hotel. At least she wouldn't have to worry about catching a cab and having to sit in that ungodly traffic again.

After a couple more minutes of internal debate, she decided to make a go of it and slip out early. At least now she wouldn't have to stop and make small talk with every person she recognized, or that recognized her, on her way out. Unfortunately, once she stepped out the room, she realized she wasn't the only one with the idea to sneak out early. The area outside the conference rooms was filled with other attendees playing hooky and who found the sessions as uninteresting as she did.

"Oh no, there's Rachel. I'm not going to be able to get out of here without saying something to her." Cheryl thought. "And she's standing right in front of the entrance too. Oh well, too late, she's already seen me."

Cheryl waved at the perky young Asian woman watching her, smiled and headed toward the door.

"Rachel, how are you?" she said giving the woman a hug.

"Cheryl Marks! Megan told me you might be here. How's everything going with First National these days?" Rachel said squeezing Cheryl tightly.

"Oh everything is fine Rachel. How are things with Jenner & Brown?" Cheryl responded not about to let one of her competitors know too much about anything.

"Oh you know. This market's crazy. But you have to do what you have to do, right?" Rachel said searching Cheryl's eyes as if trying to read them for more information.

"Well Rachel, it was really good running into you. But I'm on my way to a meeting. How long are you here for? Maybe we can do lunch if you're here tomorrow." Cheryl responded inching toward the door.

"Oh, anyone I know?" Rachel responded still trying to get a read.

"I'm just meeting with one of my clients. It was really good seeing you Rachel. I'll be here tomorrow, so if you're going to be free, just call me on my cell. Sorry, but I am really running late." Cheryl waved at Rachel and headed toward the door.

That Rachel is a piece of work, she thought. Did she really think I was going to tell her who I was meeting with? She probably already knows anyway, she thought. It was difficult to keep anything a secret in the industry since everyone was always competing with everyone else for the same business.

The air outside the conference center felt light, even though it was about ninety degrees and she was beginning to feel like she'd just stepped into a sauna. It just felt good to be away from all the industry talk, if just for a few minutes. Cheryl decided to walk back to the hotel rather than to flag down a taxi. Once she was in her hotel room, she went straight to her phone to check for messages, and then pulled out her cell phone to call the office and check her office voice mail.

Later, as she'd planned, she hurried across the hotel lobby to meet Bob Conner at her hotel's restaurant. The hotel lobby was filled with the activity of travelers checking in and out. This was one of the few hotels in Las Vegas that didn't have slot machines in the lobby because it was filled with mostly business travelers who were more interested in a nice quiet spot to hold meetings. Cheryl checked with the hostess at the restaurant door to see if Bob Conner had arrived yet. She was disappointed to find that Bob was already seated, as she liked to get to the meeting location before her guests arrived. She always felt a need to be first.

"Bob, I'm sorry I'm just getting here. I hope I haven't kept you too long?" She said extending her hand.

Bob stood up and took her hand smiling. "Oh no that's fine. I just got here not too long ago myself. Don't worry about it Cheryl, really." Bob said pulling out the chair next to him.

Bob was in his late fifties, with gray hair and a bit of a beer belly. He was wearing a light gray suit with a light blue shirt unbuttoned at the neck.

"Here sit next to me. One of the fellows at the office is going to be joining us for dinner. I hope you don't mind."

"Not at all…I'm just glad you haven't been sitting here waiting too long. So, how are you doing Bob? I haven't spoken with you in a while." Cheryl asked.

"I'm okay Cheryl. I hope you've been well too?"

"Yes I have, thanks Bob." Cheryl nodded getting all the formalities out of the way.

"I've been really busy these past few weeks working on the Braxton account getting all of the necessary information together to send out to everyone. You know that it will be coming up for renewal soon and there is a heck of a lot of interest in the marketplace for that account. Everyone wants to take a look at it." Bob smiled at Cheryl slyly. "I'm sure First National is no different. You guys want to take a crack at it as well I assume?" Bob sat back in his chair. He obviously knew he had the upper hand since representatives at every company in the country suddenly wanted to buy him dinner.

"Of course we do Bob. As you know, First National is one of the largest carriers in the nation and we currently handle some of the most prestigious accounts in the country, it only makes sense that we would pursue an account such as Braxton. We would love the opportunity to make a bid on it, and I assure you we would be the best fit for them."

"Well, we'll see. Why don't we discuss what you guys are willing to offer? As you know we are looking to place this account with a company that is able to be somewhat creative with the structure of...Uh, just a moment Cheryl. I see my colleague over there... Matt over here!" At that point Bob stood up looking over Cheryl's shoulder and began to wave.

Cheryl turned in the direction of Bob's wave. She noticed a tall young man wearing a tan suit and a blue shirt that was unbuttoned at the neck like Bob's. The man suddenly noticed Bob waving and began walking toward their table. Cheryl strained her eyes not sure if she recognized the man but felt a strange twinge of familiarity. As the man got closer to the table her eyes widened slightly.

"Matthew, you finally made it." Bob said shaking the man's hand, and then turned to Cheryl. "Cheryl, I'd like to introduce you to my colleague. This is Matthew Robinson. Matthew is one of our new brokers at Global and he's going to be working with me to place Braxton's renewal. Matt, this is Cheryl Marks with First National Insurance."

Chapter Eleven

"It's nice to meet you Cheryl. Matt Robinson." The young man said extending his hand to her.

"Hello Matthew. So, you're new at Global?" Cheryl asked slowly.

"Well, I've been on board now for a couple of months. I just moved to San Diego from Atlanta. I understand you're with First National?" Matthew asked taking the seat across from Cheryl.

"Yes…I've been with First National for the last ten years actually. I started working there after high school and worked my way through college, so I pretty much know all there is to know about the company." Cheryl replied staring at Matthew. He appeared to not recognize her. "Did you say you were from Atlanta?"

"Yes. I went to school in Atlanta and liked it so much I decided to stay there after college. I'm originally from Chicago though, so we have something in common. That is where First National's home office is, correct?" Matthew asked still not appearing to recognize her.

"Yes, that's correct. I'm from Chicago. Where did you go to school in Atlanta?" Cheryl asked wanting to know as much about what he'd been up to since high school as possible.

"I graduated from Morehouse. It was a good school, great legacy with Dr. King being a graduate, among others. But I mainly got talked into going there by my high school girlfriend." Matthew said laughing. "She wanted to go to Spelman and wanted us to be together. I had a choice between Morehouse and U. of Michigan, but she convinced me to become a Morehouse man so that's how I ended up in Atlanta. So Cheryl, where did you grow up in Chicago?"

"My family lived for a short time in the George Marshall housing project, but I mainly grew up in Ridgeland." Cheryl said waiting for the revelation to finally kick in.

"Ridgeland...are you kidding? That's where I grew up. What high school did you graduate from?" Matthew asked.

"Henry High School." Cheryl sat back in her chair and looked Matthew in the eye still waiting for something to ring a bell.

"That's amazing! I went to Henry High...Cheryl Marks.....that name sounds familiar but I can't quite place you." Matthew said searching Cheryl's face for some portion of recognition.

Cheryl could not believe that Matthew didn't know her or even recognize her at all. All her previous suspicions had just been confirmed. He'd never even known she was alive.

Bob was looking from Matthew to Cheryl. Cheryl was trying with difficulty to hide her irritation and disappointment but she was never one for hiding her emotions.

"So you two know each other?" Bob asked. "I forgot you were originally from Chicago Matt. It's a small world isn't it?"

"I do remember Matthew from high school...," Cheryl interjected, "actually we went to the same grade school too, McArthur." Cheryl turned facing Bob and away from Matthew. "Matthew and I traveled in different circles back in those days." Then she turned to Matthew and said dryly. "Don't worry about it Matthew, I was really quiet back then. You probably won't remember me." Then she turned

92

back to Bob. "Well we didn't come here to discuss me. Let's talk about Braxton shall we?"

Just then, the waitress approached the table and asked if she could get them something to drink. Cheryl wasn't a drinker but she felt like drowning herself in something. "I'll just have cranberry juice please." She said.

Bob and Matthew ordered glasses of wine and then they settled into a meal of chicken parmesan and pasta. Cheryl kept the conversation steered on Braxton as long as she could, until it turned personal again when Bob started talking about his two daughters and his grandchildren.

"Do you have any children Cheryl?" Matthew asked.

"No, I don't. I'd kind of like to be married before that happens." Cheryl replied managing to muster up a smile and still trying to hide her irritation. Then she had to ask.

"What about you? Do you have any children Matt?"

"I have one son, Timothy. He's two. My wife's not ready to go that route again any time soon. She wants to wait a couple of years and get her figure back together... but I happen to think she looks fine of course." He said laughing.

"Well of course!" Bob said laughing as well.

Cheryl just sat for a moment in silence, and then struggled to put on a smile. "That's wonderful Matthew." She then turned to Bob again. "Well, it was really good of you to take the time to have dinner with me Bob. As I said, I would really like the opportunity to bid on Braxton. Do I have a commitment from you that First National will get that opportunity?

"Cheryl, I have to tell you, you seem to know more about this account than I do. Of course, we'll give you an opportunity to bid. I'll give my assistant a call and have her overnight the information to your office. You should have it waiting for you when you get back in the office. I also have to say, from what I've heard so far, you may have a really good chance of taking this one from NRC. We'll see how it goes." Bob said grinning.

"Well Bob, coming from you that means a lot. I know Megan will be happy to hear the good news." Cheryl said.

"I'm sure she will. Let Megan know I said you are one of the most thorough account executives I have ever dealt with and I look forward to seeing what you guys can do for us."

After the dinner meeting was over, Cheryl said goodnight to Bob, letting him know she looked forward to working with him and she was confident First National would be the new insurance carrier on Braxton. But she knew of Bob's shrewd reputation as well, so she didn't take everything he said at face value. She continued to wear her forced smile as she said goodnight to Matthew and went back to her hotel room leaving him still clueless.

૭∙૭

On Wednesday, Cheryl decided to skip the last session and catch an earlier flight back to Chicago. While she was bummed by the fact that Matthew didn't have an idea who she was, she was delighted she would at least have good news to tell Megan. Bumping into Matthew after all those years had taken her back through time, but she understood at this point in her life, pleasing Megan was more important.

"It was for the best." She thought. "At least now I have Matthew Robinson closure once and for all." She turned the air conditioning knob over her airplane seat to the on position, curled up in her seat, and closed her eyes for the duration of the flight.

Once at home, she rolled her suitcase to the corner of her bedroom and tossed her tote bag on top as she usually did after a long flight.

"I'll unpack everything later. Right now, I just need to unwind a bit." She said out loud.

She was amazed at how much mail could stack up in just two days and sorted out the junk from the important stuff. She suddenly felt jet lagged and fell down across the bed. Her mind, of course, began replaying the last two days. She wanted to be thrilled by the fact that she could go into the office tomorrow and tell Megan that she would be looking at the Braxton account for renewal, and that she had wowed Bob Conner, which was not an easy thing to do. Even though Megan rubbed her nerves raw, she still had this inexplicable need to gain her approval. But try as she might, she could not get the unlikely meeting with Matthew after all those years out of her head. She understood that he was married and had a child, and hadn't even remembered he'd gone to school with her. And she kept telling herself he didn't matter. But for some reason that she couldn't put her finger on, he did still seem to matter.

After finally changing out of her travel clothes and unpacking her suitcase, she poured herself a glass of ginger ale and sat down to check her voicemail. There were as usual a number of messages from telemarketers trying to sell her a new credit card or something else unnecessary. Those she promptly deleted without listening to. Then she heard Jennifer's voice.

"Cheryl….it's Jen. I just wanted to check in with you. …Um, there's something I wanted to talk to you about. I didn't want to bother you while you were in Vegas because I knew you were going to be busy absorbing all that riveting insurance information…yeah right." She laughed and paused for a second. "But…give me a call when you get back…I really need to talk to you. Okay, thanks Cheryl. Call me. Bye."

Cheryl deleted the message. "Wonder why Jen sounds so strange?" She thought. "What's up with her now?"

There was always something going on in Jennifer's life, and ever since they were kids, she'd always been the reigning Drama Queen.

Cheryl listened to the duration of her messages and placed the phone back on the receiver to get a dial tone. She was about to pick up the phone to call Jennifer back when it suddenly rang.

"Hello?" she said.

"Cheryl….it's Tischa. I'm glad you're home. You need to come now. Daddy's in the hospital."

৯৽৶৾

The hospital seemed like it was hundreds of miles away even though it was only around ten miles from Cheryl's apartment. Since she still lived on the south side of Chicago, she only lived a couple of miles from her parent's home and closer to the hospital. But the ride from her apartment to the hospital seemed endless. She could feel her heart pumping quickly in her chest. How could this have happened? She couldn't even remember ever seeing her father sick a day in his life. Growing up, he'd always seemed so vital and strong, always the provider, the one who looked out for everyone else. Now he was lying helpless in a hospital bed after having suffered a heart attack.

According to Tischa, he had been out working in the yard all morning. Since retiring from the post office, he'd developed a passion for gardening and spent every free waking moment puttering around in his back yard. It was one of the things he looked most forward to doing after his retirement. While Mrs. Marks was sitting in the kitchen that afternoon, however, Mr. Marks came through the back door holding his arm and complaining of chest pain. When the pain began to escalate, Mrs. Marks called Tischa, who in turn thought it best to call the paramedics. When the paramedics arrived, they were able to stabilize him, but had to rush him to the hospital.

"Cheryl, there you are! Mama's in the waiting room." Tischa came running up to Cheryl as she stepped through the emergency room door. "I just stepped out to get her some water. We're still waiting to hear something from the doctor."

"How long have you been here? Have you called Pearl? What about Ralph and Carl?" Cheryl was speaking rapidly as she tended to do when she got nervous.

"I called Pearl and told her we'd give her an update as soon as we heard something else. Ralph is still out of town on some type of training for his job. I called him but told him we'd let him know more when we got more information too. Carl's with Mama in the waiting room."

"You go ahead Tisch. I'll go find Mama and Carl." Cheryl said turning and walking away towards the waiting room.

"Okay, I'm glad you got here Cheryl." Tischa called behind her.

Cheryl walked into the waiting room and looked from side to side. She noticed her mother sitting near the far corner looking worried but resigned. Carl was sitting next to her looking up at the small television screen attached to the wall. She walked over to her mother and sat in the seat next to her. Mrs. Marks looked at Cheryl and reached out and took her hand and squeezed it.

"Ma, are you okay? I ran into Tischa outside. What did the doctor say, have you heard anything else yet?" Cheryl was still speaking rapidly.

"I'm okay. I told Tischa I was a little thirsty, so she said she was going to get me some water or something. I'm still waiting to hear something more from the doctor. They took him back there a while ago. I don't know what's taking them so long to tell us something." Mrs. Marks' voice had a slight tremble, but Cheryl could tell she was trying hard to keep it together.

"I'll go see if I can find out anything else Mama now that Cheryl is here with you." Carl was obviously feeling relieved Cheryl was there and he didn't have to sit still any longer.

"Okay baby, but I don't think they know anything yet or they would have come in here and told us," Mrs. Marks said patting Carl on the arm, beckoning him to sit back down. Carl glanced over at Cheryl helplessly and took his seat. Mrs. Marks then turned to Cheryl, "I thought you were in Las Vegas for work. When did you get back?"

"I just got back this afternoon. I had just finished checking through my mail and my phone messages when Tischa called me with the news and I rushed right over here when I heard. I just cannot believe this. Daddy's never been sick, and I never heard anything about him having heart trouble?" Cheryl said questioning. "What happened?"

"He's never complained about anything before, but you know your daddy. He hates to go to the doctor. I kept telling him he should go and at least get a checkup, but he kept telling me he was fine, and going to the doctor was a waste of time and money." Mrs. Marks said with a slight smile brushing her hand across her mixed gray hair. Cheryl suddenly noticed her mother looked weary and frail.

"Yeah, I know Daddy. He always did think he was invincible, and didn't have any use for anything he didn't think was absolutely necessary. But he really should go to the doctor at least once a year at his age, Mama. He still thinks he's a sixteen-year old sprinter." Cheryl said still holding her mother's hand.

"I know baby. But trying to convince your father to go to the doctor if he doesn't feel sick is impossible. He's so darn stubborn, that man," Mrs. Marks replied.

At that point, Tischa walked back in the waiting room with a bottle of water and handed it to her mother.

"Here's your water, Ma. Has anyone been in here yet?" Tischa asked. "What is taking them so long? We've been here all afterno…." At that point, Tischa noticed her mother, Cheryl and Carl looking toward the door of the waiting room and spun around. A young doctor wearing light blue scrubs with a stethoscope hanging around his neck was walking toward them.

"Excuse me, Mrs. Marks? My name is Dr. Fields. I'm afraid I have some news for you regarding your husband."

Chapter Twelve

The sky was a dreary and cloudy combination of gray and white, and the air felt crisp and cool. Cheryl peered through the limousine window watching the array of brown, orange, and golden leaves scurrying across the freshly trimmed cemetery lawns. As the limousine pulled out of the large open gates, she let out a deep sigh. She was glad it was almost over. While she hated funerals in general, this was one she especially could have done without. Ever since the day she'd said goodbye to her father in the emergency room, she'd realized this day was coming, and she dreaded it. She knew funerals were a societal necessity, but she had a real problem with having to sit through a ceremony for hours, in a room full of people, and having to publicly display her grief.

She never forgot the time she'd watched a famous foreign diplomat's funeral on television. Thousands of people packed into an elegant cathedral. Some were mourners, however, some were probably there out of obligation or because he was a man of status, and it gave them credibility to be in attendance. She stared at the television screen as the man's family was required to sit in front of the room facing the funeral goers. At one point in the service, the diplomat's wife and daughters were overcome with emotion and tears began to stream down their faces. She remembered thinking what a shame it was that this family was unable to grieve for their loved one in private. That because of this man's stature in life, his family was being subjected to having millions of people, many who they probably didn't even know, watch as they suffered through some of the worst grief in their lives.

As the limousine pulled into the parking lot of the church where the repast was going to be held the Marks family sat in complete silence. Cheryl looked over at her mother who was flanked between Ralph and Carl. She looked as tired and weary as she did that day in the hospital, when she was suddenly forced to say goodbye to the man she'd loved for the last thirty five years. Her eyes were moist and a little red as she'd cried briefly during the service, but for the most part, she had been the pillar of strength. That was her nature. While Mr. Marks had always been a strong and capable figure in the Marks household, everyone knew it was Mrs. Marks who was the glue that really held the family together. However, it was taking every once of strength she had just to get through this day. Once everyone was out of the car, Pearl took her mother's arm from Ralph and walked into the church with her. That gesture caused a faint smile to cross Mrs. Marks' face. Even though this was a difficult time, she was at least grateful and proud of the fact she had all her children together again in one spot. Cheryl followed her family down the stairs leading to the dining area where the luncheon was being held. The First Avenue Church had pulled out all the stops. Mr. Marks had been a well-respected fixture of the church, and had served as deacon for fifteen years now. Mrs. Marks' mission group was waiting dressed in white dresses and hats, and enveloped her as she entered the room.

"Sister Marks, you all just come on in and sit down. We have a table all set up for your family up front. Just tell us what you want and we'll bring it to you. We have all kinds of good food here. Mother Johnson made sure she brought a huge pot of collard greens and cornbread, and Sister Green baked one of her famous delicious German chocolate cakes just for you."

Mattie Benson was the vice president of the mission board and had served alongside Mrs. Marks for years. She was a tall middle-aged woman with broad facial features and hips to match, and she was comfortable with being in charge. Her goal today was to make sure

Deacon Marks had a repast befitting a man who'd lived his life looking out for everyone else, including those in his family, community, and his church. And the sisters had really set it out for the Marks family that day. Long white linen covered tables of fried and baked chicken, ham and roast beef, every kind of green, cornbread, and all types of desserts lined the walls of the small dining facility.

"Children, it's good to see all of you. Pearl, it's really good to see you. I haven't seen you since you were practically a teenager. Your mother told us you were doing fine in Atlanta."

"Thank you Sister Benson. I'm happy to see you too." Pearl replied reaching out and hugging Mrs. Benson.

Pearl hadn't been home in quite a few years. She was always busy traveling to this exotic destination or that. She'd practically been to every country on earth. And she'd switched jobs a couple of times as well, and was now working as a director for a nonprofit corporation that helped to provide educational funding. It was odd that growing up, everyone thought Pearl would be married by now with a couple of kids, but she'd proven to be a real free spirit and didn't seem to have it in her to settle down, at least not yet. She had been in a serious relationship with a public school administrator in Atlanta, but as of now, they had no plans to make it official.

Mrs. Benson grabbed each Marks child, giving them one of her famous smothering hugs. She then turned her attention to Cheryl, who was bringing up the rear of the group.

"Cheryl, you are getting prettier every time I see you. Deacon Marks was so proud of you. He said you had a big job downtown and was doing really well. You should have seen how he used to beam every time he talked about you children. He loved you all so much."

Cheryl choked back the tears as she attempted to catch her breath while Mrs. Benson hugged her tightly. "Thank you Sister Benson. We were just as proud of him as he was of us."

At that point, Cheryl excused herself by saying she needed to use the restroom. She just wasn't in the mood to mingle with everyone they knew, no matter how well meaning they were. After she left the restroom, she peeked inside the dining room and noticed her family was seated at the front table delving into the sumptuous variety of soul food that had been provided for them. But she needed to get some air, and decided to slip outside for a moment. There was a fresh crispness to the fall air and she breathed it in deeply. She always used to love this time of year when everything was changing. It always gave her a warm cozy feeling, like she wanted to curl up in front of a warm fire with someone she loved, and who loved her back. She hoped she wouldn't associate this time of year from now on with the death of her father. She just could not believe that she would never hear him call her his 'Baby Girl' again. She could feel the tears beginning to well up in her eyes when she suddenly felt a warm hand on the back of her shoulder. She spun around and looked into a face that she hadn't seen in quite a long time.

"Tom! What are you doing here? Oh my god, how long has it been since I've seen you?" Cheryl's moist eyes were wide with disbelief. She hadn't seen or spoken to Tom in about three years.

Tom grabbed her and covered her with his arms. His arms felt strong and comforting around her. The last time she'd hugged Tom was the day he left for New York, but something felt different about this hug. The last time they'd hugged, they were pretty much kids. Now, Tom's hug felt stronger, yet calming, and she felt a need to cling to him a while longer.

"I know...it's been a long time hasn't it?" Tom replied taking off his tortoise shelled glasses. Cheryl could see the familiar flecks of hazel in his eyes and smiled.

"How did you know? I mean, we haven't spoken in a while."

"Well I'm here visiting my folks. I hadn't been home in a while so I promised my mom I would come home this weekend for a short visit. I was at the grocery store yesterday, and I ran into Ralph. He told me your father had passed away Wednesday, and I asked for the information regarding the arrangements. Didn't he tell you he saw me?" Tom asked raising his brow. Cheryl thought how familiar his face looked, just slightly more mature. But his eyes were still the same beautiful eyes she loved to look into long ago.

"Oh you know Ralph. He probably forgot about your entire conversation right after he left you, especially, if he ran into some hot chick on his way home." Cheryl replied laughing. "But I'm glad you were here this weekend Tom. My dad always liked you. It means a lot to us that you came."

Cheryl looked down at the ground and they stood in awkward silence for a second.

"I always liked and respected your father too. He was a good man." Tom said glancing over her shoulder briefly, and then started to laugh. "Remember when you used to come visit me at Northwestern? I can't believe he even let you come and stay all weekend because he was so strict. Even if you did tell him you were staying with your friend Colleen."

"I know, but Daddy really trusted you for some reason. I don't know what it was. I guess he saw something in you and believed that you were a decent guy." Cheryl said laughing back.

"Well, that's nice to hear. At least *he* liked me, huh?" Tom replied.

Cheryl stopped laughing suddenly and looked at Tom. For a second, she thought she saw a tinge of hurt in his hazel eyes. She realized the way she'd ended things with Tom was cold. The truth was she'd never officially ended anything. She just became gradually unavailable to him, and the result was their relationship just sort of fell by the way side.

"So Tom, how are things going for you in the Big Apple? Do you still like living in New York?" Cheryl asked trying to switch to a more comfortable subject. She didn't want to have to explain to Tom why she'd ended things with him after all that time together. How she'd changed so much since high school and how she'd set goals for her life that he just didn't fit into.

"New York is great. I'm living in a small apartment in the city. The rent there is a little steep for the size of it, but that's New York. I'm still working at the paper as a writer. I know it's not the most impressive job in the world, but it's what I love, what can I say?" Tom looked at her for a second. There seemed to be a lot of silent pauses in their conversation. "So, you ever get out to New York Cheryl? Ralph was telling me all about your new job and how much traveling you were doing lately. I know your company has that New York branch. Do you ever travel for business there?"

Cheryl paused once again. She didn't want to tell Tom that she had been to the New York branch and hadn't even bothered to look him up. She wasn't certain he was at the same number and address, or that he still worked at the paper, but she didn't even bother to find out. She was just so involved in her own life and didn't really have the time to think about him. Plus, she didn't want to start up something with him that wasn't going to go anywhere. From the looks of things, nothing had really changed.

"Um, I did have to run out there a couple of times, but I really didn't have a lot of time to do any socializing. It was basically a lot of running from one meeting to the next. I just had enough time to fly in, attend meetings, and fly back out…so how is it getting around for you in New York? Do you have to take the subway everywhere you go? No one I know that lives in Manhattan really owns a car. From what I understand it's either taxis or the subway."

"Well some people do own cars, but I pretty much take a taxi everywhere. The streets there are really narrow, plus I don't live too far from where I work. Speaking of cars, I guess now that you're making the big bucks you're driving the dream car. Let's see, what was it… a Porsche…metallic blue, right?" Tom said laughing.

"Oh my god, I guess I did use to say that a lot as a kid. Uh, no, I need to get a few more promotions to afford that car. I do have a car but it's just a little black sedan, nothing that fancy. Wow, I cannot believe you even remember that." Cheryl said laughing.

"I remember everything about you Cheryl." Tom replied. After another brief awkward pause, he looked into her eyes and reached out taking hold of her hand. Cheryl stared back at him in silence.

"Oh my goodness...is that Tom Morgan?" Jennifer asked grabbing Tom and giving him a hug. "Tom, I haven't seen you since you left for New York!" She was looking from Tom to Cheryl with a confused grin. "Cheryl didn't tell me you were going to be here." She then hugged Cheryl. "How are you doing hon? Is there anything I can do for you at all?"

Cheryl hugged Jennifer back. "No, I'm fine. Thanks just for being here. Tom just happened to be visiting his folks this weekend and ran into Ralph at the store. Ralph told him about Daddy passing away and he asked about the arrangements. Wasn't that sweet of him?"

"Yes that was. But that's Tom. He always was a sweetheart." Jennifer replied grinning at Cheryl.

"So Miss Jennifer, what have you been up to all these years? Do you still see that guy you went to the prom with, what was his name, Robert?" Tom said laughing.

"Are you kidding? No, I haven't spoken to Robert in years. Last I heard he was getting married to a girl whose father is the pastor of some huge church on the West Side. But no problem, I've moved on to bigger and better things, thank you." Jennifer said winking her eye at Tom.

"Same old Jennifer...I see you haven't changed that much." Tom said laughing.

"Oh but I have. Did Cheryl tell you I'm an associate at the law firm I worked at during high school? Can you believe your girl is a full-fledged attorney at law? And I'm doing pretty well if I say so myself.

Recently, I've been working on some of the largest, most high profile accounts at the firm." Jennifer replied with her familiar smugness.

"Really, wow that's great Jen. How'd you pull that off? Have you been out of law school that long?" Tom asked.

Jennifer stared at him for a second. "Um no, but I've been working closely with one of the partners at the firm. He has a lot of confidence in me, seeing how I was able to breeze through John Marshall as quickly as I did." Jennifer glanced over at Cheryl. She could feel her staring at her. "So Tom, how long are you going to be here?"

"Well, unfortunately, I have a late flight back to New York tonight. I wish I could stay longer..." He looked over at Cheryl. At that point Ralph walked out the church door.

"Cheryl, Mama says to come downstairs and get something to eat. You know Ma, she's not going to take you're not hungry for an answer. Hey what's up Jennifer, hey Tom man, I see you made it."

"Yeah, I'm glad I did. It was good to see everybody. I'm going to have to plan another trip back to Chicago just to catch up...or if you guys are ever in New York, please give me a call. I'm at the same number." He said still looking at Cheryl.

"Okay Cheryl, let's go." Ralph said. "I want to get some of that German Chocolate cake before it's all gone, and Mama told me not to come back without you. See you later Tom man, Jen, you coming?"

"Of course, I want some of that cake too." Jennifer said reaching out and hugging Tom. "Have a safe flight home, and let us know when you're back in town okay? Maybe we can all get together and do something?" She then grabbed Ralph's arm. "Let's go Ralph, Cheryl's right behind us." She smiled at Cheryl and pushed Ralph back in the door.

Cheryl and Tom stood looking at each other for a while longer.

"I meant what I said Cheryl...I'd really like us to keep in touch. I've missed you." Tom said reaching out and taking her in his arms again. She felt herself relaxing and closed her eyes briefly. She felt as though she could fall asleep, which she'd hadn't done that much of since Wednesday. For some reason, she felt safe and at home in Tom's arms. But she couldn't allow herself to get too comfortable. This was still Tom Morgan, the one who'd run off to be a struggling writer in New York after college. And regardless of how things felt, she knew he wasn't that ideal man she desired or needed.

"Um...sure Tom...we can keep in touch. I'll give you a call sometime since now I know you haven't changed numbers or anything. It was really good to see you again, I'm so grateful you came, thank you. Have a safe flight home, okay?" She said awkwardly pushing him back softly. "Well, I better get back in there before Mama sends both Ralph and Carl after me this time." Then she turned and walked back into the church door leaving Tom still standing on the steps.

As she walked down the stairs to the dining room she began to reason with herself. No, she couldn't risk getting Tom's hopes back up again. There was no way she was moving to New York at this point in her life and struggling with Tom in his small apartment. Not when things were going so well for her now at work. She was about to land the biggest account she'd ever gotten. She could just feel it. She was on her way up and needed someone in her life that was going with her. No, Tom Morgan was not her ideal man...but why did it have to feel like he was?

Chapter Thirteen

"Jillian, is there anything I can assist you with regarding the Miller file? Do you need me to sit in on the meeting with you this morning?"

Jillian peered over the top of her wire-framed glasses. She stared at Jennifer for a moment, and then glanced back down at the papers on her desk.

"No, Jennifer, I don't think you'll be needed to work on this one. Chad didn't indicate that he wanted you to sit in on this meeting. As a matter of fact, he specifically informed me that he would just be working with Mark and me on this one." Jillian watched Jennifer's reaction for a moment then looked back down at the papers. "The information on this account is somewhat sensitive, so we need to keep it as confidential as possible...You have quite a bit to do still with Morris and Williamson don't you?"

"Well, I believe we're just about finished with the contracts for the Morris merger. The language for the drafts has just about been completed. Same with Williamson...but I guess I do need to meet with the legal assistant to find out how the actual preparation of the documents is coming. I do have a couple of other things on my desk that I'm working on as well." Jennifer replied.

"Good. Let me know the status of those later." Jillian replied still looking down at the documents. "Sorry Jen, but I really need to review this information before the Miller meeting."

"No problem...I'll give you an update later. Thanks Jill."

Jennifer walked back to her cubicle in somewhat of a glazed stupor. She didn't know how to take the sudden change in tide. For the last month or so, she'd sat in on just about every major meeting at the law firm. Either Jillian had invited her to go on behalf of Chad, or she would receive a call from Chad's assistant letting her know Chad wanted her to attend. She'd gone to at least one dinner meeting with Chad and a major client almost every week since that first dinner meeting with John Morris. Now for some reason, Chad seemed to be shutting her out.

Not only had it been weeks since she'd attended a meeting with Chad, she couldn't remember the last time she'd had an actual conversation with him. It wasn't like someone could just meet with him whenever they wanted to. She pretty much needed to be invited. And she hadn't received an invitation lately.

One afternoon, she'd actually run into him in the lobby on her way to lunch and he was strangely cordial with her. True, there were other employees standing in the lobby, but he barely even looked at her. She'd practically almost run into him, but he just said hello to her as professional as possible, avoiding any eye contact, and turned and walked back into his office. He was obviously going out of his way to avoid her. She wanted desperately to speak with him to find out why he seemed so distant, why he was treating her in this manner. It was almost like she was just another associate, which really made no sense to her, because she wasn't just another associate. Not after what had developed between them.

After that first dinner meeting with Chad and John Morris, she was a bit confused about the sudden interest Chad had taken in her. And she'd spent that entire weekend trying to figure out what the recent turn in events had actually meant. Why was she being invited to work with him on some of the firm's largest clients, and attending after work functions with him? It was true that she was an intelligent and capable attorney, but so were a number of other attorneys at the firm.

That following Monday morning after the Morris meeting, Lynn, Chad's assistant had left her a voice mail instructing her that she would come by to pick up Chad's corporate card. Jennifer listened intently to the message as Lynn instructed her to place the card in a sealed envelope and to leave it in her inbox in case she wasn't at her desk when she came by. Jennifer did exactly as Lynn had instructed, however, when Lynn finally came by to pick up the card, she was still at her desk.

"Lynn, there you are." Jennifer said smiling at the assistant. "How are you today?"

The two of them always chitchatted whenever they saw each other. Since Jennifer had once been the part-time receptionist and was familiar with some of Lynn's duties, they had a lot in common. Jennifer would give Lynn advice or they would discuss office politics. But this day Lynn seemed different. She reached out and took the envelope from Jennifer and looked at her as though she barely knew her.

"I'm fine Jennifer. I was going to give you a call later, but since you're here, Chad wanted me to tell you that the Williamson meeting is going to be tomorrow evening at six o'clock. It's going to be a dinner meeting and he wants you to meet him in front of the elevator at about five forty. The two of you will take a taxi over to the restaurant. I'll be making reservations at LaShea's on Wacker for six o'clock. I just need to confirm with Chad that you're free. Should I tell him you are?" Lynn asked still looking at Jennifer with the same blank expression.

"Oh, that should be fine. Chad did mention that to me last week, and I told him I thought I would be free...so, I guess you can confirm for me. Thanks Lynn." Jennifer said still looking at Lynn for some degree of amicability.

"Fine, I'll let Chad know. Thanks Jennifer."

Lynn then turned and walked away without extending the conversation any further. Jennifer just sat looking at her back as she walked away. She didn't understand what Lynn's problem was. Nor could she recall saying anything to her or anything happening between them that would warrant such an attitude. But she decided to shrug it off. She wasn't going to let Lynn's funky mood put a damper on her good fortune. She was going to another dinner meeting with Chad! She had been chosen, for whatever reason, to work closely with Chad Phillips, and she was going to milk it for whatever it was worth. It was beginning to feel as though she was living in somebody else's life. She sat at her desk smiling, hoping nobody walked in her cubicle at that moment and caught her smiling to herself, but she couldn't help it. Then she grabbed her notes on the Williamson file and started to review them, trying to take in as much information as she possibly could.

"So, did I hear that right?"

The voice startled Jennifer and she glanced up quickly. Rachel Lopez was standing in the entry of her cubicle. Even though she was no longer a paralegal, she still worked in the cubicle next to Rachel's.

"Did you hear what?" Jennifer responded cautiously. She knew Rachel was the biggest gossip in the office. She never forgot her first day as a paralegal, and how Rachel had given her the lowdown on everything Phillips, Willis and McKenzie, including Chad and a couple of female attorneys that no longer worked there. And she didn't want to be the new subject of the office Daily News.

"Oh, I thought I heard you were going to some big meeting with Chad and the Williamson people. Is that true?" Rachel asked slowly. Jennifer could tell she already knew the answer.

"Well, Jillian thought it would be a good idea for me to get more exposure on some of the more high profile accounts. She's been mentoring me, and has a lot of confidence in my work. Since most of those accounts have Chad's involvement, than yes... I will be working with him too. Jillian is involved in most of them though." Jennifer said trying to diffuse the situation by interjecting Jillian's involvement as much as she could.

"Oh, I see." Rachel responded. Jennifer could tell she wasn't really buying her explanation. "Well, that's good for you I guess. You're a good attorney, and it would be a shame for anything to jeopardize that." Rachel responded and walked back to her desk without giving Jennifer an opportunity to respond. So what was that supposed to mean? Were people already talking about her and Chad? The only reason she was at the John Morris meeting last week was because Jillian had asked her to attend, and then elected her to go to dinner in her place. Was it her fault that she was a young single woman who didn't have anything else to do on a Friday night? Besides nothing had happened anyway...

She convinced herself everything was strictly innocent, even though she realized the special attention that was being bestowed on her by Chad Phillips, the chief partner of the firm, was suspect in appearance. Yes she was intelligent and ambitious, but there were others at the firm just as smart and eager. What was it that was so special about her? Once again, she decided to brush everything off and concentrate on the matter at hand. The Williamson meeting was tomorrow and she needed to spend the rest of the day and night consuming as much information about the client as she could before the meeting.

The next evening, she agreed to meet Chad in the elevator lobby just as she'd done the previous week. But this time, she felt better prepared for a late evening meeting because she'd spent extra attention on how she looked. She was wearing her black tailored pants suit, the one she'd wished she was wearing the night of the impromptu Morris meeting. For some reason, she considered it her power suit and felt more confident whenever she wore it. She'd also gotten a last minute appointment at Marissa's and had a fresh manicure and pedicure. While it wasn't the most important thing in the business world, she knew what worked for her, and placed a lot of emphasis on her appearance. She knew it was shallow, but she just felt empowered when she knew she looked good. As she walked to the elevator, she tossed her long sandy hair behind one ear, exposing the gold stud in her earlobe. Jennifer knew she was an attractive woman, and had no problem using it to her advantage.

When she walked into the lobby area this time she noticed Chad wasn't there yet. No one else was in the lobby either, so she decided to walk over to his office and let him know she was there already. Chad was still sitting at his desk with the phone to his ear. She noticed his desk was already cleared, and figured he was being detained by a last minute phone call. She stood in the doorway of his office waiting for him to notice her, as she didn't want to interrupt him. After a couple of seconds, Chad glanced up at her. His gaze fixed on her for a brief second. She smiled and waved and turned to walk away because she didn't want him to think she was listening in on his conversation, but he beckoned her to come in. She came in and sat down on one of the leather chairs across from his desk. To her amusement and surprise, Chad began making faces at her and began gesturing as though he was trying to rush the individual on the phone to hang up. She laughed at him and covered her mouth, trying not to make any noise. She couldn't believe how funny and laid back Chad seemed when he was with her. She, like everyone else, thought he was way too reserved. But she had obviously misjudged him. Finally, after a few minutes, Chad apologized to the person on the phone and let him know he had a meeting he needed to get to. He hung up the phone and grinned at her.

"Wow, can you believe that guy? I mean, don't get me wrong, he's a great guy, but I can never get off the phone when he calls me. I knew better than to pick up the phone at this late hour but I needed to speak with him about sending us a new retainer."

Chad was standing up reaching for his overcoat as he talked. He continued talking while putting on his coat and grabbing his leather case. Jennifer thought she had never seen him so relaxed before and wondered why his sudden change in mood. She decided not to read too much into it. Maybe this is just the way he is after work, she thought. He'd probably be just as much fun and just as relaxed with anybody else. As they entered the elevator, once again Chad stepped back and let her enter first.

"You look very nice tonight Ms Thompson." She heard him say as she stepped in front of him.

The comment sort of took her off guard and she nearly stumbled. While she was used to being complimented and basically thrived on the attention, to hear it come from him, her boss and a man she'd obsessed over for years, well she didn't quite know how to take it. She'd long put away those silly thoughts years ago and basically concentrated on her career at Phillips, Willis and McKenzie. So, she decided to not make a big deal of it, and told herself to remain calm and stay professional as she was obviously misunderstanding Chad's attention.

"Why thank you Mr. Phillips. You look rather nice tonight yourself." Jennifer replied calmly.

Chad was wearing a tan cashmere wool overcoat, and a navy blue pinstriped suit with a starched white shirt and burgundy silk tie underneath. The cuffs of his shirt were engraved with his signature monogram of CSP. Jennifer often wondered what the S stood for. His black, and now slightly mixed gray, curly hair was neatly combed backwards away from his face, drawing attention to his steel blue gray eyes. As they stood across from each other in the elevator, Jennifer concentrated intently on not staring.

Once in the taxi, Chad kept the conversation basically on the Williamson account, filling Jennifer in on David Williamson, the head of Williamson Ltd. and a couple of his key people. Just as they were stepping out of the taxicab, however, Chad's mobile phone rang.

"Chad Phillips…Dave are you at the restaurant already? Oh no, is that right? Well, I'm sorry to hear that Dave, I was looking forward to sharing a bottle of wine with you tonight. Yes, we will have to do that. No problem, we can reschedule something for next week. I'll have Lynn give you a call and set something else up tomorrow. Have a good night Dave."

Jennifer stood watching Chad. Apparently the Williamson people weren't going to be showing up. She stretched her neck to see if the taxi they'd just gotten out of had moved too far down the street for them to catch up to it. She didn't want to have to stand around on the corner and flag down a taxicab as it was getting pretty chilly out. She was just about to take off after the cab when Chad put the phone back in his pocket.

"Well Jen, as you probably heard, Dave Williamson is not going to make it tonight. Poor guy had some kind of emergency. I told him not to worry about it, he's usually pretty reliable. We'll have to try to set the meeting up for next week. That is, if Lynn can find anything free on my calendar." Chad then paused for a second, looked into the restaurant window and back at her. "Well, we do have reservations for tonight and since we're already here we might as well go on in and have something to eat. Are you hungry Jennifer? I'm famished. I didn't get to take a lunch break…meetings all day."

Jennifer thought for a second. She realized how hard Chad worked. Everyone at the office knew that his schedule was usually full and his day consisted of one meeting after another. Either he was busy meeting with the other partners and attorneys, or he was meeting with clients. Being the person responsible for the welfare for an entire company couldn't be easy. She glanced over at him and suddenly realized how tired he looked. Maybe that was why he seemed to turn into a different person once he stepped out of the office building. It was as though once he was out of the office, some type of weight lifted off of him, and he was free to be himself. She also didn't want him to have to eat alone. There was something that always seemed pathetic to her about people she saw eating alone.

"Sure Chad, I could eat something. And you definitely need to eat. We worry about you sometimes, you know, you really work too hard." She responded. She realized she was beginning to sound like his mother or something, and noticed how he looked at her, almost as though he was grateful for her concern.

As they shared dinner that evening, Jennifer felt as though she was with a different man. It wasn't like she was sharing a meal with Chad Phillips her boss, the high-powered attorney, but just Chad a man she'd known for a long time. At one point during the evening, Chad took off his suit jacket and loosened his tie exposing the top of his neck. She found herself strangely drawn to that spot of his neck, and tried to keep from staring whenever he spoke. After dinner, they just sat and talked sharing a bottle of red wine. She was thoroughly enjoying Chad's company and his comfort with her, and she felt totally relaxed with him. At one point she kicked off her black snakeskin pump and let it dangle off the tip of her foot. She felt so comfortable she almost touched his pants leg with her toe, but had enough restraint to realize that wouldn't be a wise choice.

There was one thing on her mind though. Chad didn't seem to talk at all about his wife. During the meeting with John Morris, John had asked Chad how Natalie was doing, which she knew was Chad's wife's name. Chad's reply was the standard "Oh, she's fine John", but there was no further elaboration. Jennifer was dying to know what the story was regarding their marriage, and after a couple of glasses of wine, she felt comfortable enough to go there.

"So Chad, tell me about Natalie. I heard John Morris ask you about her the other day, but I don't really know much about her. How long have you guys been married? I've never heard that you have children. Is that right?"

Chad looked at her as though he'd been abruptly awakened from a deep sleep. He looked down at his wineglass and leaned on the table with one arm, taking a deep breath, he looked up at her.

117

"Natalie and I got married right out of college. We were really young and didn't really know a heck of a lot about what we were doing. We'd dated practically all through college and it was one of those situations where everyone expected us to get married, and we did what was expected. After we got married, we decided to hold off on kids and concentrate on our careers. I was in law school, and Nat had started her nursing career. We did decide to try to get pregnant after I started the firm, but it was difficult. Nat had a couple of miscarriages a few years back. It's been so painful for her not getting pregnant. So, we decided to take a break for a while."

Jennifer wasn't quite sure what Chad meant by "taking a break for a while." Did he mean taking a break from trying to get pregnant or from each other, and she wasn't sure she wanted to know the answer.

"So, is Natalie still working as a nurse?" Jennifer asked.

"Yes, she loves what she does, so she won't quit. I told her the firm's doing well and she doesn't have to work. She's a supervisor at Northwestern, and she works really long hours. There's somewhat of a nursing shortage, so she's pretty much always on call."

At that moment, Chad's usual intensity was gone and Jennifer thought she saw a glimpse of vulnerability and loneliness in his eyes. They both sat silent for a moment. It was practically the only pause in the conversation all evening. Jennifer glanced down at her watch because she was beginning to feel a little uncomfortable, and didn't know what else to do. Chad noticed her checking her watch.

"It's getting pretty late, huh, maybe we should get going?" Chad paused for a moment as though he was pondering over something. Then he looked back at her and said. "Jen, rather than have you take a taxi home alone tonight, I'd feel better if I saw you home. I can quickly give my car service a call and have a driver pick us up in front of the restaurant." Chad asked while reaching for his cell phone. He paused for a second waiting for an answer from her.

"Okay...that sounds good Chad, thank you. But you don't really have to…

"No, I insist. It's not a problem at all." Chad said.

"Then, I'm ready when you are." Jennifer didn't really know if it was a good idea. She just knew she wasn't ready to say good night to him just yet.

As Jennifer sat in the car looking through the tinted glass windows at the people walking up and down the streets of downtown Chicago, and the brightness of the lights gleaming against the tall buildings, she began to feel like she was in some sort of movie, and she was watching it take place. It could have been the amount of wine she'd drank that night, or the fact that the man she had been infatuated with for years was sitting less than an arm's length from her, and was seeing her home after an intimate dinner.

She thought about the taxi ride she'd shared with Chad after the Morris meeting. How he'd told her he'd wanted her to start working more closely with him and get more exposure at the firm. The end of that evening had left her feeling both excited and confused. She didn't know what to make of Chad's newfound attentiveness towards her. Was it that he saw some sort of unique potential in her, or was there actually something else at play? Could it be possible that Chad's interest in her was not just professional, but personal as well? It was almost impossible to believe, but was Chad as attracted to her as she was to him?

As the car pulled up to the front of her apartment building, they sat for a moment in silence. They'd practically sat in silence the entire ride home. Jennifer suddenly felt as though she didn't need to make small talk with him, but for some reason, felt totally comfortable with the silence. In her mind, they were completely and totally in sync with one another. Regardless of whether it was all in her mind or not, as Jennifer turned and looked into Chad's eyes, the thought of saying goodnight to him at that point felt almost unbearable. She didn't care anymore what Chad's intentions towards her were. As she sat looking at him, years and years of pent-up and suppressed feelings came flooding to the surface. She was about to say goodnight, when she saw herself reach out and place her hand on Chad's leg, and heard herself ask...

"Chad, would you like to come upstairs to my apartment for a while?"

Chad looked down at her hand for a second as it lingered. Then he reached out and took her hand in his and looked back up at her.

"Yes, Jennifer, I'd like that very much." He whispered.

$\approx \infty$

Suddenly, the sound of her telephone ringing snapped Jennifer out of her thoughts.

"Jen, I know we just discussed this a moment ago, but I just spoke with Chad and I need you to bring me your final analysis on the Williamson file as soon as it's completed, okay?" Jillian said. "How soon do you think you'll have that completed?"

"I...haven't had an opportunity to meet with the assistant yet. I just stopped by my desk to pick up some notes. I'll run over there now and get back to you. Is that okay? "

"That should be fine. Chad is anxious to wrap Williamson up so as soon as you get everything completed let me know." Jillian replied.

"Okay Jill, I'll get back to you soon, thanks."

Jennifer placed the telephone down on the receiver and placed her forehead in her hands. Chad was asking for the Williamson file back, and he was talking to her through Jillian. It was pretty clear to her what he was doing now. For the last couple of weeks he'd been distancing himself from her. He was not only going out of his way to avoid her, but he was wrapping up all the loose ends, and he was putting her back in her place.

Chapter Fourteen

"Miss, do you have a ticket?"

The conductor's question startled Cheryl, and she glanced up quickly from the papers she had spread across her lap.

"I'm sorry. I didn't notice you standing there." She said as she fumbled through her tiny overstuffed Coach purse in search of the train ticket. "I know it's in here somewhere. Oh, here it is. Sorry about that." She handed the ticket to the conductor, who was glaring at her now with complete disdain and impatience.

The conductor snatched the ticket and punched it, then handed it back to her without a response. "Well, I guess he got up on the wrong side of the bed today too. Don't even mess with me today Mister because I'm right there with you." Cheryl thought to herself.

She placed the ticket back in her purse and apologized to the woman sitting next to her for reaching across her. The woman muttered a response without even looking at her. I guess everybody's in a fowl mood today she thought. She glanced at her watch. Okay, I have approximately twenty minutes to get it together. She was going to be releasing her final quotation on Braxton that morning and she needed to make sure she had a good grasp on all of the terms and conditions. This was the most complex account she'd gone after since becoming an account executive at First National and she needed to make sure she'd left no stone unturned and that there were no hidden surprises. Agreeing to provide coverage on an account of that size was difficult. There were so many pieces to the puzzle and if the policy wasn't drafted just right, the result could be disastrous for First National. She didn't want to be the account executive responsible for the company having to pay out millions of dollars in claims. And that fear always hovered over her like a huge dark invisible cloud.

On the other hand, she also needed to make her proposal as attractive as possible in order to seal the deal. She realized she wasn't going to be the only account executive bidding on Braxton and she needed to include every bell and whistle available in her quote. Megan had already scheduled a meeting with her that afternoon to go over the wording of the final quote letter before sending it to Bob Conner's office. One good thing though, she at least knew Bob was going to be giving her quotation serious consideration. He wasn't just going through the motions with her and having her do all that work for nothing, only to realize that he had no intention of giving her the business in the first place. She just needed to do her part to deliver. Megan and the boys in senior management were breathing down her neck on this one, and she was really feeling the pressure. She'd actually lain awake that morning at two o'clock going over the specifications of the account in her head, which always happened whenever she was feeling the pressure cooker at work. She'd wake up in the middle of the night thinking about everything that was on her desk, and try to figure out what to do with it.

"The train is now approaching Millennium station." The computerized voice over the intercom jolted Cheryl out of her thoughts and back into reality. She glanced back down at her watch. Where did those twenty minutes go? Then she jammed the papers back into the huge brown folder and shoved it into her tote bag.

"Excuse me." She whispered to the woman sitting next to her as she stepped over her to get out to the aisle.

The woman, who had dozed off into a brief nap, glared up at her obviously put off for having to move and let her squeeze by. She'd already ticked the woman off when she reached across her earlier, and asking her to move so she could get to the front of the train before everyone else wasn't helping matters much, but she really didn't care. She liked to be the first one off the train, and if that meant irritating her seatmate even further, then she might as well put the icing on the cake.

Once outside of the train station Cheryl stopped for a second to get her bearings and breathed in the fresh air, at least as fresh as it could possibly be in downtown Chicago. Should she walk to the office or should she wait for the bus across the street? The walk would only take her about fifteen minutes, but her tote bag was extra heavy that day because of the huge Braxton file inside. She decided to go ahead and take the walk. Sometimes that bus could take forever to show up and when it did show, it would take even more time getting through all of the heavy downtown traffic. The truth was she loved walking. It was the only time she could actually think clearly. As she walked, she loved looking in the shop windows and making mental notes of items she would pick up on her lunch hour or on her way home from work. Too bad she never actually got to fulfill those wishes, as she usually only had enough time to grab something to eat at lunch, and by the time she left work, everything would be closed.

By the time Cheryl walked into her office building, her back felt as though it was breaking in two, and her right shoulder felt like it was two inches lower than her left from the pressure of the heavy tote bag. She knew she shouldn't take that long walk in three and half-inch heels, but she had somewhat of a complex about her five foot four and a half inch height and the heels just made her feel taller and more powerful.

"Hey Ms Marks, how are you today? You look like you have a load there." The doorman said holding the glass door open and allowing Cheryl to enter the building's lobby as the wind whipped her backwards.

"Thanks Paul. You're right, I took a couple of files home last night and now my back is killing me. I appreciate your help though, thanks again."

"No problem, that's why I'm here Cheryl...just to take care of you." Paul responded winking.

Paul was a short chubby man about forty five years old with gray hair and a mustache. He'd run the security for the First National Insurance Company's downtown location for years, and no one got inside the building unless Paul and his staff approved them. One of Paul's favorite past-times was flirting with the ladies as they entered and left the tall office building, and Cheryl was one of his favorite objects of affection.

"Oh Paul, I bet you say that to all the ladies, right?" Cheryl responded waving at Paul as she continued heading to the elevator.

"Ah Cheryl, you know you're my special lady." Paul yelled behind her.

"Yeah, yeah, tell me anything Paul. Gotta run now, I'll see you later." Cheryl responded grinning as she stepped onto the elevator.

Paul could be a bit of a nuisance, but everyone knew he was perfectly harmless. Cheryl actually enjoyed flirting with him on occasion. It helped to take some of the edge off and relieve the stress and pressure of the day. But she didn't have time for chitchat with the security guard today. All she cared about right now was getting upstairs and dumping that darn file off on her desk.

"Good morning, how are you?" Cheryl grinned and waved to the other employees walking past, trying to be as cordial as possible on her way to her cubicle.

Once she got to her desk, however, she peeled the tote bag off of her shoulder and dumped it on her desk. It had actually made an impression across the skin of her shoulder blade. She fell down onto her chair without taking off her coat and sat for a moment rubbing her shoulder, than kicked off her heels and rubbed her feet. Being a hotshot senior account executive was not always what it was cracked up to be. Sure the money was good and there were a lot of perks that went along with the position, but it also cost a lot too. Her mother used to always quote the scripture, "to whom much is given, much is required." And on days like this, she had only one response for her mother. I hear you Ma.

She glanced over to her telephone and saw there were ten messages registered on the caller I.D. Well, at least there are only ten phone messages this time she thought. She grabbed the receiver and pushed the button to replay the messages. The familiar tone through the receiver indicating the first message was marked urgent caused her to take a deep breath.

"Cheryl, it's Megan. I just wanted to follow-up with you this morning. We have a meeting scheduled for this morning to go over the quote for Braxton with Chuck. We need to meet first to make sure we have all our ducks in a row. I don't want to go in to see Chuck if you don't have everything in order. You know we need his approval on everything before we can release the proposal to Bob Conner. Come by and see me when you get in."

Cheryl looked at the display on the phone. The message came in at six thirty that morning. It was just like Megan to get into the office at the crack of dawn. She glanced at the clock on her desk. The minute hand barely approached eight o'clock. When did the meeting get moved up from this afternoon to this morning? She thought she'd at least have time to go through all of her phone messages and emails before having to contend with Megan, but she guessed she was having no such luck. And if she didn't get herself together in a couple of minutes, she knew Megan was going to be calling again, or probably stopping by to let her know she was ready to see her. It was interesting the way their relationship had developed, or rather deteriorated, over the past few years, especially since the new head of the department had taken over. She had once admired Megan and her go-get-it style. Now their time together basically consisted of Megan barking orders at her, and her going out of her way to avoid

Megan whenever possible. Her job responsibilities were complex enough without having her adding more fuel to the fire.

After listening to the rest of her phone messages and skipping over the ones that didn't seem important, she bent down and pulled the huge brown folder out of her tote bag. She then grabbed a memo pad and headed off for Megan's office, brushing her wind tossed hair down on the way. She hadn't even taken a moment to visit the ladies' room and had no idea how she looked. When she got to Megan's office she peered in through the glass window. Megan was sitting at her desk reading an open email. She was wearing a brown pants suit, and her long black hair was pulled back into her signature bun at the nap of her neck. It was an elegant style and made her look polished and sophisticated, but Megan had beautiful hair, and Cheryl couldn't remember the last time she'd seen Megan with her hair down. Cheryl tapped on the door and Megan spun around in her chair when she heard the noise. She had obviously been waiting for Cheryl to get into the office. Cheryl didn't know how she was able to do it, spending so much time in the office, but she looked pressed and well put together. She guessed that was why she wore the bun. Once it was firmly secured at the nap of her neck, she didn't have to worry about her hair the rest of the day. That was Megan. She only had need in her life for what was absolutely necessary.

"Well there you are. I was wondering when you were going to make it in." Megan said slanting her eyes at Cheryl, obviously not satisfied with her eight o'clock arrival, and gesturing to her to sit at the round table in the corner of her office. "Do you have the file with you?"

"Good Morning Megan. Yes, of course, I have the file." Cheryl responded pulling out a chair from the table and sitting down. "I have the numbers that were given to me from the actuarial department as well. Why don't you take a look at them and let me know if you think we should go out with those numbers or not. I think they may be a bit too high, so if we can shave anything off that would be great."

"Well, you know Chuck will have to approve any deviation from the actuarial number. This account is way out of my authority. But tell me what you think we should do."

Megan leaned in and grabbed the spreadsheet from Cheryl's hands. She turned around quickly and grabbed her reading glasses from her desk, then spun back around to the table. "Wow, this is a huge number. Who worked on this for you, Jack Barnes or Tammie Wilson? You know, Jack can be so anal on these types of accounts sometimes."

"Yes, it was Jack, that's why I think we really need to shave something off of those numbers if we are going to be competitive on this at all." Cheryl responded.

"Well tell me...what have you heard? Do you have any idea where the other numbers are coming in?" Megan asked.

"I actually don't know. I've asked Bob several times, but you know Bob. He's an old school broker and as straight as they come. He'll only tell me we need to release the best number we have on the first time out. I do know there's a lot of competition and NRC is not about to let this one walk away without a fight. I think we should at least shave ten percent off the top, and get permission from Chuck to take another ten if necessary. That's my opinion." Cheryl responded eyeing Megan to see if she agreed. Megan could be so hard to read sometimes.

"Um...I agree. Let's go see Chuck. I think we have everything we need. How's the file? Do you have a good grasp on all the coverage?"

"Yes, pretty much. There are a couple of agreements included in the file that I'm still waiting for Legal to sign off on." Cheryl responded.

"Well let's take care of the numbers part, and follow-up with legal on those agreements. Make sure you have their sign-off before releasing the final quote." Megan spun around again and reached for her phone.

"Terry, hi, it's Megan. Is Chuck in his office yet? Good, could you please tell him Megan and Cheryl Marks will be coming down to talk to him about Braxton. Great, thanks Terry." Megan slammed the phone down on the receiver, jumped up and headed for the door. "Let's go, Chuck's ready."

Cheryl snatched up all the loose documents and shoved them back into the file, and scurried down the hall after Megan. Megan was holding tightly onto the actuarial document. She was going to go through the numbers with Chuck line by line repeating every thing they had just discussed, and of course, making it sound as though she came up with everything herself. And that was fine with Cheryl, since Chuck made her, and just about everyone else in the department nervous, so the sooner they were able to get in there and state their case and get out, the better.

Chuck Miller was the president of the entire department, and he was a well-respected yet rather impatient man. He made Megan look like Mother Teresa. It was rumored around the office that he had made a couple of vice presidents cry, as he could be somewhat brutal in his no nonsense approach. Megan, however, loved the opportunity to have to deal with Chuck. The more exposure she got with him the more opportunities she had to impress him with herself.

"Chuck good morning! May we come in?" Megan said standing in the doorway revealing her perfect set of white teeth.

Chuck looked up from his computer, obviously reading email. He was a tall man in his fifties with gray temples. Today he was wearing a tailored starched white shirt that was unbuttoned at the neck. He obviously didn't have any client visits because he was dressed more casual than usual. The office had a business casual dress code unless there were clients visiting. Since Chuck was usually meeting with clients, he was usually dressed in a suit and tie. Cheryl was glad Chuck was dressed casually that day. He looked a lot less intimidating when he was dressed down.

"Sure ladies, come on in and have a seat." Chuck said pointing to the chairs in front of his huge desk.

Cheryl noticed his office was extremely neat and clean. There were no loose papers scattered across his desk and floor which was characteristic of the other employees' offices and desks.

"So, we're ready to quote on Braxton I see?" Chuck said turning to Cheryl and smiling. He knew the account executives were uneasy around him and tried to put them at ease. The only thing, if you didn't have your stuff together when you came to see him, he'd end up tearing you apart piece by piece.

"Yes we are Chuck. And hopefully, in a couple of days we'll be placing the coverage on it as well." Cheryl responded smiling back and trying to sound as confident as possible.

"Well, that sounds good. There's a nice premium on this account if the previous numbers I've seen are any indication. Why don't you show me what you have?" Chuck said still smiling at Cheryl.

"Well Chuck, here is where the actuarial numbers are coming in." Megan jumped in reaching across Cheryl to hand Chuck the document. "As you can see, it looks like they have only had about two claims to exceed one million dollars in the last ten years, and their current attachment is five million dollars, so they have an excellent loss history. We are recommending they keep the same attachment and here is the number the actuaries are coming up with. We would like to shave an additional ten percent off of that number, and keep an additional ten percent in our back pocket if it becomes necessary. Here is the analysis of the overall account that Cheryl has put together. It's pretty detailed." Megan turned and looked at Cheryl, at least giving her some credit.

Chuck reached out and took the analysis from Megan and glanced through it. The room fell silent for a second.

"So what were the circumstances of the two million dollar claims? Was the insured at fault at all?" Chuck asked looking at Megan. Megan paused for a moment. In her haste she'd forgotten to read that part of the analysis or ask Cheryl about it. Cheryl could see Chuck beginning to get a little irritated. He always expected a prompt answer to his questions.

"The two claims involved were actually brought by the same claimant and involved the negligence of an employee of the insured who is no longer with the company. As a matter of fact, those claims were closed back in 1998. There have been no other claims of that significance since then. There's a detailed write-up about them in my analysis for file documentation." Cheryl said pointing out to Chuck where to find the information. Chuck took a moment and read the analysis.

"Well, everything looks fine to me. I'm fine with the numbers you have put together here so it's okay to release the quotation today." He then turned to Cheryl. "Good job Cheryl..." He then signed the analysis form and handed it back to Cheryl. "Is there anything else you need from me?"

"No Chuck that's all I have. Thanks so much for your input." Cheryl said reaching her hand out to Chuck.

"Good luck with this one Cheryl. Bye guys." Chuck said and turned back around to his computer giving them the cue that it was time to leave.

"OK...thanks Chuck." Megan said as she got up and headed for the office door. Cheryl followed her out struggling with the huge file. When they got outside the door, Megan handed Cheryl back the actuarial document.

"Here, take this. Let me see the final letter before you send it to Bob. Also, make sure you get the sign-off from legal on those agreements you mentioned earlier. I have another meeting to get to." She then spun around and rushed back down the hall to her office.

Cheryl stood for a moment in the hall struggling with the heavy file and watching Megan scurry down the hall, and shook her head. She apparently hadn't gotten as much attention from Chuck as she was hoping for.

Chapter Fifteen

Cheryl looked at the clock on her desk. It was three o'clock already and she hadn't heard a response from the legal department about the Braxton agreements yet. Megan had insisted she at least get a response from them before speaking with Bob Conner, and she was not about to leave the office that day until that quotation was in Bob's hands. That darn Dave Nelson! Cheryl wasn't one to use curse words, but she felt like she could come up with a few choice ones at that moment. Dave was the corporate attorney assigned to work on her department's accounts, and like Cheryl would hear the kids say on occasion, he could be a real donkey sometimes. She really disliked dealing with him, but he was a necessary evil. For one thing, he had a serious problem working with women and loved to patronize them whenever an opening to do so presented itself. Dave wasn't a total jerk though. He was, like everyone else, doing what he could to handle the fact he was expected to do the work of three people. Cheryl tried to cut him some slack since she could relate, but she couldn't allow her work to suffer because Dave was overworked. He just needed to man up and get with the program.

"I know what, I'll give Jennifer a call." She said out loud hoping nobody heard her talking to herself.

Jennifer's firm specialized in that type of thing. Megan also knew Jennifer, and First National had on occasion outsourced a couple of things to Phillips, Willis and McKenzie when it was necessary. At least if she got some type of signoff from them initially, she could feel comfortable enough to release her quote, and First National's legal people could confirm the analysis she got from PWM later. Unfortunately, when she dialed Jennifer's number, her voice mail kicked on.

"Hey Jen its Cheryl....what's up girl? I haven't spoken to you in a couple of weeks. Where are you hiding? I know I've been swamped at work and haven't had a chance to go out to lunch in a while, but we haven't even spoken to each other since my dad's funeral. Anyway, I need some help with a large account I'm working on and I really need you to call me as soon as you get this message. So please, *call* me. Thanks Jen."

Where was Jennifer? Cheryl had been so busy lately she hadn't even realized how long it had been since she'd really had a conversation with her friend. She thought back to the day of her father's funeral. So much was going on then, with her father's sudden passing and Tom showing up the way he did. She didn't really have a lot of time to spend with Jennifer that day. But she had noticed there was something strange about her then, she just couldn't tell what. She recalled how Jennifer had gone on and on about her new responsibilities at work when Tom asked her about her job. It was something about the way she looked when she was talking about how much new exposure she was getting at the firm, and the partner that was showing special interest in her. She'd known Jennifer a long time and she could tell there was more to the story than she was letting on. Then again, it could just be a new boyfriend or something. Jen was never at a loss for male attention and tended to become scarce whenever there was a new man in her life. Hopefully, she had just stepped away to go to the ladies room or something. She really needed to hear from her, or somebody who could help her soon.

After about an hour of opening and responding to emails, her phone rang. She snatched it up after the first ring.

"Cheryl Marks. May I help you?"

"Yes, Cheryl Marks you may. This is Dave Nelson. I'm just calling to let you know I've reviewed the information you sent me, and I don't really see anything wrong with the agreements. They appear to be using the standard language, so if you guys are okay with providing the coverage, than everything is fine with me."

"Great! Thank you so much Dave. You don't know how much I appreciate your help with this!" Cheryl had learned since working with Dave that the best way to get something out of him was to feed his ego. "Is it possible that you could just do me one last favor? I need documentation for my file, so if you don't mind, if you could just send me a quick email, you know just confirming our conversation, that would be wonderful!"

"Uh…I guess I could send you something quickly. It doesn't need to be anything fancy does it, because I really don't have time to prepare a formal report…?" Dave asked.

"No, not at all, just send me a quick email. I really need to get it today though Dave, or else I'm not going to be able to release my quote." Cheryl responded holding her breath. She didn't want to push Dave too far or she knew he would shut down.

"Okay then. I'm sending it now."

"Thank you so much Dave. You are a lifesaver!" Cheryl responded hanging up the phone.

"Wow girl, you were really pouring that on thick. Was that old nutcase Dave Nelson you were speaking with? I could hear you all the way over by my cube."

Cheryl looked up at the attractive woman standing over her desk.

"Girl, I know, but that's the only way I can get Dave to be cooperative. I needed him to write an email and I needed him to do it now. You know how Dave is with women. I figured out how to work him though. Just stroke his ego a little and make him feel like he's some kind of god or something." Cheryl responded laughing.

Alicia Mason was about forty years old, the only other minority woman account executive in Cheryl's department, and the two women had bonded over the special circumstances of being double minorities in a white male dominated industry. Cheryl didn't know what she'd do without Alicia at First National. To have someone around that really got her and she could thoroughly relate to. It didn't seem to matter to Megan if she was the only minority in a room, in fact, in some ways it made her feel as though she was special or something. But Cheryl liked to have a little family around whenever possible.

"I hear you girl. At least we know it's not just us he treats that way. Good old Dave is an equal opportunity misogynist. Tammie was telling me the other day how she hates to have to ask him anything because he always ends up talking down to her." Alicia responded.

"I know, she mentioned that to me too. I don't know, in a way I understand why he's so tense sometimes though. I mean the man is just as overworked as the rest of us." Cheryl glanced quickly at her computer screen. "Uh oh, there's my email from my boy! Let me get this quotation letter done before Bob Conner leaves for the day. Megan will have a set of calves if it doesn't go out before I leave today." Cheryl said laughing.

"Oh yeah, I heard you were going after this huge account. I'm sure Sister Girl is riding you hard about that one. You know, I'm hearing rumblings about her being considered for something really big. At least she's busting her butt to be considered. But we'll talk about that later, go ahead and finish your letter. I need to finish a couple of things too because I do not want to miss my train this evening." Alicia said waving over her shoulder.

Cheryl watched Alicia walk away. She didn't know how Alicia was able to have a regular train schedule. She would most likely still be working at seven or eight o'clock that evening. Alicia didn't seem to let the pressure bother her as much. For one thing, she'd made it clear she wasn't interested in any more responsibility. After all, she was an account executive at one of the largest insurance firms in the country, which in itself was a big deal. And she was happy with where she was. She, on the other hand, had sealed her fate years ago when she was an assistant begging for more responsibility, and trying to learn the ins and outs of the insurance industry. Now she was beginning to feel as though her position was wearing her out.

∂∞∽

"Hey guys...you happy to see me?"

Cheryl pressed her nose against the large twenty- gallon aquarium in the corner of her living room. The multicolored fish darted back and forth quickly through the water in excitement. "You have a good day? Mine was a real bear."

Cheryl found watching the fish school throughout the lush aquarium helped to relax her after a long difficult day.

"I know you're hungry. I'll get you something to eat as soon as I get settled okay?"

After changing into her favorite pair of cotton pajamas, she searched the freezer for one of her convenient microwave dinner selections, and decided on the roasted turkey with potatoes. It wasn't the healthiest choice, but given it was eight-thirty at night she didn't have time to prepare anything fancy. She pulled the meal out of the box and once she peeled back the cellophane wrapper, placed the plastic tray in the small stainless steel microwave. Then she dialed into on her voicemail and walked back over to the aquarium where the fish were beginning to congregate at the top of the aquarium impatiently waiting to be fed. As she sprinkled the food into the top of the aquarium, she listened to her messages.

"Hey Cheryl....it's Jen. Sorry I didn't get a chance to get back to you today. I actually wasn't at the office this afternoon when your call came in, so I'm just getting your message now. I had a doctor's appointment and skipped out a little early. I hope you ended up getting what you needed from someone else. Sorry I couldn't help hon. I'll try calling you back later okay?"

Well at least she knew now she was still alive. Wonder if she's coming down with a cold or something, Cheryl thought. Her voice sounds a little nasally like she's congested or something. Oh well, she said she'd call me back, Cheryl thought, so I'll just wait to hear back from her. She waited for the next message to play.

"Hi, it's Mama."

Cheryl glanced back at the fish finishing up the small flakes of food she'd dropped in the aquarium earlier. Her mother always called at least once a week if she hadn't heard from her by then.

"Haven't heard from you yet this week, so I thought I'd give you a call. I have some good news for you. I'm assuming you haven't talked to Tishca yet. She and Steve are getting married! Steve surprised her for her birthday with a diamond ring! Can you believe it? Your sister is getting married! Give Tischa or me a call for all the details. I know she mentioned she was going to ask you to be a bridesmaid, so we have a big wedding to start planning."

That bit of news caused Cheryl to sit down. Tischa was getting married. For a while, she was beginning to wonder if any of the Marks girls would be taking that walk down the aisle any time soon. Tischa had just turned thirty years old, so she was sure to have been tightening the screws on poor Steve by now. She was happy for her sister though, and glad to hear her mother sound so happy about something. She'd needed something good to look forward to after the death of her husband. And Tischa and Steve were the perfect match. Everyone always knew they would end up together.

At least Tischa had found her soul mate. She, on the other hand, had yet to reach that point in life. She wasn't quite sure if she would recognize him when he showed up, but she just refused to settle for anything less than The One. Her mind flashed back briefly to that day when she was a child on Diamond Row...

While she was thinking the last message began to play.

"Cheryl....it's Tom Morgan. I was just thinking about you and decided to give you a call...actually, I've been thinking about you since I saw you in Chicago. I was just wondering how you've been doing. I hope everything is going okay...Anyway, give me a call sometime. And if you're ever out this way, you know, at the New York office or anything let me know. Maybe we can have dinner or something. I'd love to see you Cheryl."

Cheryl sat staring at the telephone. She'd thought about Tom a couple of times after seeing him at her father's funeral. It was nice to rekindle some of her old feelings for a while. Seeing Tom made the events of that day more bearable, and she appreciated him for that. But she wasn't a kid anymore, and had changed so much since then. She glanced around her Hyde Park apartment thinking about exactly how much her life had changed over the years. She'd never even imagined she could afford to live in a high rise building like this one when she was a teenager. Now she made more money than most of the people she grew up with. Definitely more than Tom did. She really wished Tom the best. She wished that he would one day meet a girl who would love and appreciate him for what he was. She just believed in the deepest depths of her heart that she wasn't the one.

Chapter Sixteen

"Ms Thompson, please complete the attached form and return it to me. Is your insurance and other information still the same?"

Jennifer took the brown easel from the young lady sitting behind the desk and reviewed the information.

"Yes, it looks like everything is the same." She said handing the form back to the young woman.

"No, you need to keep this with the other information. I just need you to complete the updated medical history form and return everything back to me together." The young woman then looked over Jennifer's shoulder. "May I help the next person please?"

Jennifer rolled her eyes at the assistant and took the form to the nearest seat in the reception area. She didn't understand why she had to complete the same form over and over again every time she visited the doctor's office. It wasn't like she didn't come to the same office every year. By now, they should know everything about her. She hurried through the medical history form and walked back to the reception desk handing it to the medical assistant.

"Thank you Ms Thompson. Please have a seat and Dr. Levine's nurse will be with you shortly." The assistant then reached past her for the next patient's form.

Jennifer shook her head at the assistant and returned to her seat grudgingly. I bet she really enjoys this part of the job, she thought. Probably makes her feel real special having the authority to make everybody wait. I don't have time for this, I'm an attorney. I have a real job.

Jennifer sat back down in the same chair she sat in previously and looked down at her watch. Her appointment was scheduled for twelve o'clock noon, and she'd hoped she wouldn't have to take longer than her usual lunch hour to complete it. She'd been Dr. Levine's patient for the last five years, mainly because he was a good physician and had been referred to her, but also because his office was right downtown. If she took an early lunch hour, she could get all her doctor appointments out of the way without having to take time off from work to get them done.

After about ten minutes of fumbling through old issues of People and Time magazines, she glanced back down at her watch. She was just about to return to the reception desk to ask how much longer it would be when she heard someone call her name.

"Jennifer Thompson?"

"Yes, I'm Jennifer Thompson." She said to the short blonde woman holding her medical file.

"Right this way Ms Thompson."

The nurse was pointing toward the large swinging doors that led to the examination rooms. "I'm just going to take your weight and blood pressure quickly. After that, we need to get a urine sample from you. Once you have it, please stop by the lab and drop it off. Then come back to Room A and change into the gown lying on the examination table. Dr. Levine will be with you shortly."

Okay, here we go. Now the fun starts, Jennifer thought. If it was one thing she hated more than waiting, it was peeing in the small cup. She always felt awkward holding the cup over the toilet and trying to make sure the urine went into the cup and not the toilet.

She also had a problem with walking through the long hall from the ladies room to the lab holding a cup of her urine. She almost hated that as much as the stirrups, but of course, when it came to total humiliation, the stirrups trumped everything else.

After managing to muster up a cup of urine and dropping it off at the lab, Jennifer searched through the long corridor for Room A. When she finally found it, she peeked inside. At the center of the room was a long vinyl table with a paper gown placed on top of it. She put the gown on quickly and waited shivering in the cold sterile room for Dr. Levine to come in. This wait usually stressed her out more than the one in the reception area. It's a good thing they take your blood pressure before this part of the process, she thought. She could feel her pressure slowly rising the longer she waited for Dr. Levine to make his arrival. After about another five minutes, Dr. Levine finally walked into the room.

"Well, hello Jennifer. How have you been?"

Dr. Levine was a short bald man who reminded Jennifer of her grandfather. That was one of the reasons she was so comfortable with having him as her gynecologist. Dr. Levine had been around a long time, and he had just about seen, and done it all. He was also well respected in the medical field, and had privileges at a number of the more prestigious hospitals throughout the Chicago area.

"I'm fine Dr. Levine. At least, I think I am. I don't know, you tell me." Jennifer said jokingly.

"Well now…let's see." Dr. Levine looked down at Jennifer's chart. He had so many patients that he hadn't had a chance to review her file yet. "So I see you've taken a urine test…Was your blood drawn yet Jennifer?" Dr. Levine asked raising his thick gray eyebrow.

"No sir, the nurse didn't draw my blood today." Jennifer responded.

"Tell you what. I'm just going to take a quick sample."

Dr. Levine then reached over to the workstation next to him and grabbed a syringe. After he'd drawn the blood, he called the nurse to take the blood sample to the lab.

"Okay Jennifer, time for the part I know you really hate. Just try to relax and we'll be done in a couple of seconds."

Dr. Levine had a way of making his patients feel at ease even though they were about to be completely and totally violated. Jennifer turned her face towards the wall and took a deep breath. After the examination was finally done, he asked Jennifer to get dressed and meet him in his office and then left out of the room. Jennifer always felt a sigh of relief when she could get up off of that table. The only thing, usually, Dr. Levine would tell her everything looked fine before he left, even if he wanted her to stop by his office afterwards. Today, he seemed to leave her hanging. She was sure everything was fine though.

Jennifer got dressed as quickly as possible, then walked over to Dr. Levine's office and sat down in the chair across from his huge desk. He wasn't in the office yet, so she kept herself occupied by studying the wall behind the desk, which was lined with an impressive array of Dr. Levine's degrees and awards.

"Oh you're here already, sorry for the wait Jennifer. I just needed to check a couple of things out with the lab." Dr. Levine said sitting down in the huge leather chair behind his desk.

He was watching her intently, and he seemed a bit distracted. Jennifer was beginning to worry. She'd been sitting in Dr. Levine's office with him on a couple of other occasions when he'd been interrupted with disturbing news about one of his patients. Sometimes x-rays or scans he'd ordered had come back showing cysts or tumors, or blood tests had revealed something unusual. As she sat waiting for Dr. Levine to tell her what was on his mind, she could feel her heart began thumping in her chest.

"Is everything okay, Dr. Levine? You didn't say." She asked.

"I'm sorry, Jennifer, everything looks fine. I should have said that. I'm assuming you knew you were pregnant though. Is that right?" Dr. Levine asked.

Jennifer looked at Dr. Levine, her eyes began to widen, and she looked like a doe caught in a set of headlights. "What? I'm pregnant?"

"Yes dear. You appear to be a little over five weeks along. I just assumed you'd taken a home test and was just coming to confirm the pregnancy. So, I take it you didn't know."

"No, Dr. Levine, I didn't know." Jennifer replied.

❧∞❧

Jennifer stood in a trance as the elevator doors opened up into the lobby of Phillips, Willis and McKenzie. She hadn't even realized she'd made it back to the office so quickly. The last thing she remembered doing was leaving Dr. Levine's office. Now she had walked all the way to her office and hadn't even been conscious of it. As she walked past Chad's office, she looked inside. As usual, he was bent over a pile of papers on his desk with the telephone to his ear. She paused for a moment then walked over to his assistant Lynn's desk. Lynn looked up at her blankly, indicating her attitude towards her obviously hadn't gotten any better.

"Um…Hi Lynn, how are you today?" She asked trying to sound as cheerful as possible.

"I'm fine Jennifer, how are you?" Lynn responded blandly.

"Good…I really need to see Chad some time today. Do you know if he has anything free on his schedule? It's really important that I speak with him." Jennifer asked.

"Well, I'm not sure that's going to be possible. Chad's working on something really important today, and he asked that he not be disturbed. Can one of the other partners help you?" Lynn responded trying to feel her out for more information, and also rubbing it in

145

that she was no longer the "it" girl at Phillips, Willis and McKenzie in case she didn't already know. Jennifer tried to remain cordial. Lynn had the upper hand in this situation and she needed to get past her in order to see Chad.

"No Lynn. The other partners would not be able to help me with this. I really need to see Chad and it's really important. Can you please let him know that Jennifer Thompson needs to see him today?" She was trying not to sound desperate.

Lynn sat back in her chair eyeing Jennifer closely.

"Well, I'll try and let him know but I can't promise anything. You'll need to check back with me later, he's on an important call right now." She responded smugly.

"Fine, I'll call you in about an hour, thanks."

Jennifer walked to her cubicle. Who did Lynn think she was anyway? She was just a secretary, and she was an attorney at this firm. Furthermore, once Chad found out what it was she needed to tell him that would put an end to Lynn's nasty attitude towards her. There was no way he was going to allow the woman who was carrying his child to be mistreated by his assistant. That thought caused her to pause. She was actually carrying Chad Phillips' child!

Her mind went back to the conversation they'd shared the first night they were together. Chad seemed so disappointed when he spoke about how difficult it had been for his wife Natalie to get pregnant. How they had basically given up. She couldn't wait to tell him that after all this time she was going to give him what his wife hadn't been able to. Chad would be elated when he found out the news. She was sure he was going to be.

Jennifer spent the next hour pretending to function normally by staring at file documents, not really able to concentrate on their content. She hadn't really been able to concentrate on anything since she'd left Dr. Levine's office. She was pregnant and she didn't know yet how to process that information. She at least knew one thing for sure. She needed to let Chad know the baby was his. She hadn't been with anyone else since that first night she'd spent with Chad after the Williamson meeting. There was no way she could even think about anyone else after that. Chad was it for her, and he had been since she'd first met him. Never in a million years did she think she'd wind up the mother of his child. She glanced at the clock on her desk. It was ten minutes after two, and she'd spoken to Lynn over an hour ago. She decided enough time had passed and to give her a call. Surely she'd had enough time to speak with Chad by now.

"Hi Lynn…It's Jennifer again. Were you able to ask Chad if he had some time to see me this afternoon yet?"

"Chad's been in his office all afternoon. I haven't had a chance to ask him anything." Lynn responded.

"…Lynn, this is pretty important. I need to speak to Chad today. Do you mind going in his office, and if he's on the phone can you just hand him a note letting him know I need to see him?" She asked.

"I can't do that. When Chad doesn't want to be disturbed, he means he doesn't want to be disturbed, and I'm not about to put my job in jeopardy because you want to see him."

Jennifer sat holding the phone for a moment. Lynn was obviously playing hardball. She knew Lynn was able to slip Chad a note without really disturbing him and she knew she'd done it before.

"Lynn, I'm not trying to jeopardize your job in any way. I'll just check back later, thanks.

Jennifer slammed the phone down. Lynn had worked her last nerve, and she'd just about taken all she could take from her. She couldn't wait to let Chad know how she'd been treating her. Girlfriend would be lucky to still have a job after she got finished with her. After another hour passed by, Jennifer was pretty much seething. She wasn't any good at work this afternoon. There was no way she could concentrate on her job, not until she'd shared her news with

Chad. She looked at her telephone. After deciding she wasn't in the mood for another phone confrontation with Lynn, she decided to just walk over to her desk. When she got to the reception area, Lynn was on the telephone, and it was obviously a personal call. She stood in front of her waiting for her to acknowledge her, but Lynn continued to talk, actually turning her head away from her slightly. Jennifer was fed up by now, and she was not going to continue to let Lynn disrespect her. She walked over to Chad's office, and knocked on the door even though it was open. By this time, Lynn was calling out to her, but it was too late. Chad looked up from the document he was reading.

"Yes, who is it?" He asked.

She walked inside the door and stood at the entrance waiting for Chad to ask her to sit down. He sat staring at her for a moment. His blue gray eyes suddenly turned from intense to cold and annoyed.

"Hi Chad, I wanted to talk to you." She said smiling at him.

It had been a while since they'd actually had a conversation, but now that she was in his office looking at him the old feelings began to take over and nothing else mattered. The time they'd shared together had been so special, there was no way Chad didn't reciprocate those feelings she told herself.

"Jennifer, I'm really busy. I thought I told Lynn I didn't want to be disturbed. Is she out there?"

"Yes Chad… Lynn is at her desk. She was on the phone, so I just walked in. I hope you don't mind." She said still waiting for Chad to invite her to sit down.

"Well I do mind. I'm busy and I don't have time to speak with you." Chad said. "Whatever it is you need to speak to me about will have to wait."

Jennifer looked at Chad. It was almost like the man in front of her was unfamiliar. He wasn't the same man who she'd shared intimate dinners with just a few weeks ago. Nor could he be the same man who'd made love to her in her apartment afterwards.

"Chad...I really need to talk to you..."

"Jennifer, what the hell is wrong with you? I said I don't have time to talk to you today! What about that don't you understand?"

By this time, Chad was looking furious and Jennifer noticed the tips of his ears were beginning to turn red. She was completely startled by Chad's reaction and could feel the tears began to well up in her eyes. She couldn't believe Chad was speaking to her in that manner. She turned to walk out of the room, then stopped suddenly, and turned back around. She stood speechless for a moment, looking Chad squarely in the eyes. Then she suddenly turned and reached for the door to his office. As she was closing it shut, she could see Lynn peeking in. After she'd closed the door, she walked calmly over to the chair in front of Chad's desk and sat down.

"I said I needed to speak with you, and I'm going to do it. I know you've been avoiding me for the last few weeks. Maybe you've decided our relationship was a big mistake or you're targeting someone else here, I don't know. But we have a little problem Chad."

Jennifer sat back in the chair and folded her arms across her chest. By this time, Chad was sitting silently staring at her. His facial expression was a mixture of shock and confusion. After a moment of silence had passed between them, she leaned in towards the desk and said,

"I'm pregnant, and it's your baby."

Chapter Seventeen

The silence in the room was deafening. Chad continued to stare at Jennifer as though she had spoken a language that was unfamiliar to him and he was waiting for further clarification.

"What...What did you say?" He asked. He'd heard clearly the words Jennifer had spoken but he felt the need to ask the question anyway because he really didn't know how else to respond.

"I said, I'm pregnant, and I'm carrying your child." Jennifer repeated.

The thick blanket of silence continued to fill the room. Chad pushed his chair away from his desk as though he needed more space. He was looking like he was having difficulty breathing. His usual air of intensity that commanded fear and reverence from his employees had dissipated, and his shoulders appeared to slump downwards as he sat staring at the papers on his desk.

Jennifer just sat staring at Chad. The man who always appeared powerful and in control suddenly seemed anything but. She hadn't been totally sure how Chad would take the news of her pregnancy, even though she'd managed to convince herself he would be overjoyed. And why shouldn't he be? He'd told her himself how he and Natalie had tried for so long to get pregnant and how painful it had been to come up empty over and over again. Now he was going to have the child he'd longed for, and she was going to be the woman to give it to him. She had been concerned about Chad's recent dismissive behavior towards her, but now that she was alone with him in his office, sitting across from him, with the rest of the world outside, all she felt was a sense of deep overwhelming affection.

"Chad, I know this is a little shocking to hear. I just found out today myself and, believe me, I was just as shocked as you are. I just thought you should know as soon as possible since it is your child. Don't worry, I don't intend to broadcast it to anyone, at least not until we're ready." Jennifer reached out across the desk to place her hand on Chad's arm. "It's okay Chad. It'll be okay. We'll work this out. It'll be okay."

Chad looked up at Jennifer. His eyes were wide and empty as though he was looking at her but thinking of something, or someone else. After staring at her for a moment he spoke.

"Are you positively sure you're pregnant? And are you sure it's mine?"

The initial feelings of love Jennifer felt towards Chad were now slowly developing into fury and rage. How dare he ask her that question? She knew that was usually the first cop out the brothers on the street would take when they found out their women were expecting, but she hadn't expected that from him. What did he mean was she sure it was his baby? What kind of woman did he think she was? Now, he had gone from being evasive and dismissive to down right cold.

"What the hell do you mean am I sure it's yours?" She lashed out. "Yes Chad, I am sure I'm pregnant and I'm sure it's yours. I haven't been with anyone else since I was with you, and I'm insulted by your question. If you need me to take a paternity test to prove it's yours, then that's fine too."

Chad's eyes widened even further at Jennifer's reaction. He appeared to be just as shocked by the way she was speaking to him, as he was by why she was speaking to him.

"Jennifer…I…I didn't mean to imply anything…I just…what do you want to do?" Chad asked sounding just as confused as he looked.

"Well…I realize we don't want this getting out just yet, so we have to be discreet. I've heard it's not good to really tell anyone until the first trimester is over anyway, I mean you never know what could happen. But in the meantime, I guess I'll need to decide what to do about my job here. It may get a little uncomfortable working at the firm after I start to show. I haven't had a lot of time to digest everything yet, just finding out today and all…" Jennifer was speaking rapidly.

"So, you intend to keep the baby?"

"Of course I intend to keep the baby!" Jennifer responded shocked and insulted further by Chad's question. "Chad, this is your baby I'm carrying here. You finally have an opportunity to be a father. Think about it, this is a blessing in disguise. You deserve a chance to be a father… don't you want to be a father Chad?" She asked trying her best to reason with him.

"Yes Jennifer! I want to be a father. Just not like this. Look, we need to talk about this. I know it's your decision what you want to do about the baby, but I really don't want this information getting out. It would kill Natalie if she found out. I can't have this getting back to her." Chad said.

Jennifer could hear the desperation in his voice. She couldn't believe she was sitting before him sharing with him what should have been welcomed news. That she was carrying his unborn child. That after all this time, he was going to be a father, but all he seemed to be interested in at this moment was his wife.

"Are you kidding me? This would kill Natalie? I'm sorry Chad, but right now, I'm more concerned about my baby than your wife!

"Jennifer, calm down, we can figure this out." Chad was obviously trying to keep her from creating a scene. "It's clearly your decision, and I am prepared to support you financially in whatever decision you make. If you decide to have the baby, I fully intend to support it, but I need to keep this information away from Natalie." Chad was pretty much pleading by now.

"Would you quit talking to me about Natalie? Look, I don't want to hurt her, and we didn't plan on this happening. But, I love you Chad, I've always loved you and I want to have your baby."

Chad sat speechless staring at Jennifer. He looked tired and worn as though the conversation had exhausted every once of strength in his body. After a long pause, he gathered enough strength to speak.

"Jennifer, I have the utmost respect for you. You are an intelligent young woman, but I love my wife. Natalie and I have had our problems, but we love each other, and I have no intention of ending my marriage. I don't understand what it is you want from me."

Jennifer sat back in her chair. By now, the conversation had exhausted her as well. It was at that moment that she finally realized her fantasy was over. There was never going to be a fairy tale ending between her and Chad. It had all been in her head. Yes, Chad wanted to have a child, just not with her. She sat looking at Chad in silence. The man who she once thought was larger than life, now appeared broken and small. Suddenly she pushed the chair back and stood up. As she turned to walk out of the office, she could hear Chad calling out behind her.

"Jennifer, we haven't finished discussing this. I need to know…what it is you want from me."

Jennifer opened the door to Chad's office and called back over her shoulder.

"I don't want anything from you Chad."

As Jennifer walked past Lynn's desk, she could feel her gaze fixed on her. She walked past her in silence to the glass doors that led to the long corridor leading to her cubicle. Once she reached her cubicle, she sat down in the chair behind her desk and stared at her computer screen. Suddenly, she reached over and turned off the computer, pulled out her desk drawer and took out her small black leather handbag. After placing the purse on her desk, she calmly stood up and put on her long black wool coat and tied the belt snuggly across her waist. As she was closing the desk drawer, she could hear Rachel Lopez call out to her over her cubicle wall.

"Jennifer, is that you?" She could tell Rachel had obviously heard something by the tone of her voice.

Ignoring Rachel, Jennifer headed towards the elevator lobby. As she stood in the lobby waiting for the elevator to come, she could still feel Lynn staring at her back. Finally, the doors swung open and she stepped inside. Once inside the elevator, she leaned back against the wall and watched the doors close slowly across the large gold block letters reading Phillips, Willis and McKenzie.

The bus ride home was almost unbearable. Since she'd left work earlier than normal, only the local route was running. The bus she normally took only ran during rush hours so it took her almost twice as long to get home. Jennifer entered her apartment building door. She lived in a newly refurbished brownstone, not too far from Cheryl's high rise building in the Hyde Park area, and as she approached the building that afternoon, it seemed especially warm and welcoming. It felt good to be home, away from all the chaos of downtown, Phillips, Willis and McKenzie, and Chad. She pushed any thought of Chad to the back of her mind. She told herself she was not going to think about what happened that day. She didn't want to think about it anymore.

She walked into the bathroom and filled the bathtub with warm water, adding lavender scented bubble bath to the water. A glass of wine and a nice long soak in a warm bath was just what she needed to wash off everything. As she soaked in the warm water, she leaned her head back against a plush folded bath towel and watched the bubbles shimmer and burst, as soft jazz music flowed out of the small radio on top of the medicine cabinet. After the bath, she was feeling more relaxed and mellow. She put on her terry cloth bathrobe, took the half-empty glass of wine into the kitchen and refilled the glass. Then she went back into the living room and curled up on her large navy blue velvet sofa. She absolutely loved sitting in her living room because it made her feel like a queen in her castle. It was her favorite room in the house, and where she'd spent the most time and money decorating. Whenever she had guests over they would go on and on about what a great job she'd done with her place. If there was one thing she was known for, it was for being a woman of style and taste. Jennifer sat for a moment looking around her apartment. Then suddenly, she burst into tears. What had she done? She'd just walked out on her job without a word to anyone. And she was pregnant by a man who could care less about her. She didn't want to give up her law career after she'd worked so hard to get to where she was, but she couldn't continue to work for Chad Phillips either. What was she going to do?

After she'd cried for what seemed like hours, she decided to check her phone messages and go to bed. There was a message from Cheryl. She apparently needed her to do something for her at work, something about reviewing contracts. She picked up the phone and dialed Cheryl's number. Her voice mail picked up so she left a message.

"Hey Cheryl….it's Jen. Sorry I didn't get a chance to get back to you today. I actually wasn't at the office this afternoon when your call came in, so I'm just getting your message now. I had a doctor's appointment and skipped out a little early. I hope you ended up getting what you needed from someone else. Sorry I couldn't help hon. I'll try calling you back later okay?"

In a way, she was glad Cheryl wasn't there. She would probably be able to tell there was something wrong with her, and she wasn't ready to discuss this with her. Cheryl was one of her closet friends in the world and she'd do just about anything for her, but she just

156

couldn't talk to her about this. Even though the two of them had a lot in common, in some ways they were like night and day. For one thing, Cheryl was still a virgin. Most people would have a hard time believing that, given the fact Cheryl was a young, attractive, successful woman, but Cheryl took her Christian faith extremely serious, and sex just as serious. She'd never really said it, but she knew Cheryl had yet to be intimate with a man, not even Tom Morgan who was her longest and closet relationship. She'd had other relationships after Tom, but she always made it clear she was saving herself for the man she would marry.

Throughout the years, the two of them had countless chick talk sessions about their ideal men and what they wanted for their lives. Jennifer had been raised going to church every Sunday just as Cheryl, but once she reached a certain point in life she made the decision it was okay to test the waters a little. She would make fun of Cheryl's idealism sometimes, at how she expected her white knight to swoop in one day and carry her off somewhere to live happily ever after. But now, given her current predicament, she was beginning to think that maybe Cheryl had the right idea. She just wasn't ready to hear it from her. While she knew Cheryl would do her best to be a supportive friend, and would help her in any way she could, she just wasn't in the mood to feel judged by her.

Jennifer was about to move her pity party to her bedroom, when the telephone rang. She didn't care to talk to anyone, but she thought it might be important, or Cheryl calling her back, so she sighed and answered the phone.

"Hello?" she said softly.

"Well hello, is this my long lost girlfriend whom I haven't spoken to in about a year?"

Jennifer couldn't place the voice for a second, and then she recognized her friend's voice.

"Charity... Is this you?" She asked.

"Oh, she does remember me, huh? I was beginning to wonder if you and Cheryl had dropped off the planet or something. I haven't heard from the two of you in almost a year." Charity said laughing.

"Has it really been that long Charity? I thought I spoke to you a couple of months ago." Charity was still exaggerating as usual.

"Okay, it hasn't really been a year, but it's been at least six months. Anyway, how are you doing girlfriend? How's everything with the job, Ms Attorney?" Charity asked.

"Oh, everything's fine." Jennifer wasn't ready to tell anyone that she most likely didn't have a job any longer. "How's everything with you and Mike and the kids? I bet the two of them are so big by now. How old is little Mikey, about five months?"

"Mikey is five months and Callie is three years old now. Can you believe it? Did you get the pictures I sent you? We'll be scheduling our appointment for our holiday picture soon, so I'll be sending you one of those too. Can you believe it's almost Thanksgiving? What are your plans for the holidays?'

Jennifer hadn't even thought about the holidays. Charity had become a typical housewife, excited about her kids and Mike and her holiday photos. As she listened to Charity she longed to have a taste of her perfect suburban life. While Charity didn't have a big time career like Cheryl, or even her for that matter, she had a wonderful man who loved her and a perfect set of kids. Who would have thought Charity of all people would end up the most settled out of their little clique.

"The holidays….is it that time already? I haven't even thought about that Charity. I guess that's the life of a housewife, you have to be on top of those things. You know, I am just amazed by you. You sound really happy and I'm happy for you." Jennifer said.

"Well, we would love to see you and Cheryl sometimes. You two are the single people so it's easier for you to travel. We have plenty of room in our new house, so anytime you guys want to visit, just let me know. I'm always talking to Callie about her aunts Cheryl and Jennifer. She's beginning to think I made you two up since she hasn't ever seen you."

"Well tell her we're real. Who knows, I may take you up on that offer Charity. I need to get out of Chicago for a while anyway." Jennifer replied.

"Then why not come down for Thanksgiving if you're not doing anything! I love to cook everything I can think of then, and you have a couple of days off during that time don't you? Maybe you can bring Cheryl with you."

Jennifer thought about it for a second. Thanksgiving was in a couple of weeks and getting out of Chicago right now was just what she needed. She wasn't sure what she was going to do about a job, but she was pretty sure she wasn't going back to Phillips, Willis and McKenzie. Her little discussion with Chad that afternoon, at least the parts Lynn could make out, and her early exit was probably all over the office by now. And she really couldn't bear facing Chad anymore anyway. She needed to get away to a new environment, where she could clear her head and figure out what she was going to do next.

"Well, I don't know about Cheryl, she's always so busy now, but you know what Charity, I would love to spend Thanksgiving with you and Mike and the kids, so I guess you can start planning that meal now, and save a place for me at the table."

Chapter Eighteen

"Have you gotten any feedback from Bob yet? You do know the expiration date is in a couple of days. Have you heard anything?"

Cheryl looked up to find Megan leaning over her desk. Oh god, she's here again, she thought. It's amazing how this woman can sneak up on you. I mean, I know the girl is thin, but this is ridiculous.

"Yes Megan, I do know the expiration's soon, and no, I haven't heard anything yet. I've left a couple of messages for Bob, but he hasn't gotten back to me yet. I'm sure he's being bombarded with other quotes and questions, and is just busy trying to sort everything out. I expect to hear from him some time today... or else I'll try calling him again."

"Well, we need to hear something soon. Chuck is expecting me to give him an update on that account in the managerial meeting today. I'll just have to try and smooth things over by telling him you will be hearing something today. I don't have to tell you what a hot button this is. Senior Management is expecting us to deliver this account." Megan was standing over her now with her arms folded.

"I understand Megan. If I don't hear anything in a couple of hours, I will give Bob another call."

"You should call him now." Megan said sternly. She then turned and walked away as quickly as she appeared.

Cheryl could feel the bubbles in the pit of her stomach, and she suddenly felt ill. She'd been nervous about this for a couple of weeks now. Everything in her had been poured into getting Braxton. Now the renewal date was in a few days, and she hadn't heard a peep out of Bob Conner. Anyone who'd been in the business long enough knew that was never a good sign. She felt like she was in a ship sinking in deep water without a paddle, and didn't know what to do next. She'd already left a couple of messages for Bob, and Megan was sweating her to contact him again.

Megan was known to be pushy, and had no problem imposing herself on other people whether they wanted her or not. That was the reason she sent all her phone messages urgent even though most of them weren't. She always sent them that way because she wanted to make sure her call was the first one received and, therefore, the first one answered. But her aggressive behavior usually irritated the heck out of people. And Cheryl absolutely hated when Megan instructed her to do something that was out of her comfort zone. While she understood the need to be assertive, she had a real problem with coming across too aggressive or just plain pissing people off. Megan, on the other hand, only cared about what she needed to accomplish and if other people didn't like her methods, than too bad.

But Megan wasn't her issue right now. Cheryl wanted, and needed, to land the Braxton account. She realized not getting that account was going to have serious implications for her. Because of the amount of premium it could bring into First National, her quote had gained the attention of even the president of the company. She wouldn't get fired or anything if she didn't get it, but she just couldn't stand the idea of looking as though she couldn't produce in front of senior management. Sometimes, she wished she hadn't even gone after the darn thing in the first place. Then she wouldn't have this huge knot twisting in her stomach right now.

Cheryl just felt there was too much going on at one time, and she liked to keep her life as simple as possible. And the drama just wasn't at work. Now her family was going postal over Tischa's upcoming nuptials too. This was the first Marks family wedding and her mother was beside herself helping Tischa with all the planning. Cheryl had agreed to be a bridesmaid, but having to squeeze in multiple visits to bridal shops for the perfect chiffon dress, and then periodic fitting appointments, was taking a toll on her already overbooked schedule. And Tischa was being almost impossible. It had required an excursion to just about every available bridal salon in Chicago, and the surrounding areas, to find a dress she deemed fabulous enough for her bridesmaid's dress. Being in the fashion industry, Tischa had good taste, so Cheryl was at least happy that there were no oversized sleeves or ruffles involved.

To add to the chaos, Tischa had chosen the Saturday after Thanksgiving as her wedding date. Tischa had been planning her wedding ever since she'd first met Steve, so other than the dresses, she knew exactly what she wanted, and was able to put the wedding together in a couple of weeks. She figured since it was a holiday weekend, everyone would still be in a festive mood after a couple of days off from work. And normally, that would have been a lovely idea, but it just so happened that Braxton's renewal date was the Friday before Tischa's wedding. Cheryl was just worried that if, God forbid, she ended up not getting the account, it would put a damper on the whole holiday weekend for her, including Tischa's big day.

And then there was Jennifer. She'd been acting so odd lately and Cheryl had no idea why. She couldn't recall anything happening between the two of them that would cause her to be so distant. The last thing she remembered was calling and asking her for help reviewing Braxton's legal agreements. Jennifer wasn't in the office when she called and hadn't gotten her message until she'd gotten home that night. When she did call, the tone of her voicemail was strange. She remembered thinking her voice sounded congested, almost like she'd been crying. Jennifer told her she'd had a doctor's appointment that day, which was why she wasn't in the office when Cheryl called. So Cheryl automatically began to worry that she'd found out some disturbing news or something. But when she asked Jennifer later if everything was okay, she said she was fine. Cheryl was hesitant to believe her at first, but later decided she was probably worrying over nothing. At least until she got the call from Charity the following week asking if she was coming to Atlanta with Jennifer for Thanksgiving weekend.

Cheryl didn't understand why Jennifer wouldn't tell her she was going to see Charity and Mike, especially since they'd talked about visiting them in Atlanta for years. It wasn't so much that Jennifer was going without her. Since Tischa's wedding was during Thanksgiving weekend, she wouldn't be able to go anyway. It was just the fact she never even mentioned it to her. That was the part Cheryl couldn't understand, because she and Jennifer pretty much told each other everything. And given everything that was going on right now, she really needed to talk to her friend. Cheryl thought back to their days growing up in Ridgeland. While she and Charity were closer back then, over the years, Jennifer had become her go to person whenever she needed to sort anything out. She was just so laid back and easy to be around. Even though some people found Jennifer shallow and somewhat conceited, there was always an air of lightness about her that Cheryl found refreshing, and she had this uncanny ability to always make everything seem less serious than it was.

Cheryl then reached for the Rolodex next to her telephone and searched for Bob Conner's number. She didn't want to be a pain and leave Bob another message, but she had left him two messages and he had yet to return either call. She paused for a moment holding Bob's business card, then took a deep breath and decided to suck it up and call. Once again, she listened as the phone rang and rang and finally rolled over to his voice mail. Before the voicemail could pick up, she pressed the star key and then the zero to be transferred to the receptionist.

"Global International, make I help you?" The perky voice on the other end said.

"Yes you may, I've been trying to locate Bob Conner. I've left him a couple of messages, but he's yet to return my call. Do you know if he's in the office today?" Cheryl asked.

"Yes, I believe he is in today, I can put you back in his voicemail and you can leave another message, or can someone else help you?

Cheryl paused for a moment.

"Um…yes maybe someone else can help me. Is Matthew Robinson in the office?" Cheryl asked holding her breath. She wasn't sure if she actually wanted to speak with Matthew or not, but she was desperate. Before she had anytime to really think about it, the receptionist switched her over to Matthew's extension.

"Matt Robinson."

Cheryl suddenly forgot what she wanted to ask when she heard the smooth baritone of Matthew's voice.

"Matthew, or Matt, I guess you prefer Matt?" She asked trying not to sound too confused.

"Either one you're comfortable with is fine with me. May I ask who this is?" Matthew replied politely.

"Sorry! This is Cheryl Marks with First National, how are you Matt? I haven't spoken with you since we were in Las Vegas." She said smiling.

"Oh, is this Cheryl Marks from Ridgeland? Hey Cheryl, I'm doing just fine, how's it going with you? How's everything in my home town?"

"Everything is fine Matt, but you know things would be a lot better if you guys would tell me Braxton is going with First National. I haven't heard from either you or Bob since I sent our quote. And I've tried calling Bob over and over and haven't heard back from him. What's going on Matthew?" She asked holding her breath.

"…Well, I have to tell you Cheryl, there is a lot of competition on this one and the current carrier NRC is really putting up a fight to hold on to it." Matthew replied. Cheryl had heard this line before and knew where it was leading.

"Matt, I have to get this account! What can we do to make that happen? If need be, I'll go to my management and get them to approve shaving something off our number." Cheryl didn't want to tell him she had the approval already to take an additional ten percent off. The client sometimes got offended if they didn't get the best number on the first quote, but it helped to have something in your back pocket. "I just need to get an idea where we need to be…"

"Cheryl, you probably need to know also that the client is leaning towards staying with NRC. Your quote was very attractive. First National is comparable to NRC in your services and form, but the current carrier does have the privilege of getting the last look."

Matthew didn't seem to be willing to give her any information on the numbers. NRC obviously had an in with Global and they weren't willing to share much with her, which was probably why Bob hadn't returned her calls.

"Matt, I want this account and I'm prepared to do what I need to get it! I'm willing to take this all the way up to the head of my department. I just need to get an idea from you as to where we need to be. True NRC is a good company, but not as good as First National. NRC's services and form cannot touch ours. I can fax you a comparison of the two forms documenting that if you'd like. We are the ideal insurance carrier for Braxton Matt, not NRC." Cheryl said firmly.

There was a brief second of silence. Cheryl couldn't tell if her hard sell had worked on Matthew or if he was irritated by her persistence. Matthew still wasn't saying anything and she was about to speak again.

"Tell you what Cheryl, I like your style. Wow, you're a pretty assertive young lady. That must be the Ridgeland in you." Matthew said jokingly.

Cheryl felt flattered by his compliment, but she pushed that thought to the back of her mind. She didn't have time to be flattered with all her hard work on the line.

"Bob has a strong relationship with NRC, but if you guys were to send a revised quote right now, he'd have no choice but to present it to the client. It has to be soon though because they're making a decision tomorrow due to the holiday." Matthew said.

"Thank you Matt! I'll send it to your attention to make sure it gets to Bob, but please Matt, you have to give me some idea where we need to be. Just put me in the ballpark... please."

"...You didn't hear it from me, but you're going to need to come down at least another twenty percent to steal this away from NRC. Good luck with that Cheryl. I have a client meeting right now, so I have to run." Matthew said.

"Oh by all means, go ahead, and thanks Matt. I really appreciate your help."

Cheryl placed the phone back on the receiver and stared at the copy of her Braxton quotation letter as if the longer she stared at the piece of paper on her desk she could miraculously will a solution to her problem to drop into her head. She needed to shave twenty percent from her quote and she had no idea how she was going to do it. Why did she have to pour it on so thick with Matthew? She made it sound as though she had First National's management in the palm of her hand. But the truth was she had no idea if Chuck would agree to taking anything else off the number that she'd quoted. He had agreed to another ten percent, but not twenty. And she didn't even know if the twenty would be enough. Bob Conner had obviously made some kind of inside deal with NRC to keep Braxton with them another year. But she wasn't about to just let all her hard work slip through her fingers, not without a fight.

She grabbed the letter, leapt off her chair and headed for Megan's office. Megan's empty chair was turned facing the door of the office like she had just made one of her typical bolts out the door. Where the heck is she when I really need her, Cheryl thought, then turned around swiftly and walked over to Alicia Mason's cubicle.

"Alicia, have you seen Megan? I need to talk to her like right now." Cheryl asked.

"I haven't seen her since about an hour ago. She told me she was running upstairs to a meeting with administration and then she was going straight to the managerial meeting. She wanted to know if I needed her for anything, but you know I was like, uh, no Megan, if I need you, I know where to find you, thanks." Alicia said laughing.

"I hear you, but I do need her, and I need her now. I have to send Bob Conner's office a revised quote, and it has to be right way. I just need to get permission to revise the number." Cheryl said.

"If you're talking about that large account you've been working on, don't you need Chuck's approval to change the quote?" Alicia asked grinning slyly.

Cheryl rolled her eyes at Alicia. The thought of having to go to Chuck without Megan caused her stomach to churn again. At least when Megan was with her she had some type of buffer. No one ever volunteered to meet with Chuck it was more or less a command performance. But there were certain issues that required the head of the department to sign off on and this happened to be one of them.

"Don't roll your eyes at me girlie. That's how it is when you make the big bucks, you have to work on the big accounts, and those accounts always go through Chuck." Alicia said still grinning.

"Uh excuse me, but my bucks are not that big first of all. Second, I don't mind meeting with Chuck. I mean, he's always been decent to me. It's just all the stories flying around, you know, I'm always nervous I'm going to slip up on something and he's going to chew my head off, like he did to poor Bill in claims."

"I know. That's what everybody thinks. Believe me I don't envy you having to meet with him. What are you going to do?" Alicia asked.

"...If I don't find Megan soon, I'm just going to have to talk to Chuck by myself. I don't have a choice." Cheryl said then waved and headed back to Megan's office.

As Cheryl walked towards Megan's office, she called upon every ounce of psychic power she wished she had. Unfortunately, when she looked inside the door, there was Megan's empty chair mocking her, and making it clear her abilities were lacking, for she'd failed to conjure up any sign of her. Cheryl looked down at the letter in her hand. Where's all that confidence you had earlier with Matthew now, she said to herself. You wanted to be like Megan, well now's your chance. She wouldn't let anyone stand in her way of getting what she wanted. Cheryl then took off towards Chuck's office trying not to think so she wouldn't be able to convince herself to turn around. His assistant was sitting at the desk next to his office.

"Hi Terry, is Chuck in his office? I have a hot quote that needs his attention." Cheryl asked.

"Oh, hello Dear..." Terry was in her late fifties, and called everyone under forty by the name Dear. "Unfortunately he isn't. He went into the managerial meeting about ten minutes ago. They're meeting in the large conference room on the other side of the floor."

Well this day could not get any worse, Cheryl thought. That meeting was known to last for hours and by the time the participants who were subjected to attend got out of there, they usually headed straight for their offices, and then the elevators. Cheryl's mind was racing a mile a minute. She could go ahead and change the quote herself and send it on to Matthew. After all, everyone really wanted this account, and if there was ever a time to violate her authority, it would be now. She would just have to make an executive decision. Yes, she should do that, she thought. Then she stopped in her tracks. Right Cheryl, good idea. You should make the decision to change the quote yourself, and then you also need to decide whether to start cleaning out all your stuff from your desk today, or wait until tomorrow when everyone else finds out. She always thought one of the most humiliating things in the world was to watch someone who'd been terminated having to clean out all their junk from their desk, while their manager and a security person stood over them until they were done. And Cheryl thought it would take her quite a while to clean everything out that she'd accumulated over all the years she'd been an employee of First National, so termination right now was not an option.

After a few seconds of walking and talking herself into remaining sensible, and employed had passed, Cheryl looked up and realized she'd walked all the way to the door of the large conference room. She stood outside staring at the closed black door. Then she pressed her ear up against the door and listened to the sound of muffled voices inside. The room could hold as many as twenty people, and with all the department heads in attendance, it was most likely filled to capacity. She continued to stand in front of the door, as other employees passed by looking at her, some with looks of curiosity, and others, concern. She'd hoped she hadn't been talking to herself out loud, as she tended to do whenever she was trying to sort things out in her head. It was also pretty clear to everyone who passed by, that since all the managers were meeting in that room, she obviously had some serious issue that needed to be discussed with one of them.

Cheryl realized she couldn't continue to stand in front of that door for the next couple of hours. She didn't have a couple of hours to stand there. She finally decided it was time to stop being a chicken and open the door. She'd just have to live with whatever the consequences were. She said a quick prayer, took a deep breath and opened the door as slowly and quietly as possible. Chuck was sitting at the head of the long conference table. Megan was sitting two seats away from him. Of course, she couldn't be sitting near the door, Cheryl thought. Then at least she could catch her eye and ask her to step out of the room. But Megan was typically sitting near the head of the table, and there was no way she was going to get her attention without disrupting the entire meeting.

Cheryl continued to stand at the entrance of the large conference room hoping she could catch Megan's eye, but her eyes, of course, were fixed on Chuck, who was addressing the group. Cheryl's heart felt like it was about to beat out of her chest, but she continued to stand in the doorway. Finally, after what seemed like an eternity, Chuck caught a glimpse of her in his peripheral vision. He suddenly stopped speaking and stared at her. His expression was a mixture of surprise and annoyance, and Cheryl could feel her heart began to beat even faster. At that point, Megan turned her glance in the direction Chuck was looking. When she saw Cheryl standing in the doorway, she slanted her eyes, in obvious disapproval. Cheryl realized it was time for her to speak or close the door. She ignored Megan's disapproving stare, and looked directly at Chuck.

"Excuse me Chuck, I hate to disturb your meeting, but I have an issue that's extremely important and time conscious. It's regarding the Braxton account."

Chapter Nineteen

There was a second of silence in the room. Cheryl continued to stand at the door waiting for a response from Chuck.

"...Cheryl, what is it you need?" Chuck said after another short pause.

Cheryl's breathing felt labored. She began walking towards the front of the room.

"I'm so sorry, guys, but this is sort of important." She said to the other managers as she headed towards the front of the room.

"No problem. We needed a break." She heard one of them say as she walked up to Chuck. The room suddenly burst into laughter. The comment caused a slight grin to spread across Chuck's face to her surprise.

"I'm sorry Chuck, but I need to revise my Braxton quote right away, and I need your permission to do it. I know you've already given me permission to take off ten percent, but I have it on good authority that if we can come down another ten, we have a really strong possibility of writing this account. The problem is I need to get the quote over to Global within the next hour. That's why I needed to interrupt the meeting. Otherwise, I wouldn't have disturbed you." Cheryl said.

"Do you feel comfortable with taking another ten percent off Cheryl? Does the loss history and exposure count justify the decrease?" Chuck asked.

"Yes, Chuck I do feel comfortable. As we discussed in our earlier meeting, other than two past losses as a result of an employee who is no longer with the insured, this account has an exemplary loss history. This is a large account, but based on the premium and losses, I think another ten percent is doable." Cheryl replied quickly, then reached out and handed Chuck the quote letter. Chuck reached out and took the letter, reading the terms she'd included on the letter. After a moment of silence, he looked up at her.

"Well, in that case, I'm fine with the revision." Chuck then grabbed a pen from the table and wrote on the letter, then handed it back to Cheryl.

"Thank you so much Chuck. I'll just get out of your way now. Thanks again guys." She said as she quickly headed towards the door. As she was walking, she heard Megan's voice.

"Be sure and give me an update before you leave today Cheryl." Megan said.

"I will." Cheryl said without turning around.

≈•≈

The next morning, Cheryl couldn't get into the office soon enough. It wasn't like she was able to sleep the night before anyway. True to form, she'd awaken that morning about one thirty and every emotion and unresolved issue came flooding to her mind, leaving sleep all but impossible. She'd decided to give up on trying to fall asleep about four o'clock and by six o'clock was headed to the office. Since it was the day before Thanksgiving, the office would be closing early, and she wanted to have ample time to get everything she needed done before the holiday weekend. She was also anxious to find out what the verdict was on Braxton once and for all. The last few days had taken their toll on her and she was resolved to putting the matter to rest, regardless of the outcome.

One good thing had come out of it though. Her bold move the day before had turned out to have surprising results. She had no idea what would happen when she walked into Chuck's meeting the way she did. It was as though all of her reserve and common sense had left her being and the adrenaline had taken over, carrying her into that room. She didn't know what the result would be, but she knew she had to open that door and go in. Never in her wildest dreams could she imagine doing that, or that she would address Chuck the way she did and walk out of there with her head, and dignity still intact. Not only did Chuck not bite her head off then, he was even more civil towards her later that day.

The meeting had gone on longer than usual, and by the time it was over, most of the other staff had gone home for the day. Cheryl, of course, was still sitting at her desk when Chuck walked through the office on his way to the restroom, which he usually did at the end of the day to check out which employees were still working, and who had skipped out early. Cheryl was finishing up a phone call, when she saw him walk past and wave. As she waved back, she could feel her heart start fluttering again. Even though he had received her well earlier, she never actually felt totally comfortable with him. So when he stopped by again on his way back to his office, she did her best to suppress the queasiness she suddenly felt.

"Cheryl, you're still here. How did everything go? Did Bob give you a response yet?" He asked.

"No Chuck. I haven't heard from Bob yet. I talked to Matthew Robinson though, who is working with Bob on Braxton. He was the one who gave me the tip to decrease the number by twenty percent. I think NRC has an in with Bob, but Matthew is trying to work with me. I don't know what's going to happen yet though Chuck." Cheryl replied.

"Well Cheryl, regardless, you have done a good job with this account whether you get it or not. Do you want me to give Bob a call? I've known Bob a long time. You know we used to work together in Seattle a long time ago." Chuck said grinning.

"No, I didn't know that! Sure, I could use all the help I can get Chuck. Please feel free to intervene." Cheryl replied starting to feel more at ease.

"No problem, I'll light a fire under old Bob. I'll tell him to stop ignoring my account executives." Chuck said winking.

"Thanks Chuck, but if you don't mind, please don't tell him about my conversation with Matthew Robinson. I don't want to cause any friction between the two of them."

"I understand. Well you go on home now Cheryl and I'll let you know about our conversation tomorrow." Chuck said still grinning.

Cheryl looked at Chuck and smiled back. She was beginning to look at Chuck in a new light. He was actually speaking to her like someone who was trying to support her instead of the big bad wolf everyone made him out to be. Apparently, assertiveness, with just a touch of aggression, was something he found appealing in his staff.

"Thanks Chuck, I think I'll do just that. Have a good talk with Bob and I'll speak with you tomorrow."

When tomorrow finally came, Cheryl wanted to know, once and for all, what old Bob was thinking. Was Chuck able to touch base with him at all, or did he avoid him like he'd been doing with her. It was highly unlikely that Bob would ignore a call coming from someone in Chuck's position, so she was sure they'd had some type of conversation, but she had no clue what it was. All she knew was, she had done all she could do and whatever the outcome, she just needed some type of closure. Chuck had seemed pleased with the work she'd put into it, so even if the outcome was going to be negative, she'd made some type of impression with him.

She figured she might as well give Megan an update too. Since she now had some level of communication with Chuck, dealing with Megan didn't seem so bad. Just as she was about to get up off her chair, her phone started to ring. She paused before she answered it then decided she might as well get it over with.

"Cheryl Marks." She said.

"What's up Cheryl? How's it going?"

Cheryl paused for a brief second then answered.

"Jennifer? What's up with you? I thought you'd be on your way to Atlanta by now?" She said.

"I know Charity told me she spoke with you last week and told you I was going to visit them." Jennifer replied.

"So, why didn't you tell me you were going, or ask me to go with you? We've always talked about going to visit Charity and Mike together, and now I hear from her that you're going down there by yourself. What's up with that?" Cheryl said. She was trying to keep her composure being at work, but she wanted Jennifer to know she was just a little pissed off.

"I know...I just needed to get away from Chicago for a while. No offense, but I just need some time to think by myself right now. To figure things out..."

"Figure out what things? Jen, are you all right? I know there's something going on with you. I've known you a long time and I can feel it. What's going on?" Cheryl asked.

"I'm pregnant." Jennifer said.

There was a long moment of silence. Cheryl knew there was something wrong with Jennifer and had prepared herself for something major, but she wasn't expecting this. She waited to select her response carefully before answering. While she was shocked by

Jennifer's response, she wanted her to know she wanted to be there for her.

"Jen, why didn't you tell me? How long have you known?" She asked.

"I found out that day I told you I had a doctor's appointment. Believe you me…I was just as shocked as you are. I thought I was just going for my regular visit, and then Dr. Levine tells me I'm pregnant. I didn't know how to take it. And then, there's Chad…."

"Chad? What does Chad have to do with this?" Cheryl asked. Jennifer didn't answer right away.

"…You're not going to believe this, but Chad is the father." She said.

"Chad is the father!" Cheryl realized the pitch of her voice had risen, and made an effort to lower her voice. She didn't want Jennifer to think she was being judgmental. Now she understood why Jennifer hadn't told her what was going on. "Jennifer, tell me everything. How did this happen? I mean, I know how it happened, but I had no idea you and Chad had anything going on. How did *that* happen?"

"Well, I told you Chad had asked me to start working with him on some high profile accounts at the firm. I started attending a lot of after work meetings with him. One night, our client didn't show up, so we just ended up having dinner alone. Chad saw me back to my apartment and one thing just led to another. I can't believe it happened myself sometimes. I mean, the way I used to trip over Chad when I was younger, and now I'm pregnant with his baby. It feels like I'm in some kind of bad dream or something." Jennifer said. Cheryl could hear the sadness in her voice.

"Jen, what did Chad say? You have told him, haven't you?" She asked.

"I don't care what Chad has to say! I told him and he started tripping about, was I sure it was his baby, and he loves his wife and is not about to end his marriage, after everything he told me!" Jennifer said. Now her voice was beginning to rise.

"Jen, I'm sorry. I wish you had told me earlier. You've known this for weeks and you didn't say anything. What are you going to do?" Cheryl asked.

"...I don't know. I just couldn't tell you. I guess in a way I was ashamed. I mean, I should know better. I knew Chad was married, and all I could hear was how you used to tell me to get over him back when we were teenagers, and now, here I am a grown woman and I do something stupid like this. Chad may have wanted to sleep with me, but he could care less about me or this baby. And now, I may not have a job either." Jennifer said.

"What? Chad can't fire you because of this. Jennifer, you're an attorney. You know better than that. Take his butt to court. He has to pay, whether he wants it or not. You're his employee. He can't get away with this." Cheryl said furiously.

"I know. Chad didn't say he was going to fire me. It's just that, I feel so stupid, I don't want to face him and I kind of made a little scene and walked out. It wasn't really a scene, I just talked to him in his office, but I'm sure his secretary overheard some of our conversation. The way he treated me, I don't want anything from him. I don't want to have anything to do with him, or his firm. I did call in the next day and let Jillian Reed know an emergency had come up and I needed to take a couple of weeks of vacation, she's always been so good to me, but I'm pretty sure I won't be going back." Jennifer said. Her voice was breaking.

"Jen, what are you going to do about the baby? You are going to keep it aren't you? And you need to get support from Chad." Cheryl said.

"I don't know what I'm going to do right now, but I have to tell you, I am leaning toward having an abortion." Jennifer said quietly.

"What! Jennifer you can't kill your baby. I know it seems hard right now, but it's your child we're talking about here. Forget about Chad! If he doesn't want to be a part of the baby's life, you have me and Charity and Mike. You know we'll help you. Plus, your folks will help you. They'll do anything for you." Cheryl was talking quickly. She had to convince Jennifer to keep her baby. She knew that was why Jennifer hadn't told her in the first place, because she knew she'd go straight to her pulpit, but she didn't care.

"I know that's your position Cheryl. I've known you a long time too, but I can't have a baby right now. I don't even know if I have a job, and I'm not about to depend on Chad. It's just not the right time for me. I want to have children one day, but not like this." Jennifer said.

While she was talking, Cheryl could see the light on her phone start to blink, indicating she had another call coming in.

"Jen, I have a call coming in that I need to take, but promise me you'll think really hard about this. You don't want to do something now because you're mad at Chad that you'll regret later." She said.

"Go ahead and take the call. I need to head for the airport soon anyway. I just wanted to call you before I left. I mean you never know what could happen and I didn't want to leave without talking to my girl." Jennifer said laughing. Their talk had obviously done her some good. "Have a good Thanksgiving Cheryl, and enjoy Tischa's wedding. I'll talk to you when I get back."

"You have a good one too Jen. I'm so glad you called me. Love you, and have a safe trip. We'll talk when you get back."

Chapter Twenty

"This is Cheryl Marks."

"Cheryl, this is Bob Conner."

Cheryl could feel the familiar fluttering in her chest beginning to flare up. She took a minute to catch her breath.

"...Yes Bob?"

"I just wanted to give you a call regarding Braxton."

"Yes...I've been trying to get in touch with you...."

"Well, I had a long conversation with Chuck Miller last night. You know Chuck and I go way back. We were both agents at Johnson and Tanner in Seattle about twenty years ago. You were probably still in diapers around that time." Bob said with a chuckle.

His jovial and easygoing demeanor at least helped Cheryl to gain her composure. It doesn't matter what he tells me, she told herself. I did the best I could, and I just need to know one way or another, so I can move on.

"Oh, I'm sure I wasn't quite in diapers, Bob. You and Chuck are not that much older than I am." She replied.

"No....it's true Cheryl, the two of us have been around a long time. We've got a lot of experience under our belts, which is not a bad thing. You need that in this business." Bob said.

Cheryl let out a sigh. OK, here it comes, she thought. She knew a lot of the older brokers had issues with young account executives handling their larger accounts. She prepared herself to hear Bob's excuse for not giving her the business due to her lack of experience.

"I agree Bob. There's no substitute for experience. That's why I've always enjoyed working with people like you and Chuck. I feel I've learned a lot over the past few years at First National. You know we have quite a few seasoned people working here." She replied.

"Well Cheryl, let's get to the reason I called. As you are aware, the client asked us to market their account this year. It wasn't so much that they were dissatisfied with their relationship with NRC, but they wanted to get a feel for what else the market had to offer. After reviewing a number of competing quotes, the client narrowed their options down to NRC's and yours. I have to tell you, I was on the fence regarding which way to steer the client. Your quotation had everything the client was looking for, but I was a bit concerned about your experience. But after speaking with Chuck last night, I feel comfortable with First National taking over the insurance coverage for Braxton. Chuck assured me that you guys handled your accounts as a group effort, and Chuck really thinks highly of your abilities as an account executive. He informed me that you were one of the shining stars on his staff. So, congratulations Cheryl. You have yourself a new account."

"Oh my God!" She squealed not caring who heard her. "Thank you Bob...I wasn't quite sure where you were going at first, but thank you so much! We look forward to working with you on this account, and I'm sure Braxton will be more than satisfied with the service we can provide. Wow... again thank you for the opportunity!" Cheryl said.

"No, thank you for all the hard work you put into this Cheryl. You did a fantastic job, I must say. I'll send out an email to you confirming everything and copy both Chuck and Megan on it. Once again, congratulations Cheryl. I look forward to working with you and have a wonderful holiday. Oh, one other thing. We'll have to set up a face to face meeting between you and the Braxton people. I'll give you a call next week and we'll talk about that then."

"Great! I look forward to it. You have a good Thanksgiving too Bob. I'll talk to you next week."

Cheryl sprang up from her chair and ran directly to Megan's office as soon as she placed the phone down. When she got there, Megan was talking to someone on her phone, so she just stood in the doorway and waited for her to hang up. She was too hyped up to go back and sit down. Megan looked at her in her normal annoyed fashion and continued talking. Cheryl continued to stand in the doorway. Megan finally concluded that she wasn't going anywhere and wrapped up her conversation. She hung the phone up and glared at Cheryl with a look that read "this had better be good".

"I got Braxton!" Cheryl squealed. "Bob Conner just called and told me!"

"What? Congratulations!" Megan said. If it was one thing that put her in a pleasant mood it was putting a multi-million dollar account on the books.

"Good job Cheryl!" Megan said, then immediately turned around and grabbed her telephone and started dialing. "Chuck is at home today, but we can call him anyway...Chuck, hi, it's Megan. I have good news for you. We got the Braxton account!"

Cheryl stood back and listened to Megan rattle on to Chuck about how "we" got the Braxton account. While she knew Chuck's late night conversation had a lot to do with tipping the scale in her favor, she couldn't think of a lot Megan had contributed, other than spouting directives at her. This served her right anyway, she thought.

No matter how much she moaned and complained about Megan's heavy handed style, she still had this juvenile need for Megan to pat her on the head and tell her what a great job she'd done. After another fifteen minutes of talking with Chuck and presenting her strategy for handling Braxton, Megan hung up the phone.

"Chuck says to tell you congratulations. I know everyone's going to be running out of here soon due to the holiday, but make sure you send a binding letter to Bob before you leave today, and send out an email letting everyone that should know we got the account. We also need to talk to Bob about setting up a meeting with the Braxton people so we can introduce ourselves to them. I'll put together a list of First National people that should attend the meeting with us, and you can check everyone's schedule for a time when it's convenient for them. We probably will need to make travel arrangements too." Megan said grabbing a memo pad from her desk.

"Megan, Bob and I already discussed that. He's going to set up a meeting with the Braxton people, and we're going to be discussing that in more detail next week. Bob's also going to send out a confirming email to me and copy you and Chuck. I'll send the binder after I receive his email." Cheryl said.

"Oh, well we'll wait to hear from Bob then. In the meantime, it doesn't hurt to start checking the schedules of these people." Megan said handing a sheet of paper to Cheryl.

Cheryl reached out and took the paper from Megan.

"Fine, I'll do that. Oh well, I just wanted to let you know the good news. I guess I'll go back to my desk now and check to see if Bob has sent that email yet. If I don't see you before you leave today, have a good holiday Megan." Cheryl said and walked back to her cubicle.

Leave it to Megan to put a buzz kill on her getting the most important account she'd ever gotten. But she wasn't going to let her spoil this for her, not this time. She felt like a huge dumbbell had just lifted off of her chest. All she had to do was wait on Bob's email, and then send out the binder, and she was out of there. There was a long holiday weekend coming up, and not a minute too soon either. And then there was Tischa's wedding on Saturday. She was actually going to be able to enjoy the weekend for a change and not worry about what was going on at work for once.

It had taken a while longer but she finally got the email from Bob Conner. As he'd promised, Bob had copied Megan and Chuck on the email along with a number of other people, some she didn't even recognize. When it came to an account generating that kind of money, a number of people obviously had a vested interest in it. At the end of Bob's note, he indicated the client was going to be having a meeting at their law firm's offices in New York in December. He thought either the client could stop in Chicago on their way to New York, or they could all meet at First National's New York office at that time.

Cheryl knew Megan and Chuck were not going to want to put the client through any unnecessary changes. If they were already going to be in New York, and since First National had an office there, most likely the meeting would be held in New York. That news obviously made her think of Tom. He had asked her to let him know whenever she was going to be in New York so they could get together, but as usual, she quickly put that thought out of her mind. No, she wouldn't be letting Tom know she was going to be in New York. She didn't want to open that can of worms, not now.

When Cheryl had finally completed Megan's last minute directives, she gave her "to do" list a final run through. It looked like everything the queen had commanded had been completed. Just as she was about to clean off her desk and go home, Terry, Chuck's assistant, came walking up to her holding a large floral arrangement. Her eyes widened when she saw the bouquet in Terry's hands.

"Oh good, Dear, you're still here. These were dropped off on my desk by mistake." Terry said grinning.

Cheryl couldn't believe that Chuck had gotten her flowers. She understood Braxton was one of the largest accounts they'd ever written, but account executives usually didn't get flowers for bringing in accounts. They were usually compensated in other ways.

"Oh my goodness, are those for me? Why am I getting flowers?" Cheryl asked reaching out and taking the basket from Terry.

"I don't know Dear you must have been a really good girl, or else a really bad one." Terry said laughing. "Enjoy." She said and waved and walked away.

Cheryl was a little startled by Terry's comments. The flowers obviously couldn't be from Chuck or anyone else there. But who would be sending her flowers? She placed the basket on her desk and picked up the white envelope attached to the arrangement. She took the card out of the envelope and read it, and then sat staring at the message on the card.

"To a very smart and determined young lady... Congratulations, Matt Robinson."

❧∞❧

The holiday weekend was filled with all of the last minute scrambling to make sure Tischa's wedding went off without a hitch. Thanksgiving at the Marks family home was more hectic, and crowded, than usual since the wedding was in a couple of days, and there were a number of out of town extended family members staying at the house. Some of the relatives hadn't been to Chicago before and after a huge family dinner on Thanksgiving Day the Chicago Marks family hosted a day of sightseeing and shopping on Friday. Cheryl, of course, had been designated the official tour guide since she had an extensive knowledge of downtown, and every shopping area within a fifty-mile radius. By the time Saturday finally rolled around though, she was beginning to feel wedding weekend burn out. As soon as she saw Tischa walking down the aisle of The First Avenue Church in her elegant ivory silk strapless wedding dress, however, all the hassle of the busy weekend seemed worthwhile. As Cheryl and Pearl stood at the front of the church waiting for Steve to reach out and take Tischa's hand once she approached the altar, Cheryl couldn't help but feel overwhelming happiness and longing at the same time. While she was happy that her sister had found a man to love her and vow to care for her the rest of his life, she couldn't help but wonder if that day would ever come for her.

The large reception room of the church had been transformed into a beautiful candlelit banquet hall with vases of large pastel flowers lining the head table, as well as each individual table. Soft romantic music played as one hundred and fifty of Tischa and Steve's family and friends feasted on roasted chicken and beef, and a number of other delicacies prepared by the church's catering service. After the cutting of the seven layered flower and pearl adorned wedding cake, Tischa and Steve took to the center of the floor and performed their first dance as husband and wife as a rendition of the Luther Vandross song "Here and Now" played softly in the background. As she sat alone watching Tischa and Steve dancing, Cheryl thought she'd never seen Tischa look as beautiful or as happy as she looked that night. The feelings of longing began to rise once again just as her mother walked over and took the seat next to her at the table. Mrs. Marks was beside herself with wedding excitement and was thoroughly enjoying her duties, and the attention, of being the mother of the bride, as she hadn't sat down most of the evening. She was beaming and looking just as beautiful as Tischa in her beaded floor length powder blue evening dress. A large ivory orchid was attached to a silver elastic band across her wrist.

"Baby, doesn't your sister look absolutely beautiful tonight?" Mrs. Marks asked.

"Yes, Mama, I don't think I've ever seen Tischa look this happy before. I'm so happy for her and Steve." Cheryl replied still watching Tischa and Steve dance.

"You know what baby?" Mrs. Marks asked softly.

"What Mama?" Cheryl asked back.

"God has a special man for you out there too, and when it's time, He'll reveal him to you. Just be patient and wait on Him."

Cheryl looked over at her mother and smiled. "Thanks Mama." She said.

She'd heard all this before, but for some reason, tonight she really needed to hear it again.

Chapter Twenty-One

"Be sure to call us when you get home tonight, okay?" Charity said, reaching out and grabbing Jennifer and hugging her so tightly she almost lifted her off the ground.

"Okay, okay!" Jennifer said laughing. "I'll call you as soon as I get in the door. Don't worry about me I'll be fine."

"You better. And don't wait so long next time to visit us. I don't want Mikey and Callie to be grown before they see you again. Next time, Cheryl better be coming with you too…and try not to worry about the other thing. Regardless of what Cheryl thinks you have to make the decision that's best for you. It is your life. I'm a mother myself, but what's right for me is not necessarily right for you. I understand what you're going through, and I think you're making the right decision." Charity said reaching out to hug Jennifer again.

"Charity, you just don't know, this weekend was just what I needed. Sometimes you have to get away to get a new perspective on things. Now I just need to figure out how I'm going to make a living." Jennifer said holding on to Charity. "I guess it's a good thing I hadn't taken a vacation yet this year, and I did have the sense to save some money all those years, so I can afford to take a couple of months off if I need to. Okay! I have to go or I'm going to miss my plane. Love you, Charity, kiss Mike and the kids again for me!"

Jennifer then kissed Charity on the cheek, grabbed her small black suitcase and rolled it to the door of the airport. Then she turned around and waved again at Charity who was still standing near her car waving. After she stepped through the automatic doors, she turned around once more and saw Charity finally get into her car and drive off.

As she stopped to search the overhead monitor for her gate number, Jennifer reflected on the past couple of days. The weekend had been re-energizing for her. As she'd promised, Charity had roasted or baked anything and everything she could get her hands on, and had surprisingly turned into quite a skilled cook. Jennifer kidded her that she had lots of free time to hone her skills while Mike was at work and the kids were in day care. But the truth was, Charity worked part-time as a school counselor in Atlanta, and then rushed to pick up the kids from daycare, and then made time to plan and prepare a nice warm meal after work each day. Not to mention the days she had to take the kids to their doctor visits, shopping, or Callie's ballet classes. Charity's life was pretty full. As a matter of fact, Jennifer didn't know how she was able to do everything she did and keep her sanity. She couldn't imagine having to work and run a household the way Charity did, much less doing it by herself.

Yes, the weekend had been what she needed to figure everything out. And the first thing she'd figured out was that she was not ready for motherhood. Now she just needed to tell Cheryl. She'd hoped to be able to tell her prior to the procedure, since it would be nice to have someone with her when she went to have it done. Cheryl was her closest friend in Chicago, but she wasn't sure she would be receptive to her decision. As a matter of fact, she'd already made it clear that she wouldn't be. She'd asked her to take her time and think about it first, and she had. She'd even discussed everything in detail with Charity who had been instrumental in helping her to make up her mind. Charity just seemed to get where she was coming from.

Even when they were kids, she and Charity would sometimes withhold things from Cheryl they didn't want her to know. They loved her as a sister, but her standards had always seemed so much higher than theirs. The two of them had always been the bad girls in the bunch, and Cheryl had always been the good girl. It wasn't like Cheryl went out of her way to make them feel guilty about the things they got into, they just did. Sometimes, she'd actually try to do or say something that was out of her character, just to fit in, but she could never pull it off. And the odd thing was they didn't really want her to. Cheryl provided them with balance, but sometimes her idealistic advice was too much to swallow. Charity, on the other hand, was more of a realist, and this time, Jennifer felt she needed a more realistic point of view. Cheryl always believed that no matter how bad things got, God would work everything out, but Jennifer just didn't believe she had the same in with God that Cheryl had.

After finding her gate number on the monitor, Jennifer walked through the airport towards the gates. The airport was filled with thousands of travelers making their way home after the long holiday weekend. She liked to be at the airport early so she had about an hour before she needed to board, even after waiting in the long security lines. Since she was flying on a no frills airline, she decided she'd stop in one of the snack shops to have something to eat before boarding the plane. The pregnancy was obviously increasing her appetite, giving her yet another excuse to end it. She wasn't ready to be a mother, and she didn't want to end up looking like a little tub of lard either.

After surveying the food options at the airport, Jennifer settled on grabbing a slice of pizza because the line in that particular restaurant looked the shortest. She stood behind a young girl who appeared to be about twelve years old. Jennifer noticed the girl had a mane of thick black curly hair, and would occasionally turn around looking over her shoulder as if she was searching for someone. Jennifer kept glancing at the girl trying not to stare, but she kept thinking that the girl reminded her of someone, she just couldn't place who it was. When she got to the front of the line, the girl ordered two slices of pizza and two colas. After the cashier rang up her order, the amount came to ten dollars and thirty cents. The girl only had a ten-dollar bill and was about to give one of the colas back, when Jennifer stepped up and offered to pay for the rest of her order.

"I can give you thirty cents." Jennifer said smiling and handing the girl two quarters.

"Thank you ma'am…my mother is sitting at one of those tables over there holding a seat for us. I can wait for you to order and we can find my mother and get your money back. She didn't think our food would be over ten dollars." The girl said smiling back at Jennifer.

"Oh that's all right." Jennifer replied. "You don't have to worry about it. Go on to your seat, you don't have to wait for me." Then Jennifer noticed the girl's order on the counter. "Can you handle all that? I see you have two cups to carry with your pizza. On second thought, why don't you wait for me, and I'll help you carry your food to your seat."

"Thank you, my mother's sitting right over there." The girl said pointing behind Jennifer.

What a polite young lady Jennifer thought. She seemed so mature, even though she couldn't be over thirteen. The girl stood to the side smiling and waiting while the cashier filled Jennifer's order, then they made their way in the direction of her mother's table. As they approached the table, Jennifer saw a small woman, who appeared to be about her age sitting at a table waving at the girl. She was looking at her with a curious maternal glare. The girl bounced up to the table and handed her mother the pizza and the cola she held in her hands. Then she reached over and took the other cup from Jennifer and placed it on the table.

"Thank you ma'am," she said. Then she turned to her mother. "Mommy, you didn't give me enough money. I had to borrow fifty cents from this lady. She offered to help me carry the food to the table."

"I already told her I don't want the fifty cents back. I just wanted to help her carry the food to the table since she had a load. Don't worry about it really." Jennifer said waving at the woman to keep her money.

"Are you sure? I didn't think two slices of pizza and a couple of drinks would be over ten dollars. These airport prices are ridiculous aren't they? I guess we aren't used to flying, so I had no idea." The woman said. Jennifer couldn't help but notice the girl looked so much like her mother, who also looked familiar to her. "Would you like to join us? There aren't a lot of free seats in here, and that's why I was holding this one. Miss Tiffany here didn't want to hold the table or else I would have paid for the food myself."

"Um…I guess I should sit with you guys. I don't like to stand up and eat, if that's okay with you." Jennifer said sitting down at the table across from the lady and her daughter. Then she reached her arm across the table. "Hi I'm Jennifer Thompson. I'm just waiting for my flight back to Chicago."

The woman sat and stared at her for a moment, then leaned in a little closer.

"Jennifer Thompson from Chicago…Jen is that you?"

Jennifer's eyes widened. "I thought you looked familiar too…."

"I'm Vanessa. We went to school together remember? From Ridgeland…"

"Oh my goodness…" Jennifer yelled. "Vanessa! I'm sitting here looking at you thinking that I knew you, but I just couldn't place you. I haven't seen you since we were sixteen. That was about…"

"Twelve years ago. I'd just gotten pregnant with Tiffany when I last saw you." Vanessa said turning to Tiffany and running her fingers through her curly hair. "See what a big girl she is now?"

"That's right. I heard you had a girl. How have you been Vanessa? Where are you living now? Are you back living in Chicago?" Jennifer asked.

Jennifer had a million questions for Vanessa. She couldn't believe she was sitting across from her after all this time. She and Vanessa had gone to grade school together and had almost been inseparable at one time, at least until she got pregnant and left Chicago, and before they'd just drifted apart.

"Well, I've been doing fine. Of course, things were a little difficult at first. I mean I had a baby at sixteen, but you know what, it turned out to be the biggest blessing of my life. I don't know what my life would be like today if I didn't have my Tiffany girl here." Vanessa said smiling at Tiffany and reaching out to touch her hair again.

"Ma..." Tiffany said gently pushing Vanessa's hand away.

"She is such a pretty girl too Vanessa. I kept looking at her in line and thinking she reminded me of someone. She looks just like you did when you were around twelve. And she's so polite and well mannered. You've really done a great job with her." Jennifer said.

"Well, like I said, it wasn't easy at first. It was just Tiffany and me for a while. My uncle and aunt helped me a lot when I was a teenager. Remember I moved to Alabama with them after I got pregnant. Then my parents ended up selling their house and moving to Florida after I got out of high school, which is where we're coming from now. We spent Thanksgiving with them. I ended up going to college at night and working during the day, so at least I was able to finish college and get my degree." Vanessa said taking a bite of pizza.

"Wow, that's really good Vanessa. What kind of work do you do?" Jennifer asked.

"Well my degree is in Psychology. I worked as a school counselor for a couple of years in the Birmingham school system. But I quit doing that a few years ago." Vanessa said.

"Oh, you're kidding! Remember Charity? She's a school counselor too, even though she only works part-time. Actually, I'm just coming back from visiting her and Mike now. Do you remember how crazy she was about Mike Fields when we were going to Henry? Well they ended up getting married, and they have two kids now, can you believe that?" Jennifer said.

"I do not believe it. Charity and Mike ended up getting married after all. I guess you can find your soul mate, even when you're just a teenager. It took me a little longer, but thank God, I finally found mine too." Vanessa said grinning.

Jennifer suddenly looked down at Vanessa's hand and noticed the large sparkling emerald cut diamond ring on Vanessa's finger.

"Vanessa! That is some ring you have on your finger there. I mean that is a piece of rock girl! How long have you been married?" Jennifer asked. She had so many questions she hadn't even realized she hadn't taken a bite of her pizza.

"Well I met my husband Ken when Tiffany was around three. He had just graduated from theology school and was the guest speaker at our church in Birmingham. My pastor asked him to join our church staff, and after he was there about a year, he asked me to go to dinner with him. He said he'd noticed me the day he first spoke at our church, but waited until he was sure it was the right time to ask me out. He said he would watch me sometimes with Tiffany, and admired the way I was taking care of her as a single mother. A year after our first date, he proposed to me. Now he's the pastor of one of the largest churches in Birmingham. That's why he's not with us. He had to fly out yesterday with our five year old son to take care of some church business, but I wanted to stay a little longer with my parents. Isn't that amazing? My husband is the pastor and I'm the first lady. Miracles do happen after all don't they?" Vanessa said laughing. "You know, sometimes you make mistakes in life, and you think it's the worst possible thing in the world. You can't see how things are ever going to work out, but God has a way of working things out far better than we can."

Then Vanessa looked down at Jennifer's uneaten pizza. "Girl, you'd better eat your pizza before you miss your plane. Tell you what, give me your telephone number, and you take mine and we'll talk when I get back to Birmingham and you get back to Chicago."

"That's a good idea Vanessa. We have to keep in touch this time. I can't believe after all these years, that I ran into you and Tiffany like this." Jennifer said finally biting into her pizza. "I can't wait to tell Charity and Cheryl!"

"Cheryl Marks? Make sure you tell her I said hello and give her my number too. We'll have to all get together some time soon. Maybe you guys can come visit our church in Alabama. I can't believe after all this time, we ran into each other like this either. But like Ken always says, there are no coincidences, everything always happens for a reason."

Chapter Twenty Two

The Braxton meeting ended up being held in New York as Cheryl suspected. Both Chuck and Megan insisted on the Chicago First National people traveling to New York, since the client was already going to be there at that time. Even though the CEO, John Richardson, was going to be in New York meeting with the attorneys, they would only be meeting with their loss control people. Cheryl was a little disappointed by that fact, since during her research on Braxton, she'd studied every single detail about him she could, and she found him to be one of the most fascinating people she'd ever read about. It would have been perfect to get a chance to actually meet him. But she wasn't going to let even that disappointment get her down. She was satisfied with the fact she had snagged the account, and if she wasn't going to get to meet one of the most brilliant financial minds in the modern business world, then she would have to make due with whatever she got.

Megan had, of course, wanted to attend the meeting with her. Some of the risk and claims people who handled the territory for First National were also going to be in attendance. At one point during the meeting, Cheryl sat back in her chair and looked around the large room. The size of the table was similar to the one that was in the conference room where Chuck Miller held his weekly meeting for the department heads. The irony was not lost on Cheryl that a couple of weeks ago, she was on the outside of the room trying to gather enough courage to walk through the door. Now, she was an active participant in a meeting of similar size that held some of the most important and influential people at one of the largest accounts in the company.

Sometimes, she still couldn't believe just how far she'd come. As she was looking around the room, her gaze fixed on Matthew, who was sitting next to Braxton's risk manager. She still didn't know how she should take the flowers he'd sent her the day she got the coverage on Braxton. It wasn't uncustomary for brokers to send account executives gifts, or vice versa, if there was a special occasion, or sometimes just to say thank you. It's just that the gift didn't come from Global or even Bob Conner, who was the broker of record on the account. And the gift wasn't addressed to anyone else at the company but her. She'd sent him a quick email to say thank you for the flowers, but she hadn't really had a conversation with him since then. She told herself not to read anything into it. It seemed like as soon as she thought she was done with them, those old childhood fantasies had a way of creeping in. And she couldn't afford to lose her professionalism over something silly. Plus Matthew hadn't treated her any differently today when they'd greeted each other. Everything appeared to be business as usual.

As the meeting drew to a close Bob Conner thanked First National for hosting the meeting at their offices and then turned to Cheryl smiling.

"Well, before we close, I just want to commend Cheryl Marks for all of her hard work in putting together an excellent program this year and making the necessity of this meeting possible." Then he turned to Braxton's risk manager and said, "As you are aware after our meeting today, First National handles their accounts on a group basis, but I have to tell you, this young lady went above and beyond what all of the other competitors were willing to do. I'm sure you will enjoy working with her as much as we have."

Cheryl was somewhat flustered by all the unexpected attention.

"Why thank you Bob, you flatter me." She said trying not to blush.

"No flattery, Cheryl, I'm telling you the truth." Bob said grinning. Then he turned to Megan. "Matthew and I have been very impressed with your staff thus far Megan, especially Cheryl."

Megan smiled at Bob and looked over at Cheryl. "We always aim to provide the best service possible Bob. We would expect no less from our staff, but thank you." Megan said.

With that, Megan reached out and shook hands with the Braxton people making sure they knew she was the Queen Bee at the table, and thanking them for entrusting their coverage with First National. She then offered to take the client along with Bob and Matthew out for lunch. The client, however, declined because they had another series of meetings with their attorneys, and then they were off to San Diego that evening. Bob and Matthew were free, so Megan took them along with Cheryl and the other First National people out instead.

After finally managing to flag down a couple of taxicabs, they decided on a casual lunch at a restaurant in midtown Manhattan. The restaurant was in walking distance of her hotel so it was fine with Cheryl, because instead of going back to the office, she could stay in her hotel room the rest of the day and use her laptop to catch up on returning emails and phone calls. Megan was scheduled to take a flight out to Dallas after lunch for another meeting so she was headed to the airport. She on the other hand, had offered to come back to the office the next morning to meet with the claims consultant assigned to Braxton to discuss special claims handling procedures. At least it would be Friday, and once that meeting was over, she planned on flying out that afternoon, and getting an early start on the weekend.

During lunch, Cheryl noticed Matthew was especially cool, at least towards her. He sat next to Megan, who was flanked between him and Bob Conner, and proceeded to dominate the conversation in her usual manner. Cheryl sat next to the risk consultant, who had recently moved to the New York office from Chicago. Even though she'd moved a year ago, she still couldn't get over the fact that even with the salary increase she'd received to move, she could only afford an apartment that was one third of the size of her lake front apartment in Chicago. Every now and then, Bob Conner would ask Cheryl a question to include her in the conversation, but Matthew would then steer the conversation to Megan, who would just pick up where she left off. Cheryl couldn't tell if he was trying to get to know Megan better, since it was their first meeting, or if he was just going out of his way to ignore her. Either way, by the end of lunch, Cheryl was feeling a little offended by Matthew's lack of attention towards her.

She was confused by her feelings and tried to hide her irritation with Matthew's ignoring her, which she knew made no sense because even though she had a childish crush on him when she was a kid, they were adults now and business associates, and he was married. She had no right, or no business getting or requiring attention from him. She just wished he hadn't sent her those flowers. They just seemed to muddle everything. Before that, she was in control of her emotions. She was proud of the woman she'd become and had long ago accepted the fact her silly crush on Matthew was part of her past. And she had come a long way since she was a schoolgirl in Ridgeland. But now for some reason she couldn't explain, she was beginning to feel like she was an insecure fourteen-year old again.

After lunch, everyone said goodbye and took off in different directions. The claims and risk people went back to the office, while Megan jumped in a taxi and headed for the airport. By that time, Cheryl just wanted to get away from everything and everyone and just crash the rest of the day at the hotel. Then Bob offered to walk her over to the hotel, and she realized he and Matthew were staying at the same hotel. Try as she might, it was difficult for her to hide the fact she was thrilled to have Matthew's company.

"So Cheryl, what are your plans for the rest of the day?" Bob asked.

"I am swamped with emails and voicemails. I'm just going to change into a pair of jeans and work on returning messages for the rest of the afternoon. It's so hard to keep up with everything when you're traveling. I know it's difficult to believe, but I do have other accounts to tend to Bob." Cheryl replied smiling.

"No! Here I thought you were totally devoted to us and Braxton." Bob said grinning. "Oh, I'm sure you're busy. By the way, I'd like for you to take a look at a couple of smaller accounts I have. Not a whole lot of premium, like Braxton, but I may be able to push them your way. Are you interested at all?"

"Of course, Bob. I'm always looking for more business. We can discuss those whenever you're ready." Cheryl said.

"Well, I have a dinner meeting with an old friend this evening and an early flight out in the morning. Matt, maybe you and Cheryl can discuss those accounts. You're free this evening, right?" Bob asked.

"Sure Bob, I'm free for dinner that is, if Cheryl is free?" Matthew asked looking at Bob.

"...I guess I should be finished with my messages some time this evening. What time were you thinking?" Cheryl asked still looking at Bob.

"What do you think Matt, around seven? That's good for you?" Bob asked.

"Seven's good for me. What about you Cheryl?" Matthew asked finally looking at her.

"That's fine. I'll meet you in the lobby at seven." Cheryl responded trying to sound as cool and nonchalant as possible.

"Good...Matt will fill you in on everything then, as I said, they aren't much but you might find them interesting. Well Cheryl, it was a pleasure seeing you again." Bob said reaching out and giving her a hug. "You have a good flight back to Chicago if I don't speak to you before you leave."

That afternoon, the clock on the nightstand seemed to be eerily skipping minutes. Every time Cheryl glanced back at the clock, another half an hour had passed by. Most of the afternoon had been spent opening and deleting emails and trying to return as many phone calls as possible, and time had just slipped away from her. She still had a number of messages still unopened and the clock was quickly approaching six thirty. And she hadn't even started to get dressed for dinner with Matthew. Not that she was in the mood to get dressed and go out anyway. The thought of staying in the hotel room in her jeans and tee shirt, and ordering room service, seemed ideal right now. As she sat on the edge of her bed looking down at her laptop, she began to wish she hadn't made any plans to meet with Matthew that night. She looked at the clock again. It was now six thirty-five. She walked over to the nightstand and grabbed her cell phone and searched her address book for Matthew's cell phone number.

"Matt, hi, it's Cheryl."

"Cheryl, you ready for our dinner meeting already?" Matthew replied.

"That's actually why I'm calling you." Cheryl said. After hearing Matthew's voice, she was having second thoughts about canceling their dinner. "Time has just gotten away from me here. I'm still sitting here in my jeans looking through my emails and I really don't see how I'm going to be able to meet you in the lobby at seven. I'm so sorry to be canceling so late, but maybe you can drop the information at the front desk for me and I'll give you a call to discuss everything sometime next week?"

"You know what Cheryl? We don't have to go out to dinner. Global has me set up in a pretty nice suite here with a large meeting section. You don't need to change out of your jeans, as a matter of fact, I was about to change out of mine, but now I don't have to." Matthew said laughing. "I'm not in the mood to go out anywhere either. Why don't you come over to my suite and I can call room service and have them bring us up something to eat. That way we can eat while we discuss the accounts."

Cheryl was startled by Matthew's suggestion. The thought of staying in and having a nice quiet casual dinner meeting with Matthew was appealing, but Cheryl found herself needing to refuse his request.

"That sounds really good Matt, but, I'm really busy, and tired and grungy. I'm not in any condition to go anywhere...."

"But you have to eat something, and I don't care how you look. Besides you couldn't look that much different than you looked earlier today, which was fine to me." Matthew said.

Cheryl didn't know how to respond to Matthew's last comment. Apparently, he hadn't been totally ignoring her at lunch.

"How do a couple of nice juicy steaks with baked potatoes and a couple of salads sound? It'll be my treat." Matthew asked. "Come on Cheryl, it'll be fun, and strictly casual, I promise."

"...Well, the steaks do sound nice. I'm actually starving..."

"Then it's settled. I'll call room service now and have everything prepared and sent up."

"Okay, but I'm still going to need a little more time. Can we make it around seven thirty?" Cheryl asked.

"Seven thirty's fine. I'm in suite number 1105." Matthew replied.

Chapter Twenty Three

Cheryl walked up to the large mahogany door and stood for a second staring at the silver plated numbers. She stopped for a moment to gain her composure, then took a deep breath and reached out and tapped underneath the numbers 1105. The sound of Matthew's footsteps approaching could be faintly heard through the door. She stepped back and waited for Matthew to open the door as her heart began racing in its usual fashion.

"Well, there you are..." Matthew said smiling as he opened the door.

He then stepped back and extended his hand directing her to enter the room, removing her large tote bag from her shoulder, and placing it on the cherry table near the door as she walked past him. He was looking stylish wearing a black turtleneck sweater and tailored denim jeans. Leave it to Matthew Robinson to look good while wearing just a turtleneck and jeans, she thought. She suddenly felt underdressed.

"Hey, you told me it was going to be really casual." Cheryl said rubbing her hands down the bottom of her purple tee shirt. Tom had given her the shirt during his senior year at Northwestern and she tended to wear it whenever she wanted to feel completely relaxed and comfortable.

"It is casual, don't worry about it. I happen to think you look really cute in your Northwestern tee shirt. You look laid back and relaxed, which is a good thing." Matthew said grinning. "Hey, I didn't know you went to Northwestern…Come on in and have a seat. The food's not here just yet, so maybe we can look over the accounts before dinner. That way we can eat in peace."

"… I didn't go to Northwestern. The shirt was a gift from an old friend of mine who went there." Cheryl said stepping into the hotel room and trying to ignore Matthew's second reference to her appearance that day.

She walked around looking through the suite in total amazement. Global used it to impress clients and as a perk for its employees lucky enough to do business in Manhattan. The front of the room was a large living area with a plush beige sofa and two large burgundy wing back chairs. In front of the sofa was a large cherry wood cocktail table, with two cherry end tables at both sides. Next to the living space was a kitchen and dining area with black and gold granite countertops, small stainless steel appliances and a round cherry table with two burgundy dining chairs. On the other side of the suite was a spacious spa style bathroom with beige and white marble tiled walls and floor. Cheryl noticed that next to the bathroom was a large bedroom area with a king size bed in the center of the room. She quickly walked back over to the living area and took a seat on the sofa.

Matthew joined her on the sofa and reached over to the documents he'd placed earlier on the table. He scooted closer to her and handed her a couple of the documents to read, while giving her a brief overview of both accounts and describing to her each document included in the submissions. As he was speaking, Cheryl strained to keep her thoughts professional and concentrate on the words Matthew was speaking. But she was finding it difficult to do, given the fact they were alone together in a hotel suite and he was sitting just a couple of inches away from her. Every now and then, as he would reach over to the table, or hand her a document, she would get a faint whiff of his cologne. It was the same cologne he wore the night she'd had dinner with him and Bob in Las Vegas. She was beginning to wonder if meeting Matthew for dinner in his suite was really a good idea after all.

After a while they heard a knock at the door, and Matthew walked over and let the room service attendant in. After everything was set up near the dining area, he reached inside his pants pocket and handed the attendant a small stack of folded bills. The attendant then left thanking him repeatedly for the generous tip.

"Wow, something really smells good." Cheryl said thankful to be distracted by something other than Matthew's cologne. "I hope it tastes as good as it smells. I feel like I haven't eaten in days."

"I noticed you didn't eat that much at lunch. Don't worry, I've eaten here before. You won't be disappointed. They have excellent food here." Matthew said reaching out and pulling one of the dining chairs from the table for her. "I think we've discussed enough business for one day. It's time to just sit down and eat!"

Cheryl sat down in the chair as Matthew pushed it back under the table. So, he had noticed her at lunch. She leaned into the table trying to concentrate on the fragrance of the food and not his cologne, as Matthew walked over to the other side of the table and took the seat across from her.

"May I pour you a glass of wine, Cheryl? I took the liberty of making the selection. I wasn't sure what your preference was." Matthew said holding the bottle. Cheryl hadn't noticed the attendant had brought a bottle of wine with the food.

"Water is fine for me. I don't really drink alcohol." She said putting her hand up.

"Really, you don't drink any alcohol at all? I don't think I've ever met anyone who didn't drink wine. That's interesting." Matthew said. Cheryl thought he looked a little disappointed.

"Oh that's good then, I've always prided myself on being unique." Cheryl joked. "But, please, feel free to indulge. I'm used to being the only one at the table not drinking. It never seems to stop any of my friends from helping themselves though."

She wanted Matthew to feel comfortable drinking without her, and her efforts appeared to be working as the evening progressed, because Matthew seemed to let loose and appeared to be thoroughly enjoying the food and wine. Cheryl sat across the table watching him as he ate and drank and tried not to stare. The rest of the evening took on a surreal vibe as she and Matthew began reminiscing about their days growing up in Chicago. As the evening wore on, Cheryl hadn't realized she'd stopped talking completely and sat staring at Matthew in silence. She was trying to get a mental grasp on the fact that this was the same Matthew Robinson who she sat next to on her first day of eighth grade. The same Matthew who was the most beautiful person she'd ever seen. This was the same guy who never even paid her one ounce of attention throughout four years of high school.

"You okay, Cheryl?" Matthew suddenly asked. "Didn't you like the food?"

"Oh no, the food was really good." She said still staring. "Everything's just perfect."

The room fell into an awkward silence as they sat looking at each other. Cheryl suddenly began to feel like she was a teenager again. She could feel all the old familiar pangs of her painful childhood crush beginning to scratch the surface.

"I can't believe I never noticed you when we were kids at Henry." Matthew said watching her closely as she looked at him.

"And McArthur...I actually sat next to you my first day of eighth grade, can you believe that? In high school you probably don't remember me because you were much too into that Donna, what was her last name? You know the pompom girl..."

"Johnson, her name was Donna Johnson...I know because I married her." Matthew said still watching her to see how she would respond to his answer.

"...Oh, you married Donna! I do remember when we had dinner in Las Vegas you saying that you married your high school girlfriend. I guess it didn't register. You two have a little boy too, right?" Cheryl asked. She was beginning to feel flustered and was having difficulty hiding her emotions. She suddenly felt her face begin to burn as the color began to rise. She put her hand to her face.

"Right, Timothy. He'll be three in a couple of months." Matthew said still studying her closely.

Cheryl suddenly realized the reality of the situation and felt like she needed to get out of the room. She stood up and walked quickly towards the living room area. Matthew followed after her.

"Cheryl, are you okay?" Matthew said sounding confused by her sudden bolt from the table.

"I'm fine. I'm just feeling really tired all of a sudden. I'll just get the information on those two accounts..."

"I really wish you wouldn't leave yet, Cheryl." Matthew said softly.

He then reached out and grabbed her hand. Cheryl dropped the documents back on the table and looked up into Matthew's eyes. He just stood holding her hand in silence.

"Matthew...I should be going...."

"Does the fact that I'm married bother you Cheryl?" He asked still looking closely into her eyes and holding her hand. "...I understand if it does. But, I just want you to know I'm very attracted to you, and I can tell you're attracted to me, too."

Cheryl looked at Matthew. She couldn't believe this was happening. Why was Matthew standing in front of her, holding her hand and telling her he was attracted to her after all this time had passed? He'd never noticed her before. Why now that he was married with a small child. She didn't need this in her life right now. She was not the same insecure teenager she once was. She had accomplished a lot for herself, and she didn't need validation from Matthew Robinson after all these years. At least, she kept trying to convince herself that she didn't. Suddenly, Matthew pulled her closer still holding her hand. Before she could speak, he bent down and kissed her softly on the lips. She felt paralyzed and suddenly couldn't move or speak. He stopped kissing her and looked down at her. Cheryl looked up into Matthew's eyes. She felt like she was having difficulty breathing. After she failed to move, he pulled her close again and began to kiss her more intensely. He let go of her hand and put both of his hands around her waist pulling her closer to him. Cheryl felt herself giving in to what was happening and suddenly put her arms around his neck holding him tightly. She felt like she was hovering over the room looking down at the two of them. As though she had lost all control over her actions and had no choice but to participate in what was happening.

Cheryl could feel Matthew leading her over to the sofa. Her heart was pounding. She needed to stop, but she couldn't. Before she knew it, she was down on the sofa. She could feel Matthew's hands on her body. He quickly reached down to her feet and easily slipped off both of her shoes. She tried to speak, but every time she did, Matthew would kiss her again and she'd end up speechless. Suddenly, Matthew jumped up off the sofa and headed for the bathroom.

"I'll be right back." He said. "Don't move… I'll be right back."

Cheryl watched Matthew disappear into the other room. She sat up on the sofa and looked around the room. She looked over at the table where they'd just eaten dinner and had no idea how she'd gotten to the sofa. The empty plates of food and Matthew's empty wineglass were still on the table. She then looked toward the bathroom door again and could hear Matthew closing what sounded like a cabinet. Then she looked toward the front door of the suite. She suddenly noticed her tote bag sitting on the table near the door where Matthew had placed it when she entered the room, and remembered the bag had come from Tischa's boutique. Tischa had picked the bag out as a gift from her parents after she finally graduated from college. Tischa thought the leather tote was much more stylish and befitting a young woman on her rise up the corporate ladder than the old black canvas briefcase she used to carry. She sat staring at the bag remembering how proud her family was of her that day, which is why she carried that bag practically everywhere she went. Suddenly she reached down and picked up her shoes and carried them over to the table where her bag was sitting. As she was walking to the table she heard Matthew come back into the room.

"Cheryl, what's the matter?" Matthew asked.

"Nothing's the matter Matthew. I just can't do this. I'm going back to my room." She said.

"Why? Is it because I'm married, or because we work together? Cheryl come on...this kind of thing happens all the time...."

"Not with me it doesn't." Cheryl said turning around facing Matthew. She noticed he had removed his black turtleneck sweater and was now just wearing a sleeveless white undershirt. "Good night Matthew, I'll call you sometime next week and let you know if I can do anything with these."

She walked back over to the sofa table and reached down and picked up the documents on the two accounts they'd discussed. Then she walked back over to the door, picked up her bag from the table and stuffed the account information in it, and walked out of the room still carrying her shoes in her hand.

Chapter Twenty Four

"Good morning Ms Marks. This is your six o'clock wake up call." The perky and pleasant voice on the other side of the phone said.

"Oh...thanks." Cheryl said and hung up the phone.

She glanced over at the clock on the nightstand next to the bed. How could anybody have that much perkiness at that time in the morning? She couldn't believe it was six o'clock already. She felt like she'd just gone to sleep, mainly because she had only been asleep a couple of hours. The last time she glanced at the clock it was four o'clock. She must have finally fallen asleep some time after that. All night, she kept reliving her dinner meeting with Matthew. It was a good thing she at least had the frame of mind to schedule a wake up call before she went to bed. After last night she'd decided to get up early so she could check out of the hotel and wait at the First National New York office until it was time for her meeting. That way, she wouldn't have to worry about running into Matthew before she checked out. And once the meeting was over, she planned on jumping in the first taxicab she saw and heading straight for LaGuardia. It was time to bid adieu to the Big Apple once and for all, and she needed badly to wash the events of the previous day from her mind.

At least now one thing really was certain. After all these years, she finally had Matthew Robinson closure, and for good this time. She couldn't believe that she had allowed herself to be put in the position she had last night. If she had ended up sleeping with Matthew she wouldn't be able to look at herself in the mirror. But the scary thing was she had come awfully close to doing it. Now she felt a lot more sympathetic toward Jennifer and her situation. It was easier now to understand how it was possible to get sucked into a moment and end up making a mistake that you could possibly regret the rest of your life. She had no idea how she was going to be able to work with Matthew after last night, but it would have been worse if they'd ended up in bed together. Now at least she still had her dignity. Matthew obviously had some issues to deal with, and she didn't care to be party to them, no matter how attracted she was to him. And it was also pretty obvious that he had cheated on his wife before. Poor Donna! And to think she used to be envious of her when they were kids, now all she felt was pity. Life could be so ironic sometimes. She had worshipped what she thought was the image of Matthew Robinson for so long, but she really had no clue who or what he really was at all.

⁊⁋

"Good morning Miss, thank you for staying with us. I hope you enjoyed your visit to New York. May I hail a cab for you?" The doorman asked.

"Yes, I will need a cab, thank you." Cheryl replied.

The doorman waved to a taxi that was already waiting in front of the hotel, and then took Cheryl's suitcase and placed it into the trunk. As the taxi pulled away from the curb, Cheryl looked back at the hotel entrance and let out a deep sigh of relief.

The claims consultant, Lydia Rosen, was in the office early also, so at least Cheryl was able to up the time of the meeting. Now she could get to the airport earlier and possibly catch an earlier flight out to Chicago. As Cheryl sat in the conference room discussing Braxton's claims procedures with the consultant she occasionally glanced out the door into the office. The building where the offices were held was modern and more luxurious than the home office in Chicago.

That was probably because First National didn't actually own the entire building but just rented a couple of floors in it. The staff in New York was a lot smaller than the one in Chicago and the office climate was much more laid back and close knit. Cheryl didn't get the impression there was a lot of politics that went on in the New York office like there could sometimes be in Chicago. Even though her trip had not been totally pleasant, she was at least grateful for the peaceful and calm environment in the office. By the time the meeting was over she felt a lot more at ease.

When it was time for her to leave, Cheryl hugged Lydia and told her she would give her a call when she got back to the office in Chicago. Her plans were to grab something to eat quickly at one of the outdoor vending carts and find a cab to the airport, but Lydia insisted on calling a car to come and pick her up in front of the building. Sometimes finding an empty cab at lunchtime in Manhattan could almost be impossible. But she would have a couple of minutes to grab something to eat before the car was scheduled to arrive.

Cheryl stepped outside the building and looked up and down the street in search of a street vendor. She hadn't eaten anything since her dinner with Matthew the night before and refused to wait and have to purchase the food at the airport. After failing to spot a cart, she decided to just start walking in the direction of the aromas of onions and garlic in the air. After finally finding a vendor selling sausages and hotdogs, she settled on a hotdog with mustard and relish. With her hotdog and suitcase in tow, she then walked back over to the front of the building to wait for the car to pick her up. It was a beautiful winter day in New York. Even though it was a little chilly, the sun was shining brightly. The thought that it was probably a little warmer than it was back in Chicago, caused Cheryl to want to savor the crisp clear weather, so she leaned back against the side of the building, took a huge bite out of her hotdog and waited for the car to arrive.

Since it was lunchtime, the streets were filled with people who were either tourists or office workers, looking for something to eat or conducting various forms of business. Cheryl watched as the people walked past, some looking uptight in their business suits and ties and carrying brief cases. She was suddenly grateful she'd only had to meet with Lydia that morning and was able to dress casual that day. She thought about years ago when she was in high school how she used to walk through the streets of downtown Chicago. She remembered how she would watch the business people in their pin-striped suits and carrying brief cases, and would make up stories or imagine who those people were, hoping to one day be one of them. Now that she was actually one of them, she wished she could let that teenage girl know to just chill out. It really wasn't all it was cracked up to be. Sometimes, when you're on the outside looking in, it was easy to imagine that life would be perfect if you could just get inside, but most of the time, getting inside didn't bring perfection at all.

Standing there alone, Cheryl suddenly felt drained and empty, as if she could no longer find any meaning in anything. She was so used to reaching for this goal or running after something else. But suddenly, she didn't know what it was she really wanted. It seemed as though everything she'd wish for or idolized in her life had either let her down or turned out to be different than she thought it would be. She finished off her hotdog and continued to lean back against the building for support. She tried to brush it off, but was having trouble shaking her sudden onslaught of overwhelming futility.

"Cheryl? What are you doing here?"

Cheryl turned to look at the man who had just walked out of the building, stopped in his tracks and doubled back. It was Tom Morgan. She stood speechless staring at him as though she had just been caught stealing change out of her mother's purse.

"I can't believe it's actually you. What are you doing here?" Tom repeated.

"I...had to come here for a client meeting. Everything was so hectic...I didn't have a lot of time for anything else." Cheryl explained quickly. "I'm just standing here waiting for a car to pick me up and take me to the airport now."

For a moment Tom just stood looking at her. Cheryl could tell he was wondering why she hadn't gotten in touch with him or let him know she was even going to be in New York that week.

"Wow...I can't believe this. I was just thinking about you the other day and I walk out the building and here you are standing...in New York! How have you been? How's everybody back in Chicago?" Tom asked.

"I've been fine Tom." Cheryl said. "Everybody's fine. Oh, Guess what? Tischa got married Thanksgiving weekend! She married her boyfriend Steve. I think you met Steve the day of my Dad's funeral?"

"What? Tischa's married, huh? I do remember Steve from the funeral. Well, tell the both of them congratulations for me will you?" Tom said. "Wow, Tischa's married..."

Tom's voice suddenly trailed off. He was looking as though he had something else on his mind.

"Yep, Tischa's married." Cheryl repeated. "It was really a beautiful wedding too. You know Tischa, Ms Fashion Plate, and Steve is just as bad. They make a perfect couple, they really do. Oh, by the way, I know you'll find this bit of news unbearably amusing. I was a bridesmaid!" Cheryl said laughing. "But at least the dresses weren't some putrid color or covered in ruffles or anything."

"Oh, that's too bad. I would have paid to see those pictures!" Tom replied laughing. Then he suddenly stopped laughing. "I'm sure you were a beautiful bridesmaid, Cheryl. Too bad I didn't know about the wedding. I would have loved to see you walking down the aisle."

Cheryl stopped laughing and looked at Tom. His golden hazel eyes were sparkling as usual against the sunlight. He was looking at her the exact same way he looked at her on the steps of the First Avenue Church on the day of her father's funeral.

"So, you haven't decided to take that walk yet, huh, Tom?" Cheryl asked trying to break the silence, but also because she suddenly really wanted to know. "...And New York is full of available ladies I hear. There has to be someone here you're interested in?"

"Oh, New York does have a lot to offer in that department. Don't get me wrong. I've dated a couple of ladies since I've been here, but no one serious. No one I'm interested in going down the aisle with...at least not in New York. What about you...you planning on taking that walk any time soon...as a bride I mean?" Tom asked.

"No Tom, I'm not planning on getting married anytime soon, either. There's no one in my life that I'm at that point with either...actually, there's no one in my life at all right now. I'm pathetic aren't I?" Cheryl said laughing nervously.

"Cheryl, you're anything but pathetic, as a matter of fact, that's the last thing you are."

Cheryl didn't know how to respond to Tom so she stared at him in her usual awkward manner.

"...I'm actually happy to hear you aren't involved with anyone right now." Tom continued. "You know when I told you I was just thinking about you? Well, the truth is, I think about you all the time. I know you probably don't want to hear this right now, while you're on your way to the airport, but I may not get the chance to see you again any time soon. Even after all these years, I haven't been able to forget about you Cheryl. And believe me, I've tried. But I don't think it's a coincidence that I ran into you today like this. I prayed that I would get the opportunity to tell you this, and now I have it. I love you Cheryl. I've always loved you and you are the only woman I've ever thought about marrying."

Tom moved closer to her as if he wanted to make sure she caught every word he was saying. He was looking deeply into her eyes and Cheryl suddenly couldn't move or speak. At that point, he bent down and kissed her softly. Cheryl could feel the tiny jolts of electricity once again. The ones she always felt whenever Tom kissed her.

"...Tom...I don't know what to say..." She finally said pulling back.

"You don't have to say anything. I just needed to say it. I just needed to make sure you heard it." Tom replied.

Just then, a silver town car pulled up in front of the building and began to honk.

"There's my ride." Cheryl said taking hold of the handle of her suitcase. "It was really good to see you Tom. And I appreciate what you told me, I really do. I just don't have a response for you right now."

"That's okay, I understand. Just promise me you'll think about what I just said, Cheryl. I mean really think about it." Tom replied.

"I will." Cheryl said reaching out and hugging Tom.

"That's all I ask." Tom replied hugging her back. He then reached out and gently rubbed the side of her mouth. "You had a little mustard on your lip."

Cheryl walked over to the car and handed her suitcase to the driver. Tom opened the car door and held it while she sat down inside. As the car pulled away from the curb and headed down the street, Cheryl turned around and saw Tom still standing on the side of the curb watching her ride away.

Later that evening, after she finally arrived home, Cheryl made her usual walk straight to her bedroom door, propping her suitcase upright in the corner of her bedroom. The trip had drained every once of strength she had both mentally and physically. She hadn't been able to catch an earlier flight after all and had ended up having to wait at the airport until the time of her original flight. Between what had happened with her and Matthew the night before and then hearing Tom profess his love for her on the streets of New York and pretty much asking her to marry him, her head felt like it was going to explode. The problem was she knew deep down inside, that she did love Tom and always had. She just didn't know what to do with that fact right now. She threw herself across the bed and lay flat on her back staring at the ceiling. It felt good to lie there and not have to think about anything if just for a brief second.

Cheryl looked at her telephone on the nightstand next to her bed and debated with herself if she wanted to go there or not. She then gave in and rolled over to the nightstand and picked up the phone and began entering her password. There was a call from Jennifer.

"Hey Cheryl…. it's Jen. I just wanted to let you know I have an appointment set up for next Thursday and I wanted to know if you could come with me. I really don't want to go by myself, and you were the only one I could think of that I'd want with me. Anyway, give me a call and let me know if you can come. Thanks."

Cheryl's heart felt like it was sinking. She'd tried her best to talk Jennifer out of what she'd decided to do, and she really didn't want to have anything to do with it. But Jennifer was her closest friend and there was no way she was going to let her go through something like that alone. She just couldn't deal with that right now. She skipped over to the next message.

"Cheryl, Megan here. I'm sure you're not off the plane just yet, so that's why I'm calling your home number. It's very important that I see you ASAP Monday morning and I wanted to make sure you knew that before you got into the office and got distracted by anything else. I have something I need to discuss with you. Talk to you then. Thanks."

Chapter Twenty Five

The weekend passed by quickly as usual. But this was one time Cheryl was fine with it because she was anxious to hear what it was Megan needed to discuss with her. All kinds of things were going through her mind. The first, of course, was had she heard anything about her and Matthew? And if she had heard anything, how did she? Cheryl couldn't believe that Matthew would say anything to anyone about what happened between the two of them. Not that anything had happened. But she didn't know if Matthew was the type to make something up or not. It wasn't like she and Matthew had been close growing up. She really didn't know him all that well at all. Could it be possible that he was doing some type of damage control, and was trying to spin what had happened in his favor before she had the opportunity to say anything?

As she stepped off the elevator and headed to her cubicle, the office seemed unusually quiet. It was rather early in the morning, and the majority of the office staff wouldn't be in until at least another thirty minutes or so. She wanted to get in early, she needed to get there early, and be waiting for Megan to either summon her or she'd just walk over to her office and get whatever she needed to tell her out of the way.

Her desk was cluttered as she suspected it would be. Whenever she was out of the office for any length of time, when she got back, her desk was usually covered with unopened mail, memos and messages, and even though she'd answered a number of them before she left New York, both her voicemail and email were full with messages. She decided to take Megan's advice and not bother to open or check anything yet because she knew if she did, she would get distracted and forget that Megan needed to talk to her. She decided not to prolong the suspense and walked over to Megan's office, but when she got there, of course, she wasn't there. She was, however, in already since her computer was already booted up and Cheryl could see her coat hanging on the hook in the corner of her office. She decided not to try and locate her since she could be any number of places and walked back to her cubicle.

As Cheryl was walking back to her desk, she noticed the other employees starting to straggle in and make their way to their cubes. She couldn't put her finger on it, but she could tell there was something in the air. Office gossip was a typical way of life at First National, she had even engaged in a huddle or two from time to time. Most of the time it was innocent and a way of passing time. But there seemed to be a lot more whispering going on today than usual and she couldn't help but wonder if she had anything to do with it. She walked over to Alicia's desk thinking that if there was something going on, she would know about it and would fill her in. But when she got to Alicia's desk, she wasn't there either. She was just about to walk out of the aisle of Alicia's cubicle when she almost walked right into Megan.

"Oh, there you are." Megan said. "I need to talk to you. Let's go back to my office."

"Okay, I came over earlier, but you weren't there." Cheryl replied.

She didn't know why but she suddenly started to get nervous. Megan looked so serious. She didn't know how she was going to respond if Matthew had made any allegations against her. And she would be completely humiliated if everyone was talking about her. Megan continued to walk in front of her not speaking as she followed behind her like a lost puppy. As they walked past, Cheryl noticed the few employees that were in the office already watching them closely. Her mind was racing and her heart was pounding. Was she getting fired or something? After all the hard work she'd put in, was this really the way her career at First National was going to end?

"Come in and close the door." Megan said not looking at her.

"Okay." Cheryl responded. "What's going on? Why did you need to see me?"

Megan beckoned her to take a seat and she continued to stand over her. Cheryl sat down and told herself that whatever happened she would be okay. She knew she'd done nothing wrong.

"I understand Bob has a couple of new accounts he's interested in us reviewing for him? How did your meeting with Matthew go?" Megan asked standing over Cheryl with her arms folded, slanting her eyes in her usual manner. Cheryl suddenly felt her breathing become labored as her chest moved up and down with each breath and her heart pounding.

"Yes he does….did you speak with Bob after you left?" Cheryl asked.

"No, Matthew called me to tell me he enjoyed meeting me." Megan replied. Cheryl leaned back in her chair and waited for Megan to finish speaking. "…He was also very complimentary of you and the job you did on Braxton."

"Is that why you needed to see me?" Cheryl asked holding the sides of the chair. Her palms were moist with perspiration.

"Well not really…I don't know if you've heard anything yet, it's probably floating around the office by now. But in case you haven't heard, I'm going to be leaving the Chicago office in a couple of months. I've accepted a promotion in Los Angeles. I'm going to be the new Senior Vice President heading up a new office First National is setting up there. Since I'm from LA and I've done such a good job turning this office around, senior management thought I was the perfect candidate to get that office off the ground. Of course I had to do some lobbying, but it was obvious I was the most qualified person for the job."

Cheryl released the air that had been building in her lungs since she walked into Megan's office.

"Megan congratulations! I was wondering what was going on... Wow, Senior Vice President! We're really going to miss you around here." Cheryl said. She didn't really know what else to say. But she was relieved the conversation hadn't taken the turn she'd been imagining it would.

"Well, I've known about the office opening up for a while, but management didn't want it out just yet." Megan said in her usual smug way. "So, as I said, I'll just be here a couple more months, long enough to make sure there's a smooth transition. And then I'm back off to LA."

"So, you're moving back to LA! I didn't know you wanted to go back there." Cheryl said.

"Well, it's not so much that it's in LA, but this is a dream job, so I wasn't about to let it just slip through my fingers. You have to make some sacrifices to get to where you want to be." Megan said.

Cheryl watched Megan as she spoke. She could see the spark in her eyes ignite as she spoke once again about rising to the top. She used to love to sit in Megan's office and listen to her rattle off about climbing the corporate ladder. For a brief moment she felt like the new assistant again studying her mentor and eager to emulate every aspect of her life. Megan always knew how to get what she wanted.

"So is Richard excited about moving back to LA? I know he has family there too." Cheryl said sounding more excited than Megan.

"...Well...no, Richard is not going to be moving to LA." Megan replied slowly. "He actually likes it here in Chicago, plus he doesn't want to leave his job right now, so no, he won't be coming...whatever,

I mean we'll have to work that out later. But I'm not about to let anything, or anyone for that matter stand in the way of me getting to where I want to be."

Suddenly Cheryl saw the fire in Megan's eyes start to dim just a little. Were she and Richard separating? She always thought Megan had a dream life...a career, a beautiful home and the perfect man to love her. But apparently, it wasn't perfect enough for her. In her quest to keep rising up, she was more than willing to drop off anything or anybody that held her down, and nothing, or nobody, was indispensable.

"...Well, I'm glad you told me Megan." Cheryl said. "Congratulations again... I hope you'll be happy in your new position."

She was wondering why Megan had made a point of telling her the news privately. They hadn't actually been that close lately. At least, she hadn't felt like they had.

"Just a second, I haven't told you the part I really need to tell you." Megan said. "As I said, the reason management wants me to stay for the next couple of months, is so there will be a smooth transition. One important aspect of that transition will be training my successor. Chuck asked for my input on selecting the person who should take my place managing the account executives for our territory, and we both agree, that person should be you. After you nailed Braxton it was obvious you have what it takes to be really successful in this business. It was an obvious choice." Megan said. Cheryl thought she saw a faint smile beginning to form on her face.

"What...me? You've got to be kidding! Oh my god, you want me to be the new Vice President of Sales?" Cheryl yelled.

"Well, Assistant Vice President. You'll have some work to do before you earn that title, but if everything goes well, you should get to that point after about a year or so. But at least you'll be on the track to follow in my footsteps." Megan said. "Now it's going to take a lot of hard work, don't get me wrong. If you thought the life of a senior account executive was tough, well get ready. As you know, it's not uncommon for me to be here working from six or seven o'clock in the morning until after that time at night. And there will be a lot more travel involved as well. Richard would be so upset at how much I had to travel, but he just doesn't understand the way our business works. At least you won't have to worry about that problem, thank God."

Cheryl sat back and listened quietly to Megan as she spoke. A couple of years ago, she would have never dreamed they would be sitting here having this conversation. Management had chosen her to follow in Megan's footsteps. Her dreams had finally come true and she was being given the opportunity to be just like Megan. But as she listened, she suddenly realized how confused she'd been all this time. She didn't really want to be like Megan at all. She just continued to watch Megan talk and not responding. She didn't know how to respond. Finally, Megan noticed she wasn't saying anything.

"So, I need to tell Chuck today if you accepted the offer or not. The big boys are a little nervous about this office and they want to make sure I have a successor as soon as possible. So, what do you say?" Megan asked.

"...Well, Megan....I can't tell you how honored I am that you and Chuck thought enough of my work here to offer me this opportunity...but...I'm going to have to decline the offer. I really appreciate it, I really do. But I can't accept." Cheryl said.

Megan sat staring at Cheryl with her mouth hanging open. Cheryl had never seen her at a loss for words before, and didn't know whether to be afraid or amused.

"What! You're turning it down? Do you know how hard I had to push to get this position for you? You've always expressed to me that you wanted more. Now I'm giving you the opportunity to move up in this company and you're turning it down?" Megan said angrily. "Why, Cheryl? Are you out of your mind? Why on earth would you turn an opportunity like this down? I can't imagine what reason you would have to do that!"

"...Because...I'm going to be requesting a transfer to the New York office...I'm getting married." Cheryl replied.

❧◦❧

It was a beautiful clear day in New York. Even though it was the end of winter, the sky was blue and the sun was shining brightly, indicating spring's impending arrival was fast approaching.

"Tom...can you please tell me where we're going?" Cheryl asked impatiently.

Cheryl never liked surprises or feeling out of control and had tried her best to get something out of Tom, but he just wasn't budging. He'd purposely had the taxi drop them off a block away from their destination to keep his surprise under wraps as long as possible.

"Wait just a couple more minutes. Why do you always have to know every last detail before you do anything? Trust me, you're going to like my surprise, I promise you." Tom said grinning. "Okay now, we're here."

Cheryl looked around and noticed they were standing on a busy street with a couple of restaurants and shops nearby. She glanced back at Tom, who by now was staring at her with the widest grin she'd ever seen him wear. Then she looked up at the signage over the building they were standing in front of and saw that it was an automobile dealership.

"Why are we standing here Tom? Are you buying a car?" She asked. "But you don't need a car where you live...we always take taxis everywhere. Plus, you're always complaining about how hard it is to drive in Manhattan."

"Well, I was thinking I might buy one. I saw one in here the other day that I really liked and I wanted to get your opinion. Come in and tell me what you think about this one." Tom said grabbing her hand and pulling her behind him as he walked into the store.

Cheryl followed Tom into the showroom and looked around at the vehicles. She noticed the floor was filled with luxury and foreign made models. She continued to follow Tom through the showroom floor wondering what they were doing in such an expensive dealership, and how on earth Tom thought he could afford a car out of there in the first place.

"Well, what do you think?" Tom asked still grinning and pointing to a small Porsche convertible.

"Excuse me? How do you think we can afford to buy a car like that Tom? Are you crazy?" Cheryl asked looking at Tom as though he'd suddenly lost it.

"Well actually, we can afford to buy it...A few years back, I made a couple of smart investments and I've gotten some pretty nice returns over the past couple of years. I mean what else was I to do with my money, seeing I didn't have a lady in my life to spend it on?" Tom said grinning, his hazel eyes sparkling. "Also, I didn't tell you because I wanted to wait until you flew out here, but my novel was recently published and now someone's going to turn it into a screen play. It's going to be a movie, can you believe it? Do you remember that day I ran into you while you were waiting for your car to the airport? Well, the reason I was coming out of your building was because I'd just left a meeting with my agent and a couple of studio execs signing off on the final papers."

"Congratulations Tom!" Cheryl squealed grabbing Tom around his neck, hugging him and jumping up and down. The other customers stopped what they were doing and started watching them.

"Okay, now we'd have to special order the color, but that shouldn't be a problem...I know it needs to be metallic blue, right?" Tom asked. "Well, what do you think? Should I have them draw up the papers on this bad boy or what? But maybe you want to do a test drive first, huh?"

Cheryl just stood silently staring at the beautiful sleek shiny car. She'd always talked about having a car like that one ever since she was a poor kid in the projects. Now all her dreams seemed to be coming true. Then she looked back at Tom and saw how excited he was. He almost looked like a little boy who'd just opened the gift he'd been begging for on Christmas day. She couldn't believe that after all these years he'd remembered her childhood ranting about one day having enough money to buy that car. She thought about how he'd waited for her and loved her in spite of all her shallowness and rejection. How he seemed to always be there at the lowest points in her life. And how she knew there was nothing he would withhold from her, or do for her if he could. Then she looked back at the car and realized all her childhood desires and insecurities that she'd projected onto that car suddenly seemed so trite and unimportant. No longer the little girl staring out of the window of the George Marshall housing complex, watching her uppity neighbors and desiring to one day be like them. She was finally able to see clearly what had been clouded for so long.

"No Tom, I don't think we need to buy that car. Besides we don't even need a car, I still have my little four-door sedan remember? And it's really dependable, plus I get good fuel mileage with it." Cheryl replied laughing.

"What.....fuel mileage, are you kidding me? But Cheryl baby, this is your dream car. It's what you've always talked about...the one you've always wanted..."

Cheryl just stood looking at Tom. He looked so confused and a little disappointed. She suddenly reached out and grabbed him and hugged him as tightly as she could. As she held him close, she looked over his shoulder at the platinum band with the princess cut diamond in the center that he'd placed on her finger the night before.

"Not anymore Tom. Besides, I already have everything I ever wanted...I had it all along."

Epilogue

Jennifer plopped down on the plush sofa in her living room holding a large cup of herbal tea. She reached down and slipped her shoes off and rubbed her tired feet, then tucked them underneath her on the sofa. It had taken a while, but she'd finally completed all the remodeling she wanted to do on her apartment. She'd decided to do a complete overhaul on her guest bedroom with a cool tropical theme. The warm earth tones and cool colors would help to block out the gloom of a long cold Chicago winter, and provide some pretense of being on an isolated Caribbean Island. Jennifer knew the whole Caribbean theme bordered on overkill, but then again, she could never do anything conventional.

The truth was she had way too much time on her hands these days, and way too much denial. It had been almost a year since she'd walked out on her job at Phillips, Willis and McKenzie and she knew it was time to get a new one. Chad had at least offered her a pretty generous severance package. It was partly hush money, but she really wasn't ready to go back to work just yet, so she accepted it. Now reality was finally setting in and she realized she couldn't hide in her faux paradise forever. The money was beginning to run out and she needed to go back to work. She also knew she should have been more conservative with her spending, but delving into the remodeling project at least gave her something else to concentrate on, and another way of masking her pain.

It seemed liked everything was going so well for everyone else in her life. Charity and Mike were thriving in Atlanta in their beautiful home with their two beautiful children. Cheryl and Tom had finally decided to stop avoiding the inevitable and were getting married. And she'd even found Vanessa after all these years, who even though she got off to a rough start, her life was just about perfect now. She was happy for her friends, she really was. It was just that when she thought about how hard she'd worked to become an attorney, and how everything had turned out for her, she felt as though her life was a one great big failure.

She knew growing up no one really expected much out of her. Sure she was always the girl everyone would go to for trivial advice. Sure, she knew how to set off an outfit with the perfect pair of shoes, or how to deal with a complicated relationship. God knows she'd had quite a few. But being an attorney was the one accomplishment in her life she was most proud of, mainly because she knew nobody really thought she could do it. And now here she was sitting in her newly remodeled apartment, sipping tea, with no way of supporting herself.

Jennifer reached over to the sofa table and picked up the Sunday newspaper to go over the employment listings once again. It wasn't as though she hadn't sent out a couple of her resumes to a few of the downtown firms. The problem was she had yet to hear from any of them. Maybe she was being black balled, or she'd taken too much time off, she didn't know. But she'd just needed some time to heal and get her head back on straight. She realized she hadn't always made the right choices, but she'd really been trying to work on being a better person lately and didn't know what else to do at this point. Needless to say, her back was against the wall and there was nowhere else to go. Well God, she thought, I know I haven't always done what I should, but I've really been trying here lately. Where's my happy ending?

Suddenly, she thought she heard a noise coming from the next room and jumped up from the sofa. Then the telephone rang. She turned and reached over to the table next to the sofa and picked up the phone.

"Hello?" She said impatiently.

"Jennifer Thompson, please."

"Yes, this is Jennifer Thompson." She replied quickly.

"Jennifer, how are you…I haven't spoken to you in a while, so I wanted to make sure it was really you. This is Jillian Reed." Jillian said.

"Jillian…you're right…we haven't spoken in a long time! How are you?" Jennifer responded wondering why on earth Jillian Reed would be calling her.

"I'm just wonderful Jen. Actually, I just opened my own law firm! As a matter of fact, I'd been working on setting it up for about a year now, one of the reasons I could never make all those late evening meetings with the guys at Phillips, Willis and McKenzie." Jillian said with a chuckle. "Well, we finally opened last month, and that's the reason I'm calling you. A friend of mine who does hiring for one of the firms downtown sent me a couple of resumes that recently came across his desk and that he thought I might be interested in. Imagine my surprise when I opened one to discover it belonged to a Jennifer Thompson formally of Phillips, Willis and McKenzie. Jennifer, as you know, I've always thought you were a bright and intelligent young lady and an excellent attorney, after all I taught you everything you know. Well, I'd like you to come and work for me at my new firm."

"Oh my god!"… Jennifer yelled. "…Jillian, I can't believe after all this time, you'd even consider me… of course, I'd love to work with you!"

"Great! I was hoping you'd say that. I'd like to set up a lunch meeting with you to discuss all the details. Are you free tomorrow, around noon?" Jillian asked.

"...Tomorrow at noon...um, sure, I can meet you tomorrow at noon. That should be fine Jillian. Where should I meet you?" Jennifer said.

"I'll make reservations at Rossi's on Dearborn. So it's confirmed, we'll meet there at noon tomorrow. Well Jen, I'm not going to take up too much of your time, as I said, we'll talk everything over tomorrow." Jillian said. "...And Jennifer, I just want you to know, I know the details of what happened with you at Phillips, Willis and McKenzie. Let's just say, it's time for a new chapter in your life and leave it at that, okay?"

"...Thank you so much Jillian. I just want you to know I really appreciate this." Jennifer said.

"I know. We'll talk tomorrow." Jillian said and hung up the phone.

Jennifer sat staring at the phone for a second, and suddenly felt an overwhelming need to tell someone special her news. She jumped up off the sofa and ran over to the spare bedroom, opened the door and walked over to the small bed in the center of the room. She bent over and looked into the crib at the small face peering back up at her. Then she reached down and picked up the tiny figure and held it to her chest. The baby curled up at her touch and snuggled against her.

"You hear that baby girl? Mama has a new job." Jennifer whispered. "She's going to be an attorney again!"

As Jennifer held her baby daughter, her mind went back over the events of the last year, her ill-fated relationship with Chad, walking out on her job, and running into Vanessa at the Atlanta airport. While she held her beautiful baby daughter in her arms and gazed lovingly into her large brown eyes, she suddenly heard the words Vanessa spoke to her that day.

"Sometimes you make mistakes in life, and you think it's the worst possible thing in the world. You can't see how things are ever going to work out, but God has a way of working things out far better than we can."

Jennifer took her baby and walked over to the large white rocking chair next to the window. She rocked her baby back and forth, looking around at the tropical themed décor of the nursery and suddenly burst into laughter.

"The world had better get ready for us Thompson girls, huh?" She said looking down at her daughter.

The baby looked back up at her and cooed as if in agreement. Jennifer then lifted the baby up and held her close to her chest feeling her heart beat against hers. As she continued to rock, she finally realized, she'd made the right decision after all.

About the Author

Sharron McKinnis Fowler is a freelance writer and marketing chairman for a nonprofit charitable organization. She previously spent nineteen years in the insurance industry including eight years as a medical malpractice liability underwriter. Sharron is a graduate of Washington College with a degree in Liberal Studies. She currently resides in the Chicago area with her husband. A Bird's Eye View is her first book.

Printed in the United States
144535LV00003B/10/P

9 781438 942162